CRIMEUCOPIA

STRICTLY OFF
THE RECORD

A Murderous Ink Press Anthology

****

I0667373

Murderous—Ink Press

CRIMEUCOPIA

Strictly Off The Record

First published by Murderous-Ink Press
Crowland
LINCOLNSHIRE
England
www.murderousinkpress.co.uk

Editorial Copyright © Murderous Ink Press 2023
Cover treatment and lettering © Willie Chob-Chob 2023
All rights are retained by the respective authors & artists on publication
Paperback Edition ISBN: 9781909498464
eBook Edition ISBN: 9781909498471

Acknowledgements

To those writers and artists who helped make this anthology what it is, I can only say a heartfelt Thank You!

Additional thanks must go to Jim Guigli,

for taking a lot of the grunt out of the grunt work

And to Den, as always.

Contents

The Florida Keys first appeared in John M. Floyd's 2016 collection, *Dreamland*
**Sneaker on the Beach first appeared in *Green Silk Journal*, Fall 2007
Please Note: This mono publication can be read in stereo by purchasing two copies at once

Shafer City Stories-
Tales of the NYPD
in East Harlem

Jesse Aaron

New York City, East Harlem, 1998. The city was still dirty and dark, a place of horror and wonder all at the same time. Shafer City Stories goes inside the minds and hearts of the cops on patrol in East Harlem's 25th precinct.

These men and women are sometimes brutal, sometimes kind, and always human. These cops are not John Wayne in a uniform; they are real people who feel the streets inside their souls.

Shafer City Stories will make you sad, it will make you angry, it will make you reflective, and most of all it will leave you with a story that you will never forget.

Let's Keep This Hush-Hush, On The QT...

(An Editorial of Sorts)

...And strictly off the record.

Of course there are going to be those who will happily point out that we've taken our subtitle this time around from James Elroy, and his rightly famous *L. A. Confidential.* However, like most Hollywood gossip columnists, "that's not strictly true."

Some of the earliest references come from the 1870s/Victorian England, and it is believed that the 'QT' in question is shorthand for *QuieT.* Not that any of the authors contained within these pages are particularly bothered, one way or the other – or quiet for that matter.

Of the 16 contained within, 12 are Crimeucopians of old – though that doesn't automatically make them a Crimeucopian Dirty Dozen.

Brandon Barrows follows newcomer *Anthony Diesso's* nicely off centre *The Bones of Angels*, with his *A Real Artist*, before *E. James Wilson* offers a swift and effective *Slam Dunk.*

James Roth, in his inimitable way, turns Noir on its head by moving us back in time and also to another side of the world, with his *The Liver Eaters.*

Jesse Aaron then brings us back on track with his *The Old Wheel Still Turns*, which also paves the way for *Jim Guigli* to give us one of his new John Moss stories in *Just a Dream.*

John M. Floyd adds a spritz of humour by telling us about *The Florida Keys*, and another new Crimeucopian, *Kevin R. Tipple*, offers up a darker humour with a politically topical twist in the form of *Sweet Dreams Are Made of This.*

Next up sees the welcome return of *Maddi Davidson*, who presents us with *A Goldy Opportunity* that shouldn't be missed, before *Michael Grimala* comes back with another of his slightly outré tales, this time involving a library setting in his *Fort Kent Public*.

Another Crimeucopian old-timer, *Robert Petyo*, brings us back into more traditional P.I. country with his *Face the Truth*, while *Shannon Hollinger* gives us a refreshing, Lemmy Cautionesque style of delivery, even though she assures us that it's all just *For the Birds*.

Despite his 95 years, *Tom Sheehan* remains actively writing, and continues to win awards for his own style and subject matter — in this case, it's all about a *Sneaker on the Beach*.

Wil A. Emerson gives us an often un-played Point of View, with the twisting *Unsolved Mystery*, which we feel acts as a perfect firebreak to *Peter Trelay*'s rather stylish Noir tale of *Vanity and Innocence*.

Finally, the last to drop down onto the turntable of this anthology's auto-changer is *Philip Pak*'s humorous piece, introducing Crimeucopia to his reoccurring character, *Jackson Blast*, in *A Lovely Place to Die*.

And, of course, every one of these tales is a guaranteed, solid gold A-Sider.

As with all of these anthologies, we hope you'll find something that you immediately like, as well as something that takes you out of your comfort zone – and puts you into a completely new one.

In other words, in the spirit of the Murderous Ink Press motto:

You never know what you like until you read it.

The Bones of Angels
Anthony Diesso

New York City, November 1929

1

Ding.

He felt stretched, a sudden pulling on his calves. The impression passed, though, and he ascended, no longer aware of flouting gravity. Waiting, he considered the elevator's Deco paneling, its copper sky, its brass and steel garden. Flower petals flashed like blades; grass curved like scythes; a silver fountain shot up where the doors converged.

"Strike you blind," he sighed, then lowered his hat brim. "And who loves Nature so much he goes out and has it bronzed?" He extended a hand; and touching the gear-shaped center of a flower, he left behind a smudge. "Aw, nuts." He stared at the bright mist for a moment, raised an elbow, and was about to rub the mark away when the elevator jerked to a stop.

Ding.

The fountain pulled apart; and in its place was a frosted glass door with ROBERT KENEALLY—FINE ANTIQUITIES painted on it. Having entered, he shut the door without a sound.

"Oh, Mr. Connell, good morning." A secretary behind a low oak desk lifted her head and smiled. She straightened up, ran fingers through her auburn hair, then across the metal-looking fabric on her thighs. She put a pinky in each ear, gave a little shake, then listened with a grin.

Mr. Connell tipped his hat. "Good morning, Ms. Daley. How's business?"

"Aw, there's nothing new."

"Nothing new," he chuckled, "not in the antique business. That's a good one." He removed his fedora, placed it on a hook beside the entrance. "Is Mr. Keneally in?"

"He is. He's been asking for you."

Connell headed for an ebony door with a big, brass knob. He noticed her perfume, its subtle trace of jasmine. "Always nice to know you're wanted—whattaya think, Ms. Daley?"

"Sure—unless it's on a poster," she answered with an eyebrow tilt. Then swiveling in her chair, she turned to face a stack of papers.

"Right you are." He snapped his fingers, then turned his attention to the tall black door. He paused, shut his eyes, inhaled slowly. "Alright; here we go." He twisted the doorknob and pushed.

*****

As if entering a dimly lit church, he at first saw nothing. The sconces near the ceiling shone upward like bowls of fire, leaving everything below in a thin, cathedral light. Between the two draped windows was a highly polished desk. On it, a shot glass of whiskey, a tumbler of water, and a little hand towel were the only props. "Good morning, Mr. Keneally," Connell began with a nod.

The man behind the desk observed him sullenly. He was half-way through his fifties, and with a V-shaped head, his hair combed back in grayish flames, and eyes that flashed with animal quickness. Every few seconds or so, he stared at the glass of whiskey on the desk, though he never once touched it during the interview. Instead, he reached for the tumbler of water, picked it up, then put it down without taking a sip. "Jimmy, you're late. You out shopping for bad habits?"

"Can't afford 'em, Mr. Keneally."

"Oh, I can. But why should I pay out? Is today your birthday?"

"Not 'til April."

"Fine." Mr. Keneally leaned forward to emphasize the point. "I can afford bad habits, but now the sport's in letting 'em alone. You see? That's how I deal with age—I give up things before they're taken away." He leaned back; the tip of his paisley, black necktie slid across the desk. "I'm getting better at parting with things – yes, sir, better all the time." He held up a hand and inspected the cuticle of his index finger. "Maybe I should part with you, Jimmy; it might solve a few problems for both of us…" He began to pick at the nail. "Or maybe we should put you in the mor—Good Lord, now will you look at that—see that? That gray beneath the nail? What makes that dirt there? I haven't shoveled for, God, I don't know how long. But there it is: the same filth against the skin, same shape, same color, everything.... Anyway, I need you to snatch a Calabrese."

Connell cleared his throat, then asked, "Which one?"

"Costanzi."

"Costan...Oh, sure. He's an accountant, works for the Italians."

"That's the one."

Squeezing his palms against the armrests of his chair, Connell leaned back, then forward. "What's the need, Mr. Keneally, if you don't mind my asking?"

"What do you think?" Mr. Keneally laughed, his laughter more the echo of a laugh. He flicked a fingernail against the whiskey glass, making a bell-like sound. The liquor quivered subtly. "Trouble with the stevedores again. The boys hiring on the docks've been less than generous."

"With that little economic dip, no one's very generous."

"*Gombeen* bastards. With jobs tight, there're oughta be business enough."

"Well, if they're not pulling their weight, why can't we talk it out with the union boys?"

Mr. Keneally squeezed, relaxed a fist. "They're taking a pinch, and if they're not coming to us, they're getting their share, or else they've got some little business of their own. And that's why we nab this Costanzi and wait—the arrangement should be good for twenty thousand at least."

"When?"

"Friday night, so late it's early." While speaking, he slid a finger across the desk, as if showing directions. "Take Sixth to Greenwich Village, beneath the El. Ryan McCoy'll be waiting with an address. Mr. Costanzi has a *geebag* in the neighborhood: you meet him as he hits the brownstone." When he took his finger from the desk, it was shaking, and the tip looked bloodless.

3

Thinking it over, Connell tapped the side of his nose as if leveling a pipe bowl. "How do we know he won't have a few of the Sons of Italy at the door instead of a waving ladyfriend?"

"Because he makes too much money. The man's not a *capo*, he's Financial Secretary, and you don't pound coffin nails into a cashbox. So that's why he'll be alone, and that's why we guide him by his elbows to the car, drive him to the lodge, give him a few drinks, and wait for payment."

Connell lowered his hands into his lap. "I'd like to help, Mr. Keneally. It's just that I'm not the man to deal with something of this…nature. You know me, I'm more of a planner, an engineer."

"So now it's games, huh?" Mr. Keneally slammed a palm on the desk, and before the noise echoed through the office, he was shouting. "Alright, now what are we playing, charades? Fine. You're some kind of animal: a dog, a skunk, a baboon–what? Let's see: you shuffle in here like you can't tell time, you ignore everything I say, and now you're gonna piss all over me and leave?"

He reached for something to throw, but found nothing worth smashing on the desk. He inhaled noisily instead, held the air in for several seconds, then let it out. He leaned back with a grin, took the chrysanthemum from his lapel and lobbed it. It bounced off Connell's chest as a brief burst of red, then landed on the floor. Convinced he'd made his point, Keneally glanced down, rubbed his hands, then stared at the whiskey shot as if it were a game piece. "You know Ryan?"

Connell bit his upper lip and nodded. "I know."

"Fine. He's going, along with a bull-moose bastard named Whitey. They ain't smart, not much–they're certifiable eejits–but they're mostly level-headed, at least as far as soldiers go."

"That's nice to hear."

"But I need a reasonable man, an intelligent man, someone with good wits and judgment, and that's why I'm handing this trashy business over to you. We're looking for money, not a war, and I have no doubt you'll find that happy little balance between extortion and respect."

Connell nodded. "I meant no disrespect—certainly not to you, Mr.

4

Keneally. You've always been generous."

"We're skin and bones for the angels, Jimmy...You'll handle this delicately, I know. I don't want things going bloody pudding on us."

"None of us wants that. I was there last month for that talk they had with Sean, when he went into the street..." As if reflected off the desk, Connell saw the incident again: the revolver raised, the green tie shredded, fluttered in the air. "Some kids were playing stickball, and they kept playing until they heard the shots. Then they stopped and watched: I saw his dying in their eyes."

"That's right, poor Sean," sighed Keneally. "He was bad for kids and traffic. And you know what did him in? The man just had to be a peacock, had to show his colors right there in the middle of the street." He shook his head, then pointed. "Here's the difference: take a look at your nails."

Connell curled his fingers into his palms and stared. Keneally slapped the desk again. "See that? If you fanned your fingers out like this, you wouldn't be around today. You're not the kind of a man to flare up, Jimmy, not like that. So what do you think? You'll do this little thing for me?"

Connell nodded. He stood up and headed for the door. "It shouldn't be a problem."

"Fine." Keneally said, steadying a palm at either side of the shot glass. "Now go on, play nice."

*****

In the waiting room Connell saw Ms. Daley sitting at her desk, her gaze lowered. She pretended to peruse a folder full of papers for a moment before finally noticing him. She smiled; he smiled back, acknowledging her effort to pretend. "Everything alright?" she asked in a cheerful voice, as if she'd never heard the noise that went on just a few minutes earlier.

"It is. It's alright. Everything's alright," he grinned while staring at the door window: ƧƎITIUϘITИA ƎИIꟻ—Y⅃⅃AƎИƎꓘ TЯƎBOЯ. He reached for the knob, and...

2

...shut the wrought iron gate behind him. The cemetery was a wet, rusty color with rain, the dying grass, the headstones pasted with dead leaves. The fedora still in his hand, Connell crouched in front of a particular monument. The stone was free from moss stains, chips, the discolorations of age. He sighed. "Hello, Maddy. It's...it's been awhile, I know. I try to come often, as often as I can, but..." He looked up, so that a droplet from an overhanging tree bough struck his forehead. "Aw, Hell. I hate it when it rains on you, I hate that. I hate it that there's so many things I can't do anything about, that I have to just stand and watch them happen. You and the baby out here in the cold." He extended an arm, plucked up a little, plush bear. It sagged like a loaded sponge, leaking rusty-colored water. "Look at this: it all just gets ruined. How cold it is out here for the baby... Damn it, Maddy. Things were always about to happen; they seemed so close. But the future passed before it came; it went faster than any of us would have thought. And what did we end up with?"

He ran a finger over her name in the stone. "Anyway, there's this little business they want me to do, snatch some gangster, keep him entertained while his cronies collect the ransom. Stupid, just—and all for what? You were so beautiful, Maddy, the way the sunlight brought the red out in your hair, those ringlets at the curve of your cheek; the way your throat tightened and you made that little cough when you were nervous. I'm sorry, Maddy, I should have let you be. I was a kid who wanted something, wanted it so badly, and...and just broke it when he got it." He touched his fingers to his lips, then tapped them on the stone. "I've gotta go. Watch over the baby, and remember: this, all this busyness that fills the day–it's only marking time."

*****

He clicked shut his pocket watch, put it away, and glanced out the car window. The towers' glass-and-steel skin was smeared with twilight. Pink and yellow light tinted the hats of passers-by, their faces in shadow as they made their way along the boulevard, so many fall leaves that floated at the corner of his eye. He glanced down, took out his pocket watch, and clicked it open.

*****

He clicked shut the pocket watch. Connell slipped it back into his jacket while driving, then nodded to the man in overcoat and black fedora. The man looked anxious, his gaze tight, though never focusing on anything for more than a few seconds. He'd finish each circuit by shifting in his seat and staring out the window of the boxy, 1925 Ajax. The street lamps sped by, *light, light, light.*

"What is it Whitey?" Connel asked.

Whitey shifted in his seat, stared out the window.

"Well?" Connell asked again.

"I don't want to talk about it."

"That's fine." Connell said and rolled his eyes. *Now he'll talk about not talking about it.*

The man met Connell's look, though with less defiance than a need to explain. *Light, light.* He grimaced at the reflected light, and as he spoke, his breath was whiskey-haunted. "Not this, Jimmy, this isn't the hell of it. Iris took little Maureen to the doctor yesterday. Bastard says she's got a heart-valve thingy, doesn't work right. They're talking about surgery. Filthy bastard. Iris is just about…well, she's in pieces."

Light, light, light…

Connell's mouth opened, but nothing came out. He looked forward, said finally, "They don't always know."

Whitey ran a knuckle along his nose and inhaled stickily. "Maybe they don't and maybe they do. But they might know, and so they know. And that's all there is to it." His lower lip began to tremble. "Five years old, my little girl. She comes in from the garden, she's got a basket full of flowers on her arm, and she hands me a violet for my jacket so I look nice to go to work, so I go off to work and…I…" He sniffed, stretched an eyelid with the palm of a hand, looking demented.

"Did you try saying a novena?"

A thread of saliva hung from Whitey's mouth. He tried to wipe it away with his index finger, though it slipped past and landed on the car seat. "I am," he replied, sliding out a prayer card from his shirt pocket. "Hourly. I'll be saying it in about 15 minutes, so I'm hoping we can time this thing just right."

Connell stared out the window. *Light, light...* "Why don't you take the night off? Ryan and I can handle this."

Whitey sniffed, regarded Connell with tear-filled, angry eyes. "You, too? You trying to hurt me, Jimmy? What in God's name have I ever done to you?"

"Alright, then." Connell lightly tapped the steering wheel. "Alright."

"Damn business. Maureen didn't do anything to deserve it; Iris didn't do anything wrong, Was it me? Damn business—you don't punish one worker for what another one does, do you?"

"No, you don't." *Light, light...* Connell thought of the time he'd had a dry cough, next to nothing, that he brought home to his wife and baby. "No, forget it. Try not to think about it."

"Fine—I'm not thinking about it." Whitey shifted in his seat, looked out the window, didn't speak.

"Try not to think about not thinking about it."

Light. "Aw, Jimmy, this is Hell."

Connell squinted. "Don't think so, no. It's only Willis Avenue."

*****

Light. While Connell drove, Ryan rode in the passenger's seat; Whitey sat in the back with the accountant, holding the side of a revolver to his chest. Ryan was talking, describing an incident to Connell. "So he figured with all the rumors of guys leaping out windows after that Stock Market plunge, well, it was as good enough time as any to send Malarkey off the roof. Heh. But going over, Malarkey gets ahold of Gil's tie, and they both go off the building together. Heh."

"Really?" Connell asked. "How do you know that?"

"Clerk saw them through a window, Malarkey still holding onto the tie, and Gil waving with a stupid look on his face. Heh."

"'Heh' yourself," the accountant scoffed. "You'll all be going over just like that."

"Shut up—I'm trying to tell a story. Anyway, Gil and Malarkey were like the Bobbsey Twins, and even when things went bad, and even hating each other in the end, they still went down together."

"Well, isn't that romantic?" the accountant said. "But you know what? You'll all be going down together, just like that." He snapped his fingers. "You're just too dumb to even know it."

"What was that?" asked Ryan.

The accountant shook his head. "You boys like stories? Well, here's one, complete with a happy ending. Your days of selling giggle water to johns and baby-kissers are over. Now that the stock market's jumping, the government'll repeal Prohibition, put a tax on liquor, and send every one of you Hibernians off to the breadline. Ha! How's that for a story? Come on, laugh at that!"

"You laugh at it, Honest Abe," Whitey growled. "Maybe we take your life story and tear out every page after 'they shoved him in the car.'"

"Isn't that cute? How many times've you used that one this month?"

Whitey bit his lip, then grumbled, "This is it."

"Like Hell. You boys have no knack for this. Your acting is terrible: the more you talk, the less scary you are–except to a language professor. You'd do better to drop me at the next corner and find another line of work."

"Puh!" Whitey fake-spat on the upholstered floor. "You open your mouth again," he said, pointing to the gun barrel, "and I'll put this in it."

The accountant rolled his eyes, puckered his mouth to an exaggerated "O".

"Now can I please finish the story?" Ryan asked. "So Gil and Malarkey, they just kept falling, twelve stories, and —"

"You and your endless stories," the accountant smirked. *"Merda."*

"Shut the hell up...So they kept falling, heh—"

"No, you shut up!" snorted the accountant. "And what are you gonna do if I keep talking, fancy pants, put a hole in me? I know better."

Gritting his teeth, Whitey pressed the revolver against the accountant's cheek. "Stop it."

"They just kept falling, heh," said Ryan. "Gil and Malarkey, Malarkey and Gil, just falling and fall—"

"Forget it," the accountant sniggered. "If you kill me, you might as well dig an extra grave and jump in. So go on: it'd be worth it to know you'll be filling a pothole by the end of the week."

"Another office clerk saw them from the window…"

Light. "Shut your mouth," Whitey replied. "Just…stop it."

"Come on, kill me, you Irish *stronzo*. Make your children orphans. Put your stupid, mick-brats into the street."

"And when they hit the concrete—"

Whitey swung the pistol. *Light.* He struck the man's face, struck again, and with a crunch, he felt the nose give way. *Light, light.* The accountant tried to speak, but only laughed. His bloodied nose and lip made numb, his words were garbled. "Yur, yur jerkuss, pers-ant."

Whitey felt his fist take orders from somewhere else. It punched the accountant in the nose, the cheek.

"Hrr, hrr, hrr, hrr."

Whitey continued to punch the man in the eyes, nose, and mouth, making his fist a greasy-looking rock. "Bastard! My only daughter, you goddamned son of a whore! You—"

"Heh, look at him go," Ryan chuckled.

"Whitey, what in hell—" said Connell, looking over his shoulder. *Lightlightlight.*

"Stop it!" The car began to veer as Connell struggled to reach into the back seat. "Stop!"

"You goddamned…heartless…"

Connell's foot down on the pedal. *Lightlightlightlightlight.*

"She's a little girl, just a little—"

Connell swung into a side alley, *light…light.* He stopped the car. *Light.*

"Stop it!"

"Whoops!" Ryan laughed. He shoved open the door, staggered from the shivering vehicle. His shoes made tap sounds as he fled into the darkness. The back of his jacket made a brief flash beneath the street light, and his shoe taps could still be heard a few seconds after he disappeared.

Connell drew his revolver. "Wait!" He aimed, then lowered the weapon, then turned his attention back to Whitey. "That's it. Listen–can you hear me? Now he's on his way to Keneally."

Tapping his shoulder, Connell tried to get Whitey away from the unconscious man. Whitey spun toward Connell, lifted his dripping fist. He held it up as the red went from his face, making the blood specks on his cheeks still more vivid. "Oh, Jimmy, I just couldn't—" he spluttered.

"I know." Connell put away his gun, pulled out his pocket watch. With his free hand, he pressed his first two fingers to the accountant's throat, felt a faint pulse.

Whitey sat down on the running board. "It's, it's all—"

"What's that?" Connell asked emptily. His fingers at the accountant's throat, he felt nothing.

"It's, it's gone—all gone!"

"It's just what you'd expect," sighed Connell, clicking his watch shut. He glanced over at Whitey who met his look with pink-rimmed eyes. "Listen, we need to split up, get out now."

"Oh God, Jimmy!"

"Did you hear me?"

"Oh, Jimmy, I missed my novena!'

3

"Yes. I'm sure. He isn't any more. It's just that…well you know, he wouldn't cooperate. I know, yes, we should have expected… Well, as a matter of fact we did expect, so tell Keneally we did what we could…I know, yes, he's going to be. Plenty. Yes, I know. No, you don't have to describe. I can imagine. Yes, I know he swore it off, and I know that's been putting him—uh huh, that's right. Picking up good habits can do that to a man. Yes, I know. Just tell him I'll see him when I'm able. I don't know. Alright, yes, I know. Goodbye."

Connell hung up the receiver, dropped a few coins into the slot, and exited the polished-oak booth. He pulled up his overcoat collar, lowered his fedora, and walked out of the drugstore onto the frozen street, the buildings looking like so many epic slabs.

A live jazz band from somewhere started on a bluesy dirge. The piano bang, the banjo, the whining clarinet, caused Connell to walk faster, out of pace with the funereal step. *I've got to. Now I've got to get to.* As if trying to keep up, the music dropped the minor, and burst into a lively swing. Connell shook his head. *No. Can't go home. Can't go to Keneally, not 'til tempers cool.* Sped up the streets, his head down, faster, the hat completely shadowing his face. *The Italians'll do us in; Keneally'll do us in so the Italians don't do him in...Poor Whitey. Yeah. Was better we split up. But can't go home. Oh Maddy, what now? We've got no place to. What can we—*"oof!"

—knocked shoulders with a man. "Oh, excuse me," Connell coughed.

The man didn't speak. He wore a gray suit that smelled of mold.

"Excuse me," Connell said again, and was shocked to see the man's jaw askew. The man tugged at his scarf, then at his tilted jaw. He removed a mask to conceal a disfigurement below his nose, something brought back from the war. The man's lips and mouth had been rubbed away, leaving only a puckered orifice. White breath issued from it as he mumbled something.

"Yes, I know," Connell replied, not knowing why. He put fingers to his hat, gave it a pinch. "Good night." He kept moving, scuttled half a block, then cut into an alley littered with empty crates. Beside a wall of uneven bricks, a raggedy man lay on his back, covered with pieces of cardboard. Connell unbuttoned his coat, then hurried to a sidestreet full of little shops.

Oh God, he thought, *is where I'm heading to is heading right at*—

"Me?" he saw himself in a bookstore window, his face above the pages of an open book. In thin light, as he read himself, he saw a figure crouch behind a parked car. He considered for a moment. *Pff:* a hole appeared in his reflection, a spidery crack in the glass. Drawing his revolver, Connell found nothing to aim at. He lowered his head, ran, so that the city swept by: streak-lamps, lit walls, gray flash, gold flash, smoke. He heard cracked glass, crashed trashcans, shoe-clacks on the pavement. He turned a corner down another alley, hid behind a stack of crates, a barrel drum.

Lamp-bursts hit the walk, where two faceless, back-lit figures stood. Connell aimed at, fired. One figure fell back: his upturned face flashed white, a twisted theater mask. The other leapt behind a wall. Connell overturned the barrel, kicked it. It drum-rolled down the alley toward the street, and when the figure leaned out to see, Connell aimed, fired, missed. The figure disappeared behind the wall again, and Connell backed into a door; he turned, struck it with a shoulder, with no success. He tried the knob, opened, and ran into door beads, tassels of a round, red, hanging lamp.

"*Shá?* What're you—"

Over him, more bubble lamps; to the left, an irritated waiter; to the right a bronze relief of ancient soldiers, and the Great Wall like a dragon's spine. Connell ran, bumped into the back of a chair. His stomach struck the top, his head hit the seat, and he nearly somersaulted to the floor.

"*Tiān a!*"

Straightening up, he staggered around the chair, around a black and pearl-gray screen, and reached a door tattooed with Chinese lettering. He snatched a spring roll from a nearby table, plopped it in his mouth, and left. Outside, thin snow-cords slithered over the boulevard.

Again the blast of streetlamps. Blind, he took a punch in the arm, not from a fist, but—a pain, bright pain. Kept running blind, heard puddle splats, the clang of garbage cans. Kept running. Connell aimed, fired at the lamp, missed, tripped over brownstone steps. Got up, took another punch, this time in his leg. Felt heat in his left calf, tightness, like a fever. Rather than slow him, it brought a surge of life, so that he bolted around the corner of a—bumped into a man fell back.

"Ooof!" The man reached out to break his fall, swung his gun away from Connell.

"W-wait," the man mumbled, his hat falling to the sidewalk. "Wait, wait—"

"Wait?" Connell regained his sight, saw blood trickling down his fingers. He fired into the man's chest, sent up smoke, pieces of fabric. "What am I waiting for, huh?" Crouching, he glanced up the street while prying the gun from the man's fingers. "Wait—always wait—for what?" he shouted at the practically unconscious man. "What the hell are we waiting for?" A screech and two approaching globes of light. "Well, here it comes!"

The car growled, sped up; an overcoated gunman struggled his shoulders out the passenger- side window. Connell fired one pistol at the cursing gunman, the other at the driver. He fired again, fired into the car hopped onto the curb. "Here—hope it was worth it!" Fired again. "There—one for the dog, one for the skunk, and one for the baboon!"

Another gunman fired from the back seat, nicked Connell's throat. Still holding both revolvers, he put his wrist to the leaking wound, leaned his other arm through the passenger side window, shot at the man in the back seat, hit the backseat, backseat, then the man—mouth, chest. "Don't know what's good or alive—just business—dead, stone-dead business!" He fired again at the man in the back seat. "Here, have some more! Plenty of business, plenty for everyone!"

4

Coughs echoed; steps clicked through the lobby, left sticky red shoeprints. "What a day." He slipped, reached out a hand against a couch, avoided a fall. He sat, looked past the Byzantine, gold-black marble, saw a man, maybe, through the glass of a rotating door. Outside, snow began to fall like the feathers of a shot dove. A reflected face in profile emerged from the frame, the muzzle of a revolver made an unintended tap on the glass. Connell struggled up from the couch.

*****

Ding.

He felt stretched, a sudden pulling at his calves. Soon enough, though, he left the ground and turned his attention to the elevator's paneling, the garden of polished steel and brass. He touched the metal foliage, left behind a print in blood, a rose petal on the copper vine.

Ding

The door was left unlocked, the waiting room dark, though Mr. Keneally's office was lit. "Come on in, Jimmy." Keneally stood at his desk as Connell entered; he leaned forward, then raised his hand as if addressing an assembly. "Ah, there he is. *Behold the man.* Late as usual."

Connell's sight wobbled for a moment, and he felt himself going away, although a force of will brought him back. "Soldiers are downstairs, probably in the lobby by now" he said.

"Buzz, buzz." Keneally sat down again, ran fingers through his graying hair. "Again you're late," he added while staring at the ceiling. "The last man to know, he always figures he's the first."

Connell rubbed his eyebrow with the base of his palm, giving him a demented look. "Where's Whitey?" he asked.

"You mean right now?" He peeked under the desk. "Nope. Guess the Italians got him."

"They couldn't have...so fast, unless—"

"Right you are." Keneally snapped his fingers and laughed. "We gave him up as a peace offering, although it didn't seem to work. You didn't leave us much of a choice, did you, boyo?"

"He's...he's us."

"Don't worry—they only got the body. Brought it over like a basket of fruit and cheese, right to the front door, with a flowery letter. We're not brutes, Jimmy—we're businessmen."

Connell slapped his arm twice, defying the pain. "Tell me you let him finish the novena."

"Oh, that. The man was saying prayers for something." He swung an arm, inadvertently knocked the coffee-cup and saucer to the floor. He continued to talk, his voice echoing from beneath the desk. "He didn't seem to hear a word we said. Of course, we weren't much listening to him, either." He picked up the dripping cup and saucer, put them on the table, tried to position them as neatly as possible. "It was a clean end, and how many of us are given that? How many of us struggle instead, our souls fumbling out of a heap of flesh and bones, like a man out of the rain, pulling off his saggy clothes?" The image appeared to haunt him, and for a moment, he seemed to stare at something that wasn't there. Afterward, he looked at Connell and smiled. "I was surprised to see you showing up alone. I don't know what you were up to in the last two hours, but the boys were told to bring you here alive—clipped if needs be—but alive."

"Clipped, but alive..."

"That's what I said. And do you know why you didn't die in the street, why you weren't lying there just like Sean? Because I wanted to hear the excuse you'd make. Nothing else matters anymore, so I've been sitting here, waiting for you to show up, look me in the eye, and tell me."

"There's no excuse. It was a bad plan, and we couldn't make it work."

"Aw, the hell you say!" Keneally threw the demitasse at the wall, shot porcelain pieces through the room. "At least show me the effort of a lie. Show me that much!" He picked up the saucer, struck it against the desk, though it didn't break. He swung again, though it kept intact. "Damn it to Hell," he whispered, then flung the saucer at the wall, where it landed on the carpet. Keneally lowered his head, and when he spoke, his voice was short of breath. "I loved you, Jimmy, loved Maddy and the baby, wept at their funeral like an old woman left with only memories."

Connell leaned against a wall, stared at the ceiling. "You were fine with the funeral, Mr. Keneally, fine with the weeping, the death and drama of it all. It was the living you never figured out, the day-to-day existence, the fears, the lying helpless, all the...God, I shouldn't have shot that man on the pavement."

"What are you talking about now, you raving *dryshite*?"

"Uh, no, it doesn't matter now. He was lying on his back."

"Is that all? You remember those beetles last summer? They'd fall off the roof, and if they landed on their feet, they'd crawl away, and if they landed on their backs, they'd wave their little legs until they died. And well, it's all like that, isn't it?" He laughed. "What were you expecting?"

"I was expecting something more."

"Oh? You didn't get your money's worth? Without me, you would have had worse than nothing—you would have had that." He pointed out the window: the snow was flying sidewise, and behind it, the moon was a wet blob in the cloudy sky. "There, out there: that's the truth of it."

"The truth?" Connell's arm and calf were becoming stiff, two slabs of inert agony. "The truth, that we sacrificed for nothing? That we believed in nothing, and believed in it with such violence that we crushed men like bugs for it? That we were finished from the start, and that our lives were in the hands of a madman staring at a liquor glass?"

"Don't blame me, Jimmy." Keneally flicked the shot-glass full of whiskey several times, so that it sounded like the hand-bell shaken by an altar boy.

Connell shook his head, ignoring the pain. "I'm not blaming you. This is a man's fault, a man's responsibility, not yours." He took the shot of whiskey from the desk and tossed it back. "You're just a holy mess, Mr. Keneally. Good night." He turned to go; the door clicked shut behind him.

"We're the flesh of the angels!" Keneally called out through the closed door. "You hear me? The flesh and bones of the angels!"

Connell staggered toward the elevator without giving a reply.

"The angels, you hear me? The goddamned angels!"

Ding.

Connell stepped back into the garden of polished steel and brass. He touched the metal foliage, leaving behind another print in blood, another petal on the copper vine. He went to his knees, felt the elevator's descent in his legs. "Maddy, there isn't much time, but there might be enough." He pulled out, clicked open his pocket watch. "All these busy chapters with no big purpose or a point, or even a decent ending...Was it just us, our time together? Was that all there ever was?" He stared at the doors, waiting. He closed his eyes and grinned with an overpowering exhaustion. "Yeah, I suppose that's it. You knew: you had it in that silent look of yours." He lay the watch and chain on the floor. "In those soft eyes, that little half-smile...Alright."

The elevator doors opened. He saw his dead wife's face, her eyes, a moment before the firing began.

A Real Artist

Brandon Barrows

The museum was crowded. It always was on Sunday afternoons, when the admission fee was waived. The older gentleman wandering the nineteenth century painters' wing didn't look as if that mattered to him, though. If his clothing was anything to judge by, he could have purchased at least a few of the masterpieces on display. Moving from painting to painting, his gray head nodding appreciatively, he spent a moment studying this canvas or a few minutes contemplating that one, appearing to enjoy them all.

After a time, he passed into the next hall and began examining a series of wildlife sketches by a once-famous artist, now mostly forgotten. The pieces were so lifelike, so engrossing, that he failed to notice the young woman until he turned and collided with her, knocking her back against the wall between two of the small, framed drawings.

Blood rushed to his cheeks and he whipped the newsboy cap from his head, twisting it nervously between his hands as if in supplication. "I'm so sorry, miss. I wasn't looking. I was just…" He faltered and settled for waving a hand towards the drawings.

The woman smiled, showing brilliantly white teeth that contrasted nicely with the olive color of her skin. "That's okay. It's my fault, too. I shouldn't have been standing so close, but I was interested in the bunnies."

"The bunnies…? Oh!" He chuckled nervously and looked to the nearest sketch. It showed a pair of hares huddled beneath a snow-covered bush, rendered so realistically that their eyes seemed to glisten moistly and individual hairs in their coats could be distinguished. "The arctic hares, yes."

He turned back to the woman and she smiled – a bright, warm spot amidst the hall's stark white walls and cold marble floors. "Not bunnies, then," she said.

Looking at her now, the man realized that she was a very young woman, barely more than a girl. She couldn't have been older than twenty or twenty-one. He noticed, too, how pretty she was. The warm skin-tone and large, brown eyes reminded him of a girl he knew in his long-ago youth. He felt himself blushing again.

"Is something wrong?" the girl asked.

"No, no." He shook his head. "I just—"

He cleared his throat and, trying to regain a measure of dignity asked, "So do you enjoy art, miss?"

It was a foolish question. He realized that as soon as the words left his mouth. But she didn't laugh or poke fun at him. Instead, her smile turned gentle, almost shy. "Yes, I do." Tucking a stray strand of dark hair behind one ear, she added, "I don't really know much about it, though. I'm a total amateur."

The man gestured towards the hallway he wandered earlier. "We're all amateurs, miss, except for those few whose work stands the test of time." His eyes shifted back to the drawings lining the walls. "After all, you can be a professional, even make a good living off your art, and still go quite unrecognized, no matter how talented you might be." His envy was plain.

"You sound very knowledgeable, sir. Are you an artist?" she asked.

The old man smiled wanly. "Yes, but… I'm afraid you've never heard of me."

She grinned, letting just a hint of mischief sneak into her expression. "Try me."

"Tom—" The man cleared his throat nervously. "*Thomas* Halsted. But you really would have no reason to know my work."

The girl shook her head. "I'm sorry, you're right. I haven't heard of you. What kind of art do you do, Mr. Halsted? Do you draw? Paint? Oh!" Her eyes widened. "I just realized I haven't introduced myself. And here I am, blabbering at you." She held out a delicate, long-fingered hand. "I'm Flora Welch."

Halsted took her hand gently, almost tentatively, as if he was afraid of damaging it somehow. "Flora? Now that's a name you don't often hear anymore."

"I guess not."

"Have you had lunch yet, Miss Welch?" It was an impulse so sudden, Halsted wasn't aware he was asking the question until it hung in the air between them. He felt heat rising to his cheeks again. He was an old man, well past sixty, and this girl couldn't be more than a third of his age. What in God's name was he thinking? He was just embarrassing himself.

"No, not yet," Flora admitted. She tilted her head forward, lowering her gaze. "Do you know a good place nearby?"

Halsted's heart skipped a beat. A broad smile stretched his cheeks. Perhaps the girl was just being polite, sensing his loneliness, but it didn't matter. Just standing near her made him feel things he hadn't in many years, and he wanted to hold onto that for as long as possible.

"As a matter of fact, I do." He offered his arm to the girl. She hesitated a moment, then looped her elbow through his. They turned towards the hall's exit.

Tom Halsted's heart hammered in his chest, so loudly he feared Flora would hear it. He hoped she couldn't feel the pulse racing in his arm. His head and feet both felt light, as if he were walking up among the clouds somewhere. He didn't notice when the girl, just before they left the museum's foyer, turned her head slightly and threw a wink at the redheaded young man leaning against the wall by the exit. Though apparently engrossed in his cellphone, the redhead nodded in acknowledgement.

*****

The mismatched couple sat at a table for two near the rear of Christos's Steakhouse. Halsted fiddled with his coffee cup and tried not to be obvious as he studied the girl across from him. Her deep brown eyes seemed to bore into him and warm his very soul as they talked. Mostly, she asked him questions about art, about things she saw in the museum and the artists who created them, and seemed to hang on his every word as he responded. He knew quite a lot about art and was grateful for a chance to impress someone.

From time to time, his eyes strayed to the chest of the simple, light blue sheath dress she wore and the way its fabric strained against her body. Each time, he tore his eyes away, ashamed and embarrassed and terrified that Flora would notice. *When did I become such a dirty old man?* he wondered.

"What do you do for work, Miss Welch?" Halsted asked, finally seeing an opportunity to learn more about his companion.

The young woman smiled. "I wish you'd call me Flora. And I'm a model – or, well, I'm trying to be."

"How do you mean?"

The girl seemed embarrassed. "I just sort of… It seems silly saying it out loud." She wiggled her fingers in a kind of meaningless gesture. "I get all dressed up, do my makeup, and take photos of myself that I put up on InstaSnap." She saw the confusion on Tom's face and added, "It's an app. An internet thing, for sharing pictures."

"Ah," he said. "I don't really have much use for the internet myself. I don't like the idea of all those different organizations keeping track of every little thing I do. I prefer privacy to convenience. Is there a good living in this InstaSnap?"

"No, not really. There can be, but you have to have sponsors and you really need a lot of followers—people who look at your pictures, I mean—to catch a company's eye, and to do that, you need something different, you know?"

Halsted nodded. "Of course. Finding patrons has always been an artist's biggest trouble. Money is such a vulgar thing, isn't it?"

Flora laughed, though Halsted didn't see the joke. "What about you… Tom?" she asked.

Hearing her say his name sent a pleasant shiver down the older man's back. "I'm a kind of artist, as I said before."

"Do you draw? Paint?"

Halsted grew wistful. It was a moment before he answered. "Not for many years, I'm afraid. I loved to paint but I just couldn't find a way to make a living from it."

"So you *do* paint." Flora leaned forward on the table, supported on her elbows. The action forced her breasts upwards inside the dress. Halsted felt his eyes drawn to them but quickly pulled his gaze away.

"You make it sound like an accusation." He forced a chuckle.

"No…" Something passed across the girl's face. "I was just thinking… what kind of things did you paint?"

"Oh, I tried all sorts. Pastorals, landscapes, urban scenes." He waved a hand dismissively. "I could never find a subject that I really wanted to make a career out of. Maybe that was my problem."

"Did you ever work with models?"

"No." Tom shook his head. "I couldn't afford to hire models in those days and by the time I could, it was years since I did any painting." As if to emphasize the point that he was no longer a young, starving artist, he examined the check, then pulled an overstuffed wallet from the inside pocket of his jacket and began counting out bills onto the table.

Movement across the restaurant caught Flora's eye. Her gaze flicked in that direction, just long enough to recognize the redheaded man from the museum, coming out of the bar on the far side of the dining room, headed towards the restrooms. She was sure he saw her, too.

A tiny smile played across the young woman's lips as she returned her focus to Halsted. "Well, it's not too late, is it?"

Something tugged at the back of Tom's mind. It was obvious what the girl was getting at, but there was no way he would allow himself to believe she was being serious and he didn't like the thought of being taunted.

Replacing his wallet in his jacket, he said, "I haven't painted in years." There was annoyance in his voice. "Besides," he took the last, cold sip of coffee from his cup, "I'm only visiting here, touring museums in this part of the country. I don't have any of the supplies I'd need to paint."

"Tom, what if…" Flora sat back. Her gaze on the table, she toyed with her water glass, running the tips of her fingers up and down it, making lines in the clinging condensation. It was an innocent, harmless act, but Halsted found it strangely erotic. "I mean, maybe we could help each other out. A painting of me, something tasteful—kind of classic?—

would really help bring in the followers. Everybody does photos and people add filters and stuff, but an actual *painting*? That's something special, right?" She looked up at last and was surprised to see a measure of sadness on Halsted's face.

She began again. "I guess I was just thinking we could help each other out. You wouldn't have to pay me and I don't need to keep the painting or anything. I'd just like a good photo of it for my Insta."

Halsted said nothing. His heart was hammering in his chest again, so hard it actually hurt.

Flora reached across the table, took one of his hands in both of hers. "Or don't you think I'm pretty enough to make a good painting?"

He swallowed against a suddenly dry throat. Her hands were smooth and warm and he imagined he could feel a faint pulse through her skin. "You're very pretty," he said softly.

Flora released his hands and sat back in her chair. Subtly thrusting out her chest, she said, "Then maybe it's my body?"

Sweat began to gather at the roots of Halsted's hair and heat came to his cheeks and ears. "No," he croaked. "Your body is lovely."

The girl relaxed her pose, then leaned forward against the table again. In a conspiratorial tone, she asked, "Then won't you please paint me, Tom?"

He imagined how it would be, the two of them alone in his hotel room for hours as he tried to capture her essence on canvas. She was right, it was a chance to try something he was never able to when he was young, a chance to finally create *real* art instead of the crass imitations he spent most of his life making. He realized that he wanted this more than anything else in decades, perhaps ever. But still, he couldn't quite bring himself to believe the girl.

"You can't be serious," he said.

Flora took his hand in hers again. "Tom, believe me, I am. I want to do this. I told you I want to be a model. So let me be yours. I'll be a *real* model, not just a girl pretending on the internet."

The phrasing was just right. It resonated with his own thoughts, exactly the way he put his own desires, and together they overcame his final objection. "I'm staying at the Tempo Hotel, in the penthouse suite." It was half-whispered, as if he couldn't bring himself to say the words fully out loud. "It'll take me a few hours to get ready. Could you come by tonight?"

Flora Welch smiled, sending tendrils of electricity through Tom's brain that radiated out into every cell of his body. "Is eight o'clock okay?"

*****

Hands on hips, Halsted surveyed the hotel suite for what must have been the twentieth time. The place was as tidy as it could be. Soft music played from the portable radio he purchased earlier and there were finger foods and bottled water, if Flora needed refreshment. There was alcohol, too, if she wanted something stronger. He wasn't sure if she was old enough to drink, but that didn't matter. Not tonight. He checked to ensure there was sufficient light on both the easel and the space where he planned to have Flora pose. Annoyed with himself, with his impatience, his eagerness, his nerves, he poured a finger of brandy into a glass and drained it in a single gulp.

He lifted the bottle again, but paused, then set it back down. It was a long time, a very long time, since he was alone with a woman. He wanted to calm his nerves, but he didn't want to embarrass himself. He moved to the huge window that looked out over the city and watched the tiny moving lights fifteen floors below. There was beauty in them, in the shifting but still somehow constant pattern. He appreciated it, but it did little to ease his tension.

He glanced at his watch; it was already twenty after eight. His mood sank. Maybe Flora was playing a prank on him after all.

The knock on the door made his heart leap in his chest. He crossed the room so quickly he nearly tripped over the foot of the easel. He took a moment to compose himself then opened the door. Flora Welch smiled in greeting, said "Hi," and moved into the room with smooth, lithe movements that sent Tom's blood pressure soaring again.

The girl was wearing the same dress as earlier, and carried the same purse, but she had added a denim jacket to ward off the evening's chill.

Tom took it from her and hung it in the closet before turning back to her.

"Sorry I'm late," she began. "My Uber driver took a wrong turn." That wasn't the real reason, and she doubted Tom knew what an Uber was, but she needed to explain her lateness somehow. It didn't matter, though; his delight at just seeing her was obvious.

"Perfectly fine." Halsted grinned, relief washing over him. She was here. She hadn't forgotten him, nor had she been teasing him. "I've just been getting everything ready." He gestured to the easel.

"Wow," Flora said and moved to inspect it. She walked all around the easel, examining it, the canvas, the paints and brushes Halsted laid out. She turned to the man. "All this for me? For one little painting?"

Halsted replied, "If we're going to do this, we're going to do it right. Here." He poured brandy into two glasses and held one out to the girl. She took it, sniffed at it, and said, "Brandy?"

He smiled. "You know your liquor."

Flora smiled and set the glass down. "I don't drink, actually. I'm not even twenty-one yet. My dad was a brandy-drinker, though." The look that crossed Halsted's face told her it was the wrong thing to say. Trying to recover, she changed the subject and, taking in the room with a sweep of her arms, said, "This place is gorgeous and it's way bigger than my apartment. I think it might even be bigger than the house I grew up in. I've actually never been inside a hotel this fancy before. It must cost a bundle."

Halsted set his glass down next to Flora's, leaving both untouched. "Money means nothing to me. I can have as much as I need any time I want it. Art is the only thing I've ever loved, the only thing I've ever wanted to make or do with my life, and yet no one will ever remember me for it, if anyone remembers me at all."

Surprised by Tom's bitterness, Flora looked at him speculatively. The mood between them was shifting again, growing tenser, and both were aware of it. For the first time, she began to doubt herself and this plan she concocted. But she was already here; it was too late to back out, and she wasn't leaving without getting what she came for. "Well," she said.

"Shall we get started?"

Tom studied the girl. The comment about her father bothered him, reminded him of their age difference, though he didn't believe it was meant as any sort of dig. It was simply a fact. She was very young. He had to keep reminding himself of that.

"Yes," he said, at last. "Let's get started." He gestured towards the area where he had pushed the plush, white sofa so it was beneath the track lighting on the far side of the room. He was glad she wore the dress from earlier as, when he envisioned the painting, he imagined the color of the sofa, brilliant under the bright lights, complementing the color of the dress to evoke a lightness similar to clouds in a bright summer sky. "I'm all set. I'd like you to stand next to the sofa."

Flora moved to the place Halsted indicated. He spent a moment posing her, then backed off and stood by the easel. He studied her again from the distance and angle he would be painting her. She looked back at him with those huge, brown eyes, and somehow it made him uneasy. The air between them was suddenly charged in a way he didn't care for at all.

"Is this how you want me, Tom?" she asked, her voice low and husky.

"Yes." He swallowed. "Yes, that's good."

"Just good?" She smiled.

He didn't know what to say, so he busied himself squeezing paints onto the palette. Getting just the right tone for her skin would be an interesting challenge he told himself, but his mind wasn't really on it.

"Tom."

He looked up and his breath caught in his throat. Flora still stood by the sofa, still in the pose he arranged her in, but the dress was gone. She used the moments he was readying his paints to strip out of it and remove her shoes. Now she wore only a sheer bra that hid nothing and a pair of panties that hugged the swelling curves of her hips as if made just for her.

"Wh-what..." he stammered.

"Isn't *this* how you really want me, Tom?" Flora stepped forward, closing the distance between them. Smirking, she cupped her breasts in her hands.

"No, I..." He shook his head in embarrassment and disbelief. "I never intended, I mean, we never talked about—"

A hardness came into Flora's eyes, something he hadn't seen before. "No, there wasn't any reason to, was there? We both know why you invited me." She began to unfasten the snaps on the bra.

And then she screamed, high and piercing, making a noise that chilled Tom Halsted all the way down to his marrow.

"What are you doing?!" he cried and moved to stop her as she flung the bra away. "Flora!"

"Help! Someone help me!" Nude except for the panties, she kept screaming, while she calmly walked to the door of the suite.

Halsted grabbed her by the shoulders, careful not to touch any sensitive parts of her body, and tried to pull her away, but it was too late. She had the lock undone and was wrenching the door open. A redheaded young man in the uniform of hotel security stood on the other side. "What's going on in here?" he demanded.

*****

Bright and early the next day, Flora and the young man, now shed of the uniform, stood together at a service window in a major chain bank, speaking in low tones as they waited for the teller to return.

"When that horny old creep saw I took my dress off, his face was the funniest and saddest thing ever, Paul." She suppressed a giggle. "I wish I could have gotten a picture."

"Yeah, I bet it was pretty funny." The man she called Paul grinned. "And when he got a look at me, I seriously thought he was gonna have a heart-attack. He was ready to pay us to go away almost before you asked for anything."

"I know it was all the cash he had, but I wish he hadn't given us so many tens and twenties," the girl complained. "What a pain in the ass."

"For three grand, I'm not kicking." Paul squeezed Flora's hip gently. "We'll get a few bigger bills and then clear out of town for a couple weeks. I don't think the old man'll call the cops, but you never know."

"No way. He'd be too embarrassed."

"You never know," Paul said again. "I gotta say, the phony security con is the best one we've ever come up with, and him being a painter was just too perfect. I mean, hooking him with the story about your InstaSnap was genius. I told you the museum was a good place to look for lonely rich guys."

"I know, he just—"

Flora cut off as a well-dressed, middle-aged man approached, flanked by a pair of uniformed guards. "Ms. Welch? Mr. Fein?"

"Yes?"

"My name's Henderson, I'm the branch manager. Could you please come to my office for a word?"

Flora's chest began to tingle. "What's going on?"

"Is there a problem?" Paul asked.

Henderson answered, "There are some questions we need to ask about the money you two brought in."

"What questions?" Flora demanded, trying to cover her fear with indignation.

The manager cleared his throat. Softly, he said, "Please don't make a scene. Just come along quietly. This is quite serious."

Henderson motioned with his head. The guards took hold of Flora and Paul and began guiding them firmly towards the recesses of the building.

"And don't even think of trying to tell me," Henderson said by Flora's ear, "that you didn't know those bills were counterfeit. I will admit it's a very good job. Nearly perfect, in fact. You certainly fooled the teller, if not my head cashier. Whoever made those bills is a real artist."

Flora's veins filled with ice. She glanced at Paul and saw on his face what must have been on hers: shock to equal Halsted's. She finally saw, too, the reason for Tom's bitterness and envy towards the artists in the museum. She grit her teeth, furious at how the tables were now turned, and decided that no matter what happened to her next, if it was the last thing she did, Thomas Halsted would get the recognition he craved.

Slam Dunk

E. James Wilson

"Paul Martin Duncan, what on earth are you doing?"

He was on his hands and knees, hiding under the table as he'd been told to do during the school training periods. Mrs Vanstone's voice sounded again. "Come on young man. It's snack time. You know the routine. Come on out, or I'll get angry." Mrs Vanstone, *English and Drama*, was not someone you messed with. Not when you're only six.

Cautiously he pulled back the makeshift cover and looked around the side of the table. Everything around him seemed normal, except for the two red dots of light that were still on the far wall. Bright, like roses. No, not roses, like out-of-focus corn poppies.

He scooted back under the table, pushing his shoulders and spine hard up against the wall, panting like a distressed animal. He knew exactly what those red dots meant. They meant he wasn't safe.

Imustnotwetmyself Imustnotwetmyself I must not wet my self.... He tightened his stomach and felt a little more confident as his muscles clamped down on his bladder.

His father had been right, of course.

"We have no time for bed-wetters in this family."

Then his father had tossed the shed key over Paul's head and he'd heard it land somewhere in the back yard behind him. "You can sleep outside until you've learned to control yourself."

It had taken three days of living in the back yard and sleeping in the shed before he'd been allowed back into the house. He suspected the reprieve had been his mother's doing. Either that, or the Johnsons from next door had threatened to call Welfare.

After that his father had become less standoffish — taking an interest in him and doing fatherly things, like baseball, fishing and hunting. He had bought Paul his first rifle — a Springline Junior .22 and a box of ammunition. "A great birthday present for any kid," his father had said.

That day he'd shot 4 squirrels, one after the other. "The kid's a Goddamn natural! Christ, Margaret, I don't see what it is you're complaining about?"

"You okay there, Slam?" Paul Martin Duncan hadn't been called by that nickname since college basketball. It had been a hybrid of slam dunk, and Dunkin' donuts. He shook his head and curled up into a ball in order to clear it, but the persistent memory jumble just wouldn't go from his brain.

"Yessir! Though I can't wait to come off this nursemaid duty and get back out into the field, sir!" 2nd Lieutenant Bosiak was a temporary, overly keen, green, desk jockey machine – doing his time before being posted back home and into some staff retinue duties.

Had Bosiak really called him Slam? Or was it a false memory? His head was hurting, but the memory carries on regardless.

Bosiak patted Paul's shoulder. "Not long now. Once this convoy is safe, then you'll be back on sniper deployment. Are you—"

A metal canister smashed through Paul Martin Duncan's glass balcony door, bounced off the back of the easy chair and landed on the worn carpet close to Paul's hiding place.

IN-COMING!

It hissed and spat like an alley cat on crystal meth – either C-S or smoke, though he wasn't going to take time to find out.

One Little Indian –

The small support convoy had just cleared the roadblock checkpoint and was

Out from under the table – keep low

Two Little Indians –

starting to climb back up the mountain track when two roadside IEDs

Deep breath, pull cushions off the sofa

Three Little Indians –

had been detonated either side of the road ahead of them – level with the logistics vehicles

Pile them on top of the grenade, not much but it'll gain some time

Four Little Indians –

Pull the AR-15 out from under the table.

Five Little Indian Boys! –

FIREBALL – wreckage and debris raining down and exploding around them as the rear vehicles crashed into the carnage.

The sudden pain in his chest had teeth as sharp as a pack of angry dogs every time he'd tried to breathe, but all he'd been able to do was gasp and hack, then fight back a wave of nausea.

"This is Charlie-Victor Five-Niner-Five. Medivac departing this location, now inbound, two PAX. ETA Xray-Sierra, one zero, repeat, one zero minutes, over."

He'd looked down at his chest, the sickly sharp metallic smell of warm blood in his nose, and saw the thin dagger of shrapnel sticking out of what had supposedly been protective Kevlar. Over the sound of the main rotor picking up speed he remembered hearing a voice say: "You're going to be okay, pal – we got you. Just hold still while this takes effect." Then someone had unscrewed the top of his skull, delved in, threw a switch and simply turned out all the lights.

Then they'd discovered the steel chassis bolt embedded in the back of his head. Emergency surgery to stabilize the damage, then into an induced coma and shipped back home.

"At least he's not going to be a *total* retard, Margaret," he remembered his father saying to his mom as he'd drifted in and out of consciousness in the local State military hospital.

The people on the sidewalks all looked like squirrels. No furry tails, but ratty faces and grasping little hands. Easy pickings, easy meat. It's what he'd been trained to do. He could see images of his father, proudly smiling and nodding his approval.

"The kid's a Goddamn natural!"

Paul Martin 'Slam Dunk' Duncan stood up in the wreckage of his 'downtown' Apartment – 9A – raised the empty AR-15 to his shoulder, walked through the broken glass of the sliding doors, and out onto the apartment's balcony again.

This time two bright red roses appeared on his chest, then two corn-poppy blossoms appeared, wetly spreading across his shirt.

The Liver Eaters

James Roth

Part One

Lieutenant Imamoto shone the beam of his flashlight into the hold of the broken-up freighter. Up toward the bow of the hold he caught sight of sacks of rice, canned goods, and bottles of sake, beer, and whiskey before the beam from the flashlight came to rest on what had the most value, medical supplies. There were soldiers on base suffering from burns and shrapnel wounds who were desperate for bandages, antiseptics, and, of course, morphine.

Lieutenant Imamoto took a deep breath, pleased with himself that he would not disappoint Colonel Fujizawa, his commanding officer, a malevolent little man who believed that the Japanese were superior to all other races, even if he had to know that Japan was losing the war. They all did. Lieutenant Imamoto believed that it was the little man's fear of being captured by the Americans that had had something to do with him issuing an order a few days before that all of the Chinese prisoners be executed to prevent them from talking.

It was Colonel Fujizawa who had tagged Lieutenant Imamoto with the name Apple Cheeks. Even if his family had for generations been apple farmers in Aomori prefecture, he resented this name. Other officers laughed at him, both to his face and behind his back, because of his baby red cheeks.

Lieutenant Imamoto's family had tended orchards along the fertile, shaded foothills of Mount Iwaki, a volcano known as the Mount Fuji of the north. Those Japanese who had never been farther north than Matsushima knew nothing of where he was from. Nothing. They were arrogant bastards. The pilots on base who were free and easy with the women who worked at the Odessa, a bar in town, were the worst of the lot; they had an air of superiority and devil-may-care bonhomie, perhaps born out of their awareness that some of them would not return from a mission, that they would die for the Emperor.

After eight years in the Japanese Imperial Army, it no longer mattered to Lieutenant Imamoto that he had wanted to be a pilot. (It was his nearsightedness that had kept him out of the pilot officer corps.) And so he had, after graduating from Hirosaki University, a school not far from his family's apple farm, applied to be an officer in the *kempeitai*, the military police, a hardline unit responsible for enforcing the Emperor's political objectives: the implementation of the Greater East Asia Co-Prosperity Sphere, meant to keep Western colonizers out of Asia. This belief not only justified Japan's invasion of China, but also Malaya, Singapore, the Philippines, Indochina, and the Dutch East Indies. Japanese soldiers were liberators who had come to free these oppressed people.

The freighter had been caught in a typhoon when heading for the channel into Port Arthur, foundered in high seas, and ended up on the rocks of a jetty. Gray waves were now lashing over its deck. Most of the crew had drowned. Those who hadn't, five of them, had been taken in by the Japanese Imperial Army and were on the airbase, being fed and afforded shelter.

As the freighter rocked back and forth, and the water in the bilge sloshed around, slapping up against the ruptured bulkheads and cracked hull, Lieutenant Imamoto pushed on toward the bow. He found his way past overturned crates of canned meats that were also of some value, considering most of the troops back on the base were getting by on a bowl of rice and piece of salted pork a day, and came to the crates of medical supplies.

"Privates!" he called out to two scrawny recruits who had stumbled and fallen several times as they followed him. Both of the privates were straight from their basic training on Honshu, young, perhaps seventeen, and sprouted a few whiskers from their chins; their new jackets hung off their bony shoulders. They weren't much more than skeletons who had a helmet tottering on their heads. The bewildered look in their eyes was a revelation to Lieutenant Imamoto that they had no idea why they were in China in the hold of this freighter. Perhaps they hadn't spent more than a month in basic training before being shipped out, had done maneuvers carrying wooden rifles, and hadn't fired a shot. Lieutenant Imamoto knew that supplies back home were tight. Rice had been rationed for years, and he'd heard that now that the B-29s were dropping incendiaries on almost nightly raids over Osaka, Nagoya, and Tokyo.

The Emperor's propaganda machine couldn't hide the truth, that a country whose people were starving wasn't going to win this war. Yes, Lieutenant Imamoto had once believed in the East Asia Co-Operative Prosperity Sphere that Tojo and his gang had touted would run off the foreign colonizers, bringing peace and wealth to the people of East and Southeast Asia, but he no longer believed in any of that. He had come to realize that he, and so many others, had been lied to, that thousands had died for no reason. The foreign invaders would conquer again. The American submarines that prowled the coast were proof of that as well. Only a couple of weeks before an American submarine had torpedoed and sunk a freighter just before it entered the safe harbor of Port Arthur. Sea-bloated bodies and slicks of oil and a few shattered lifeboats—and plenty of empty life preservers—had washed up onto the beaches and rocks and floated into the harbor on the incoming tide. No amount of propaganda about the East Asia Co-Prosperity Sphere could hide this.

There had been less than twenty-five survivors of that torpedoed freighter, most of them suffering from severe burns. Lieutenant Imamoto saw them as customers. The question for him was, how could they get their hands on something valuable enough to trade for morphine? They had only Japanese money, and it would soon be worthless. But then, desperate men could always resort to desperate means to pay him. They could venture into Port Arthur or one of the muddy villages and rob the Chinese of whatever they had that Lieutenant Imamoto could use to make trades with—jewelry, silks, leather boots; they might even extract a gold tooth from an old man if he was fortunate.

"Open that crate!" he ordered the privates. Both were holding crowbars.

The two privates rested their Arisaka infantry rifles against a rib of the hull and took the crowbars and popped off the tops of the crates. Lieutenant Imamoto shone his light into the crate, seeing bandages and splints and bottles of pills and antiseptic. Then he saw boxes of syringes and next to them the vials of morphine he was after.

"Close it back up!" he shouted.

The privates did and he had ordered them to and the three of them made their way back out of the freighter by climbing up a steel ladder up onto the heaving deck.

On a rock on the jetty stood flaccid, arrogant Sergeant Kaneda, his hands on his hips. Lieutenant Imamoto thought to himself that it was the career soldiers like him who profited from the propaganda coming out of Tokyo. His belly and jowls were proof of it. If Lieutenant Imamoto had learned anything during the war, it was that supply sergeants were the victors.

Lieutenant Imamoto shouted to Sergeant Kaneda, "Put together a detail of coolies to carry this cargo up to the lorries."

Sergeant Kaneda saluted. Lieutenant Imamoto knew that Sergeant Kaneda didn't really have much respect for him. The salute was just his reaction to an officer's orders. But what did it matter, an NCO's respect, now that the war was a lost cause? Profiting from defeat was what mattered.

Sergeant Kaneda shouted something at the Chinese in their own language—he had been born and raised in Manchuria—and the coolies walked down the rocks to the broken-up freighter, climbed aboard, and came to the hold, where Lieutenant Imamoto had remained. He yelled, "Get these crates onto those lorries before nightfall!" He faced the privates, "You two, show them your bayonets!"

The privates fumbled with their rifles, unsure, exactly, what they were supposed to do. "Look like you're going to bayonet them!" Lieutenant Imamoto shouted, slamming a heel of his boot down onto the rusting deck.

The two recruits quivered. One urinated.

A coolie laughed.

Lieutenant Imamoto raised his 8mm Nambu, steadied it with both hands, took careful aim, and pointed it at the coolie, who was now shaking nervously.

"You'd think people like you would've learned by now to be disciplined as we Japanese are. But no!"

Lieutenant Inamoto pulled the trigger, shooting the coolie through the temple. Blood spurted from the wound. The coolie fell over onto the deck, his legs kicking; he rolled across the deck and got caught up in a wad of rusting cables.

The two privates pointed their bayonets at the coolies, who now formed a line and went down into the hold.

"That's better," Lieutenant Imamoto said. "Discipline!"

The coolies were, to Lieutenant Imamoto's way of thinking, like a line of ants, all dressed in the same drab, dirty blue work clothes, and the same sweaty caps with short bills. They were all pitifully thin, their necks like those of butchered chickens. Gray whiskers covered their faces. But these men were the lucky ones. They hadn't been executed under Colonel Fujizawa's orders. They hadn't seen their fellows being tied to poles and bayoneted by fresh recruits.

"You," Lieutenant Imamoto said to one of the privates, "take this." He handed him his flashlight. "I want all of those crates on the lorries before the sun goes down, starting with medical supplies. We've got men back on base who need it! Stick them with a bayonet if they shuffle along the way so many Chinese do."

"Yes, sir!" the two privates said.

They, these two privates, Lieutenant Imamoto thought, weren't showing him any respect either. They had acted out of fear, considering they'd just seen him put a bullet through the head of a coolie. He'd take fear over respect when it came to getting enlisted men to carry out an officer's order. This coolie he'd shot had had the good fortune to die quickly, rather than serving as bayonet practice for replacements who'd never been in battle and needed to be hardened for it by bayoneting

Chinese at the orders of Colonel Fujizawa. The little man had laughed at the executions, then ordered that their livers be cut out and dried in the kitchen. He held a belief that eating human liver provided him with additional sexual prowess when he visited the Odessa.

*****

The coolies had unloaded the freighter by late that afternoon, loaded them onto a column of lorries that were now heading up a muddy coastal hill toward the airfield and *kempeitai* headquarters.

As the lead lorry, in which Lieutenant Imamoto was in, slipped around in the mud of a two-track trail, nearing the summit of a hill from which the land made a long descent to the sea, and the rocks, he heard the drone of approaching airplanes. He didn't recognize the engine of these planes as being Japanese. The sound of these engines was deeper, steadier, more guttural. The planes, too, were coming from the east, over the sea, an ominous sign.

They all searched the skies. Then a coolie shouted something and pointed. The planes were blue dots that quickly became larger and larger. Because of his poor eyesight, Lieutenant Imamoto couldn't make out what these plane were right off, unlike the others, many of whom had jumped from the lorries and were now running up the hill toward an outcropping of gray rocks. Then he saw recognized the planes. They F-4 Corsairs, launched from an American carrier somewhere over the horizon.

The Corsairs rolled over, diving onto the column of lorries. The coolies continued to run off, seeking cover behind the rocks along the summit, as did the two privates and Sergeant Kaneda. He'd been in the trailing lorry. Lieutenant Imamoto watched as he ran up the hill, a line of .50 calibers kicking up mud behind him, then one caught him in the back, cutting him in half. *He had that coming, the bastard*, Lieutenant Imamoto thought.

Lieutenant Imamoto, fearing that the pilots' next strafing runs would hit the lorries, did as the coolies and Sergeant Kaneda had and bolted from the cab and clawed his way up the hill toward the rocks. The rounds of the .50 calibers from one of the Corsairs followed him up the hill, but he managed to roll over the top of the rocks to safety as the tracers sparked.

When he peeked back over the rim of the rocks, he saw that the Corsairs had turned away, heading for the carrier, and, to his horror, that two of the lorries were on fire. He rushed down the hill to the burning lorries and saw that the crates containing the morphine could be salvaged.

"Get them out!" he ordered. He raised his sidearm, fired a shot. Several coolies went into the burning trucks and pulled out the crates, which fell and splintered in the mud.

"Gather that up!" Lieutenant Imamoto said, pointing at the vials of morphine. "Hurry, damn you! Another flight of Corsairs might be on us!"

The coolies gathered up the vials and put them in a burlap sack and lay the sack gently in the back of the lead lorry, which hadn't been hit, and the convoy headed on, cresting the hill, and from the crest of the hill descended toward the base, off in the distance.

Seeing the base, Lieutenant Imamoto now realized why Colonel Fujizawa had sent him on this mission. The two Nakajima 34 transport planes were gone. They were the only planes that had the fuel reserves to make it all the way back to Japan.

Part Two

Lieutenant Ikeda opened the door to the interrogation room and went inside. The room was windowless. The air smelled of sweat. At a steel table sat a Japanese soldier. He was perhaps twenty-three or -four, wore bottle cap glasses, was skeletal, as were most of the prisoners he had questioned, but there was an air of intelligence in his face behind the thick lenses of those glasses that many of the other soldiers, the sons of farmers and factory workers, lacked.

Lieutenant Ikeda introduced himself, adding, "I'm a lawyer who's investigating war crimes committed by soldiers in the Imperial Japanese Army. What's your name?"

"Nishida," the soldier said, "Nishida Ryu."

"Corporal Nishida?"

"That's right. A cook."

Lieutenant Ikeda doubted that this corporal, in spite of his apparent intelligence, his eagerness to talk, would know anything about war crimes. He was, like so many soldiers he had already interrogated, simply glad that the war was, for them, over.

"You're an officer in the American army?" Corporal Nishida asked.

"Yes."

"But you're Japanese. I never thought that the American army would commission Japanese."

Lieutenant Ikeda couldn't say what he was thinking, that the Army did hold back Nisei, or use them as the tip of the sword in Europe, as a sacrificial force. No. He couldn't admit to that. He had to promote the United States as the beacon of equality and freedom that had been the rallying call for the war, both in the Pacific and Europe. "I'm going to be a career officer," Lieutenant Ikeda replied.

"Really! I have an uncle who lives in Oregon. Maybe you know him. He's a farmer."

"I doubt it. America is a big place, and there are a lot of Japanese-American farmers who live there." Lieutenant Ikeda thought of his own family, who, after the Pearl Harbor attack, had been shipped off to an internment camp in the Utah desert called Topaz. Lieutenant Ikeda thought, what a misleading name for a place that was scorching hot in the summer and icy cold in the winter, when the wind rattled the thin walls and panes of glass in the windows of the dormitories. The camp was no jewel.

Thinking of the camp, Lieutenant Ikeda had to ask himself, again, if he had made the right decision to join the Army after graduating from the University of California Berkeley's law school, rather than protesting the internment of Japanese-Americans, as other Nisei had, including many of his friends, who now thought of him as a man without principles. He'd have to prove them wrong, and show that he was indeed a man with principles. He'd do so by prosecuting war criminals.

"War crimes," Corporeal Nishida muttered. "What might that be?

It's war. How can there be crimes in war?"

"Let's start with prisoners, prisoners that the Imperial Army captured. What happened to them? Where are they?"

Corporeal Nishida's expression turned from glee, the glee at seeing the war come to an end—and perhaps feeling a kinship with Lieutenant Ikeda—to a deep sadness. Lieutenant Ikeda thought he might begin to weep, and then, just before the tears appeared, he said, "I was born and raised in Manchuria, you understand, sir. I had Chinese friends when I was a boy. Their parents invited me into their homes. They fed me." He paused, choking up.

What is it he wants to say? Lieutenant Ikeda wondered.

"Prisoners?" Corporeal Nishida went on. "There were no prisoners. They were all executed and dumped in mass graves at the orders of our officers."

This news did not come as a surprise to Lieutenant Ikeda. He had suspected as much. He had just not come across a Japanese soldier who was willing to say this. They had seemed to fear not him but their officers, even if they were nowhere to be found.

"Who gave the orders? The names of the officers?" Lieutenant Ikeda asked.

"I wouldn't know. I was only a cook, you understand. My commanding officer was responsible for seeing that the bellies of the officers and NCOs, Tojo's stooges, were full. The Chinese are good people. Very humble, even if they can be a bit crude."

"I understand."

"The officers showed who they were when they boarded those cargo planes and got the hell out of here before the Americans arrived. I suppose they're back home now, hiding out. Good luck finding them, sir."

"We'll do our best."

"There was one officer, a Colonel Fujizawa—he was the commanding officer in the *kempeitai*—who had a fondness for human liver, thinking it would help him out with the Russian girls in the Odessa. We all had a good laugh over his lack of confidence. I didn't need human liver." He paused to chuckle. "Is that a war crime, him eating human liver?"

"It could be," Lieutenant Ikeda said.

Lieutenant Ikeda knew about the Odessa. His CO, Colonel Whyte, went there frequently, so frequently that word was that his table there was his office, not the office he had in the stone municipal building the German colonizers had built early in the century.

Corporal Nishida went on: "He had Chinese tied up to posts and ordered new recruits to bayonet them, saying it would toughen them up. But I don't know where the bodies are."

"Who might?"

"There was this fool junior officer, Apple Cheeks, he was called, he didn't get away. I heard he got his hands on some morphine from out of that wrecked freighter."

"Tell me about him."

"He's from Aomori, the son of an apple farmer. So he was called Apple Cheeks. He even has apple cheeks, like a country child wandering around barefoot up in Tohoku. I'm from Kansai myself. Japanese Fuji apples are the best. The apples are protected with news print to prevent birds from getting at them. Do Americans grow apples that way?"

"What's his name?"

"Imamoto."

"Any idea where he is now?"

"China is a big country. He could be anywhere. There are lots of places to hide. Maybe he even took up with the Communists."

"I doubt that. They'd execute a *kempeitai* officer."

"The Nationalists, then?"

"Don't you think they'd do the same?"

"I wouldn't know where he is. I'm only a cook."

*****

Lieutenant Ikeda entered the Odessa. It was a cavernous bar paneled with dark, oily hardwood. A curving staircase led to the upper floor, where the rooms the girls used were. A steady flow of GIs proceeded along the stairs, their arm around a girl—tall, bosomy Russians, pale

Japanese, paunchy Chinese, and broad-faced Koreans.

He found his way to Colonel Whyte's table, which was in a corner of the room, only a few steps from the bar. His White Russian girl was sitting beside him. She had red hair and was wearing a blue evening dress that had a plunging neckline. Around her long, white neck hung a necklace of silver in which were set jade stones. Sitting on the other side of Colonel Whyte was his executive officer, Major Sasser, who never said much at all, unless it was to agree with the Colonel. He was a reluctant officer, a graduate of the University of Tennessee, from a family of Southern aristocrats whose house and barn and slave quarters had been burned to the ground by Northern soldiers. He and his family had been scarred by war long before Pearl Harbor. That wound had been passed down from generation to generation.

"What can I do for you, Lieutenant?" Colonel Whyte said. "Sit down. Have a drink. Waiter!"

"Just a soda water for me, sir. I'm on duty."

Colonel Whyte grunted, "So am I, Ikeda."

"You drink!" the Russian girl insisted.

"The Japs left us with a supply of their best whiskey. Not only can the little devils fight, they can put out liquor that we both can agree on is very fine. This whole war could've been settled between military men sitting at a table having a drink together. Politicians! Damn them to hell."

"It's almost as good as Tennessee's best mash," Major Sasser said.

The girl smiled at Lieutenant Ikeda and drank. She set her glass down. "But they not make vodka," she said.

"You'll have to adjust, honey," Colonel Whyte said.

Lieutenant Ikeda sat, and the waiter brought him his soda water. He sipped it. He thought about what he was going to report, about what Colonel Whyte's reaction would be, even if he did have an idea. Colonel Whyte had never seemed very interested in his work. He was an artillery officer, West Point graduate, who had fought in all the major campaigns—Guadalcanal, Leyte, Saipan—and he was now resentful about commanding an occupation force that guarded Japanese soldiers who hadn't run off and were being kept on their former base, an airfield a few miles outside Dalian that sat in the saddle between surrounding hills. The Zeroes and Nakajima transports were now heaps of ash that the engineers had bulldozed off the ramp.

"There's this cook, sir," Lieutenant Ikeda said.

"A cook?"

"Yes, sir."

"Hold on. Igor is about to perform," Colonel Whyte said.

Igor Popov, a White Russian, a former colonel who owned the Odessa, had come to a dais holding a violin by the neck. The dais was positioned before a crackling fire burning in a stone fireplace. Igor was approaching seventy, was tall and bony, and, when he performed, wore a threadbare tuxedo and white shirt. He had a long white beard and watery blue eyes. His face was a crisscrossing of red lines. Liver spots were prominent on the backs of his large hands. His fingers were long, bony, and as white as ivory.

He threw back the tails of the tuxedo jacket and sat on a simple wooden chair and brought the violin to his chin.

"He could've been a virtuoso," Colonel Whyte said, "if the Reds hadn't come to power. The fucking Reds!" He took a long drink of whiskey and slammed the glass down, sloshing some of the liquor onto the table.

"Darling," the girl said, "you're so careless."

"Shut up," he said. "You're not my damn wife."

She looked at her countryman.

Igor began to play Vivaldi's *Spring* from *The Four Seasons*. The GIs, most of them, who had been shouting and arguing over the favors of a girl, or were playing poker, fell silent. They, and Colonel Whyte and Major Sasser, listened to Igor's performance, as transfixed by the music as children were to a lullaby.

When Igor had finished he stood and bowed. The GIs, and Colonel Whyte and Major Sasser, applauded. Lieutenant Ikeda did so as well, out of obligation.

"Who would've thought that in a mud hole like Dalian, art. Damn

46

Reds. He should be playing in a concert hall in Moscow."

"Yes, sir," Major Sasser said.

The GIs returned to their shouting and arguing, the girls to their laughter and playful banter.

"A cook?" Major Sasser asked.

"Yes, sir, a cook," Lieutenant Ikeda said. "It's because of him that we found the graves of twenty Chinese. Their livers had been removed."

Major Sasser said, "What?"

"You heard me right, their livers were removed," Lieutenant Ikeda said.

"That's a war crime?" Colonel Whyte said.

"Colonel Fujizawa, the commanding officer, from what I've learned, had recruits bayonet Chinese prisoners to death, to toughen them up, and ate their livers as a kind of aphrodisiac."

Major Sasser registered an expression of disgust. "I've heard of foolish beliefs," he said, "but this . . ."

Colonel Whyte laughed. "Little people, little cocks; that's why we're winning this war. Look at those men." He pointed at the GIs going up the stairs with a girl. "None of them need a booster. They're American men! And where might this colonel be now?"

"I'm afraid he flew out, along with other *kempeitai* officers, before we arrived."

"There you have it, Lieutenant," Colonel Whyte said. "Let the dead rest in peace. He'll never be found."

"Their livers were cut out, sir. That's a war crime."

Colonel Whyte turned to his Russian girl, "Know anything about this Jap colonel?"

"He come here, yes."

"Did you fuck him?"

"Me? Oh, no."

"You fucked him. Don't bullshit me. His cock was small, wasn't it?"

"No! He only take Japanese girls."

"Are you going to interrogate every Jap girl here, Ikeda? Whores don't talk. You should know that. Talking is bad for business."

"Yes, sir," Lieutenant Ikeda said. "But Igor might know something."

"He's not talking either. What's he got to gain by it? Give him something in return. Can you? No. This Jap colonel spent money here. That buys him loyalty in my book. Right, Major?"

"It often does," Major Sasser said.

Lieutenant Ikeda said, "There was one officer who's still here, a Lieutenant Imamoto. He was called Apple Cheeks because he was a farm boy."

"As opposed to a city Jap, a graduate of a prestigious law school."

Lieutenant Ikeda said nothing. This wasn't the first time Colonel Whyte had insulted him. He knew it wouldn't be the last, unless he transferred out, which he often thought about doing.

"Good work, Ikeda," Major Sasser said. As a Southerner, he must have seen some justice in prosecuting war criminals, even if the ones whom his family considered criminals were officers in the victorious Union's army.

"Thank you, sir," Ikeda said.

"There are war crimes, sir," Major Sasser said.

"War crimes," Colonel Whyte replied. "Isn't that a, what do you call it, oxymoron? But I didn't go to a university in California or Tennessee. West Point, 1931. How can civilian law be imposed on the battlefield? It's absurd."

"There are the Nazis," Lieutenant Ikeda said. "There are war crime tribunals taking place there."

"We're in the East," Colonel Whyte said. "It's a different ball game here, where all of these people look the same." He finished his drink. "Waiter!" he yelled, "Another. How about you, Major, need another?"

"I'm still nursing this one."

"Apple Cheeks got his hands on some morphine, and I think he's peddling it, maybe even to your men. They are the ones with the money."

Colonel Whyte growled, "I know my men, Lieutenant, and I seriously doubt that. They wouldn't touch that junk. They're drinkers."

Lieutenant Ikeda turned and saw a man come in from a back room carrying a crate of Suntory whiskey. He proceeded to place some bottles on the shelves behind the bar as the barman, another White Russian, was pouring drinks for two sergeants. Both of them had their arms around a girl, one Japanese, the other Russian.

Lieutenant Ikeda saw now that the man stocking the shelves had red cheeks. He watched a corporal come up to him and hand him some dollar bills he had taken from a shirt pocket. The man, in return, handed him a small packet of something. The corporal smiled and tucked it away in a shirt pocket and walked off.

"Something distract you?" Colonel Whyte asked. "Maybe a Jap girl?" He laughed.

"I was just admiring the woodwork of the bar," Lieutenant Ikeda said.

"Let me tell you something, Ikeda," Colonel Whyte continued. "This skirmish that is about to come to an end, it's a preliminary to the main event. And do you know what that is, the main event, Ikeda? You see Igor there?" Igor had remained seated on the chair on the dais and was now having a drink and smoking a cigarette that a GI had offered him. "The war that's coming is between us and the Reds that Igor lost out to. Just as Patton said, we're going to have to take the Reds on one day, so we might as well take them on now, while they're weak and spent and we have the muscle. Yes, that's the real war, us and those Reds. But the damn politicians. Peace shouldn't be left to a bunch of lying politicians." He tapped his shoulders with a finger. "And I'm not going to miss out on the main event. My father had stars on his shoulders, and my grandfather before him, and even his father. I'm not losing out. I want my stars! Do you think I'm going to get them looking after a bunch of Jap prisoners, investigating war crimes?"

"You might, sir," Major Sasser put in.

Colonel Whyte stared at him but said nothing.

Lieutenant Ikeda said, "Are you suggesting that we invade the Soviet Union?"

"Damn right! The time is right."

Lieutenant Ikeda thought, *You're a disgrace to the eagles on your shoulders.*

"I've got some business to attend to," Colonel Whyte said. He stood. His Russian girl smiled. "You speak truth," she said to him.

"You haven't any idea what I just said. Time for a session with this White Russian gal."

Colonel Whyte and his girl walked off, making their way through the drunken GIs. The hem of the girl's blue dress swirled around her long, slightly plump, white legs. They came to a door in the back of the room, a special room Igor reserved for field grade officers and their girls.

Major Sasser said, "You may be in the right, David, but it's best to let the whole matter pass. You should know by now how the Army works."

Lieutenant Ikeda stood. "Chinese were executed, their livers cut out and eaten," he said.

"You're going nowhere with this," Major Sasser said. "Your career in the Army will be finished if you push it."

"I know you're right, Bradford," Lieutenant Ikeda said, "but I can't ignore it."

He walked over to one end of the bar, from where he could see into the back room. In it Apple Cheeks was moving around crates of liquor. Lieutenant Ikeda slipped behind the bar and went into the room, and Apple cheeks, holding a crate of sake, stared at him.

"I know who you are. You're Lieutenant Imamoto," Lieutenant Ikeda said in Japanese. "And I know all about your CO, Colonel Fujizawa, all about his taste for human liver.

A look of momentary fear came to Lieutenant Imamoto's face. His cheeks flushed even a deeper red. He set down the crate of sake.

"What are you talking about?" Lieutenant Imamoto said.

"A war crimes court. That's what I'm talking about."

"What's that?"

"You'll find out." Lieutenant Ikeda made a few steps toward him, and suddenly he realized that Apple Cheeks could simply turn and run off. He stopped.

The two men stood there, staring at the other, neither of them apparently knowing exactly what to do, and then, after a minute or so, Lieutenant stepped back, realizing that nothing would come of Apple

Cheeks arrest. Absolutely nothing, not with a commanding officer like Colonel Whyte. And then it came to him that Apple Cheeks was, as so many others like him were, a farm boy caught up in the propaganda and hysteria of Japan's war machine. He was a victim of his own foolish decisions, just as Lieutenant Ikeda believed, now, that he was.

Lieutenant Ikeda backed up and left the room and walked through the bar and came out onto the street. Drunken GIs were stumbling along it. Several had their arms around a girl. Chinese men with braided ponytails sitting behind various street stalls shouted at them, "Buy! Very cheap! You buy! Come! Come! Girl you want? Have sister!"

Lieutenant Ikeda had no realization of where, exactly, he was going. He heard the growls of drunken GIs and the laughter of their girls and he stopped to watch two GIs arguing over the favors of a Russian girl. And then, suddenly, one raised a beer bottle and cracked it over the head of his adversary, dropping him to his knees, collapsing onto the muddy street. The victor rifled through the jacket of his slain comrade and removed his wallet, then stripped from his arm his wristwatch. He marched off with the girl in the direction of the Odessa.

"You very strong!" she cackled, her arm through his.

"You ain't seen nothin' yet, babe." He handed her some bills from the wallet.

Lieutenant Ikeda continued on along the street. A Chinese man shouted at him from the dark recesses of a shop, "You Jap lose war! Go home."

The Old Wheel Still Turns

Jesse Aaron

Retired Detective Sonny Williams stared at the opposite wall in in his living room and once again wondered where all the time had gone. The far wall was adorned with three plaques. The first one was given to him by his old partner from patrol, Vinnie Popendopolis. Vinnie had passed away six — no, make it seven years ago, almost to the day.

He wanted to be back on patrol, following the scent like a finely bred bloodhound, feeling the neighborhood and all of the players right down to his bones, a part of something, moving and reacting in a symbiotic symphony of movement with the giant being that was the street.

He wanted it so bad he could taste it. It was either that or the pasta sauce he had just eaten. His stomach was not what it used to be, and the once proud giant who could eat an entire pizza for lunch without a thought had left the building and abandoned his body.

As he got up, he let out a large sigh and a fart and he felt the pressure release in a pleasant way from his stomach. He could also feel the sad nostalgia seep out of him a little along with the gas. He slowly walked over to the mirror in the short narrow hallway that led to his bathroom and stopped to stare at his reflection.

His form had gone soft in the middle, and his arms, while still strong enough to lift his bulk twenty times each day from the floor while he did his morning push-ups, had begun to sag a little. He felt the top of his head and was reminded there was nothing left there but blotchy skin. But the most telling feature was the eyes. The dark brown that was once as sharp as a brand-new scalpel was now a dull and muddy puddle in the middle of two bloodshot overcooked egg whites. His eyes said they were tired, and the rest of his body agreed.

Suddenly he heard a loud banging in the hallway, and he nearly fell over at the sound. During his patrol days something like that would not have fazed him, but now he spent so much time in silence that it startled him, and it was another sad reminder how far away he was from being a cop.

Sonny looked through the peephole, but he could not see anyone. He stepped back and picked up his revolver from the table next to his kitchen. He then slowly opened the door while he stood to the side. As soon as the door was all the way open, he could see there was a girl laying on the ground in a curled up bloody heap about four feet in front of the entrance to his apartment.

She was moaning and holding her stomach tightly, and he could see the slow ooze of blood creep through her fingers as her life trickled away. He checked the rest of the hallway, but it was empty. He leaned down and gently put his meaty hand on the victim's arm, but she didn't even flinch. She was so absorbed in her own pain and shock that Sonny doubted she even knew he was there.

He had seen this before, and he already knew that the girl was not going to make it. Moments later, the girl slipped away, and her arms relaxed as she slowly curled up until she was almost a tight ball. She stopped moving and Sonny knew it was over.

He leaned down to stare myopically at the body and squinted to try and see a clearer image of the victim, while avoiding any actual contact. He could see blood was still pumping from the stomach wound, but he could also see something around the victim's neck. It looked like before she received the gut wound she had been choked. He cursed himself for being so stubborn about the glasses.

As he rose to his feet, he could feel his knees crack and he felt frozen by indecision, something he never would have felt when he was still on the job. Should he do a quick canvass of the building? It was possible and even likely that the perp. was still on the scene. He unconsciously reached for his radio and his shield. He was quickly reminded he was no longer a cop. He realized with a shock of fear both of these things were not there.

Sonny acknowledged with some sadness there was only once course of action. He was too old and retired too long to play this game anymore. He would have to let the real cops handle this. He quickly retreated into his apartment and called 911.

However, that did not mean he could not be a good witness. He stepped back into the frame of his apartment door and stood there to watch anyone that might flee the scene. He knew it would not be long before the first sector car showed up, but he could not resist getting involved. His common sense screamed at him to leave it alone, but he could not. The man he used to be was still running through his blood, and he knew that even if his I.D. card was stamped "retired" he could not stop being a cop, ever.

He could see that there was a blood trail leading down the hall to the apartment across from his. He knew this apartment well as he was friendly with the tenant, a retired plumber named Tommy Rantoli.

He avoided stepping in the blood trail as he walked down the hallway to the source as he knew it would become evidence. He could hear the approaching sirens and he knew he should probably wait for the uniforms, but he could not resist. Sonny banged on the apartment door where the trail ended and after about three loud knocks the door swung open quickly, startling Sonny.

Tommy was standing there with tears in his eyes and blood dripping from his open hands.

"Sonny, God help me, I killed her. I killed her Sonny. Take me in. Take me in."

Tommy turned around and stuck his arms behind his back, perfectly positioning himself to be handcuffed. His open hands beckoned Sonny to grab a hold of him and become a cop again. Sonny stood there staring at Tommy's hands, and for a brief second, he allowed himself a silent moment of joy that he was back in the middle of it. He felt like a cop again and he loved it. Then the uniforms were behind him, and he could sense the barrel of the pistol pointing at him, and he realized how different this was going to be now that he was retired.

*****

Fortunately for Sonny, the lead detective was one of the first cops to arrive. Sonny realized how lucky he was when he felt the barrel of an automatic poke him in the back and then pull away. He recognized the booming voice of his dead partner's son Mike Papondopolis as he yelled,

"Stand down! He used to be on the job! For Christ's sake, stand down!"

Sonny let out a sigh of relief, but just to be sure he slowly placed his gun at his feet, and in an even slower motion raised his hands and turned around. He could see the narrow hallway was jammed with uniforms and one plain clothes detective in the form of his dead partner's son Mike.

Mike was standing behind him shaking his head, and Sonny could see his dark eyes were blazing. Mike holstered his gun and ran a hand through his dark hair in frustration and impatience. Sonny could see he was on the scent, and when it got like that you didn't want to stop. You wanted to keep moving and running until the thing was solved, like a marathon runner in the first mile.

"My God Sonny, you almost got capped! What the hell are you doing in the hallway of a murder scene? No, wait, don't answer. Let me guess, you forgot you were retired."

Mike leaned on his hip and his squat and solid form seemed to tense up as he waited for Sonny's answer.

"Mike I'm sorry I got in the middle of this. I was just trying to help."

Mike grabbed Sonny's arm and pulled him slowly back in the direction of his apartment.

"Fine Sonny, but for now go wait in your apartment please. I've got to process this scene."

He pointed to the nearest uniform.

"You, Lang, go with him. Sit with him in his apartment while I talk to this guy. And you, Williamson, go check on the victim and let me know if she's likely, and somebody get some crime scene tape in here and secure the scene. I'll talk with you later Sonny."

With that, Mike pushed past Sonny and took Tommy back into his apartment. The rest of the other uniforms followed Mike with their guns drawn and Lang gently steered Sonny to his apartment. Sonny quickly pushed past him to get his gun from the ground and jammed it in his waistband. Lang waited for him and then led Sonny into his apartment.

Sonny sat on the couch and waited. He offered Lang a drink, but Lang refused. Lang looked like a poster boy for the Boy Scouts. He had a flame of red hair, a pale thin frame and a nervous look in his blue eyes that screamed rookie.

"So, Lang, what are you, twenty-three, twenty-four?"

"Two sir."

"Huh? What do ya mean two sir?"

"I'm twenty-two sir."

"Jesus H. Keerist. They're letting them come on the job that young now?"

Sonny let a slow whistle escape through his teeth. Other than being on the same job that he was now no longer a part of, he knew he had absolutely nothing in common with this kid.

Sonny turned on the T.V. and let his body sink back into the couch.

*****

An hour later Mike barreled through the door, looking pissed-off and tired.

"Lang, you're relieved."

Mike sighed and sat next to Sonny on his sagging couch.

"Sonny, do you realize how much trouble you could have gotten into? Do you realize how much trouble you could have gotten *me* into? Do you even think about this kind of crap, or do you just wonder around like a lost old man, getting into the middle of things?"

"Mike look, I saw some marks on the neck, it looks like she may have been strangled before she was stabbed. Can you tell me anything? Can I have one more look at the body? Please, humor an old bastard. All I've got left is those plaques on the wall, a ruined stomach, an ex-wife who hates me, and a whole lot of jumbled memories. Please?"

Mike let out a deep sigh and then leaned towards Sonny.

"Look Sonny, you how how this works. I respect you, and all the time you put in on the job. You are legend for God's sake. You were my father's partner and he loved you, so for him I'll give you what I can, even though I'm not supposed to."

He leaned a little closer and spoke a little lower, as if he was telling Sonny a deep and dark secret, and in a way he was.

"I got a confession from the old man across the hall. He's down at the station house writing it as we sit here. The victim was his son's girlfriend. He says he made a move on her, and when she rejected him, he struggled with her and she fought him pretty hard. Without thinking he just grabbed the knife from the table and before he knew it, she was on the floor crawling to the door. His DNA is all over her, and her blood is all over him. There are no other witnesses, and we got DNA and a murder weapon. He's a plumber-those guys have strong hands and arms-I have no doubt he has the strength. It's a water-tight murder collar and the case will be closed by the D.A. by the end of the week. He'll take a plea and my Lieutenant can check off another case as cleared on his monthly stats. Everyone is happy."

Sonny knew it did not feel right. He knew Tommy. He had shared a lot of beers with him, and he knew Tommy's son used to be a junkie.

"What about the son? Sal? What's his alibi? Where is he? You know he used to be a junkie? How did he react to this?"

"My partner spoke to Sal-he was at his friend's apartment all night. His buddy already corroborated it. My partner didn't see anything hinky. It's done Sonny, so please, let me finish at the scene so I can maybe get to see me kids again before they graduate high school, huh? Do not, under any circumstances, go out into the hall until Crime Scene has cleared the hallway and the body is gone."

Mike stood up quickly to let Sonny know they were done. Before he stepped out, he stopped and looked at Sonny one last time.

"Swear you won't go out into the hall. I need your word."

Sonny stuck up his hand in a mock salute.

"I promise. I'll stay in here until everything is done. I'll even mop up the blood if you like once the body is gone."

Mike glared at Sonny and stepped out of the apartment. Mike didn't notice that Sonny had his other hand behind his back with his fingers crossed. There was no way Sonny was going to let this rest. His gut told him Tommy was innocent, and he was not going to ignore twenty-two years of hard lessons and experience.

Sonny waited two hours and then slowly opened his door and peeked out. The scene seemed to have quieted down, and for the moment there was only one cop guarding the body. Sonny got lucky-it was Lang.

He slipped out his door and kneeled down next to the body to get a better look. Lang moved towards him, but Sonny put his hand up to stop him.

"There is a change in your orders. Mike changed his mind-he called me five minutes ago and he gave me permission to look. I won't touch her, I just need to get a better look at her neck."

Lang gulped and looked confused.

"Hadn't I better call him on the radio before you do that?"

Sonny didn't wait for an answer. He pulled his magnifying glass from his pocket and moved it up to her neck. It was embarrassing, but he had no choice. His close-up vision was shot, and this was the only way he could get a better look.

Sonny could clearly see a ring around the neck, and it looked like it had been made by someone's hand. He also saw a dark spotted depression in the middle of the red hoop that surrounded the victim's neck. It looked like it had been made by a ring or some type of metal object. Sonny could hear the police radios coming up the stairs. He quickly pulled out his phone and took a couple of pictures of the victim's neck.

"Not a word about this to Mike or anyone else who comes to the scene. Mike doesn't want anyone to know I'm helping-he's a little embarrassed, you understand, don't you kid?"

Lang's throat bobbed nervously as he nodded at Sonny. He put his radio back on his belt.

"Yes sir, I won't say anything."

Sonny waved to him and slid back into his apartment.

*****

Two days later Sonny heard some movement in the hallway, and when he opened his door, he could see Tommy slowly walking towards his apartment. Sonny knew he had to interview him, so he walked out to meet him. He had to know if the story was true, and was sure that if he could talk with Tommy he would get the truth.

"Tommy, how are you? They let you out?"

Tommy's face looked like a fresh side of beef. His eyes were puffy and raw, and his skin was red. The remaining thin grey whisps of hair on his mottled round head were sticking out in three different directions, and it was obvious they had worked him over.

"Yeah, I'm out on bail, one of the conditions I made of my confession. There's a cop downstairs in case I get any ideas. I go back tomorrow. I just wanted one last night in my own bed."

Sonny walked over to him and gently placed his hand on Tommy's shoulder.

"Tommy, can I come in? We need to talk."

"Well…I'm awful tired, but okay. I'm not going to see you for a long while. If you don't mind waiting while I shower, you can come in."

Sonny followed Tommy inside and was immediately reminded of how neat Tommy kept his apartment. As Tommy slowly walked to his bedroom, Sonny could see there were still blood stains on the floor. Nobody even bothered to wipe them up. As Tommy showered, Sonny got a mop and bucket from the closet and cleaned up as much of the blood as he could. He felt that Tommy deserved at least that courtesy.

Sonny opened two cold beers and waited at Tommy's small and battered metal kitchen table for him to finish up. Ten minutes later Tommy shuffled over to the table and sat down. He took a long swig from his beer and put his head in his hands.

Sonny put his hand on Tommy's arm, and Tommy responded by looking up.

"This is a hell of a thing Tommy. A hell of a thing. What do you need from me before they take you back?"

Tommy put his hand over Sonny's, and as he looked at Sonny his eyes were sad and empty. Sonny felt a chill run through him. It felt like the touch of a dead man, and for the first time he realized that Tommy was not planning on going back.

"Tommy, please. Can you talk to me? I'm your friend. I was there for you when you had all those issues with Sal. I won't talk to anyone, but I need to know how this really went down."

Tommy pulled his hand away and he stood up so fast his chair fell over.

"No! This is done! Do not try to come in here and change things! This is how it has to be. I'm an old man. I don't have much time left. The boy has a life to live. He's finally clean and he fought hard for that. It's done."

As he said those last words, he turned his back on Sonny, and Sonny could clearly see his body was shaking with sobs. He was a proud person, and he did not want another man to see him weeping. Sonny gently placed his hand on Tommy's shoulder and spoke softly to his back.

"Tommy, I understand why you are doing this, but you can't take the fall for Sal. What's right is right, and they are going to find out anyway. I want to see your hands if I can, I want to show you something."

Tommy waited until he could stop weeping and then turned around slowly and stuck out his tanned shaking hands. Sonny looked down at them and could see his hands were bare and he had no white outline from a wedding ring. He looked up into Tommy's watery eyes.

"Tommy, look down at your hands. You don't wear any rings, do you?"

Tommy looked at Sonny, and a small light came back into his eyes.

"No, that's right, I don't. I can't in my line of work, might get caught on something or fall down a pipe."

"The girl, she had a big bruise on her neck. Whoever choked her wears at least one ring. I know you don't want to look, but you have to see this."

Sonny pulled up one of the pictures on his phone he had taken of her neck and zoomed in on the spot with the dark bruise.

"You see?"

Tommy silently nodded.

"And another thing, stick out your strong hand."

Tommy looked up with interest, then stuck out his right hand.

"You are a righty. I looked at the choke marks-whoever did this was a lefty."

This was purely a bluff-Sonny could not know this from his brief examination of the body, but he had to trust his instincts.

"Tommy, I know it wasn't you. Was it Sal? Is he using again? You can tell me, even if you still plan to take the collar. I understand your pain and why you would do this, but just for me, I've got know."

Part of this was a lie. While Sonny sympathized with the practical reason why Tommy was doing this, he did not have a son of his own and would never understand the depth of Tommy's love for his own son.

Sonny sat down with Tommy and methodically picked apart his story. At first, Tommy resisted and kept trying to push the same tale he told the police. Sonny knew he was lying. He had interviewed enough suspects and victims over the years that he could tell in just about every instance if someone was lying.

It was just going to take time to pull out the truth. He was protecting his son, but Sonny knew that if he could absolve him of the responsibility of convicting his son and somehow shift this burden to someone else, Tommy might give him the real story.

Slowly, over the course of the next hour and three more beers, Sonny got him to loosen up. Finally, Sonny convinced him it was not his fault. He absolved him of his guilt, and this allowed Tommy to open up. Sonny had used this tactic many times during interviews, and it still worked. He might be off the job, but he had never forgotten how to talk to people and still understood the human condition.

Finally, like one of Tommy's clogged pipes that is finally cleared of the debris, he spilled out the whole story, and it came pouring out like a gush of clean water.

Tommy finally admitted Sal was using again, and Sal had snuck into the apartment high as a kite with one of his junkie friends while Tommy was out at the store. When Tommy came back, he walked into the tail end of the fight between Sal and the victim, who was his girlfriend. Her name was Carmen.

Tommy told Sonny he loved Carmen like his own daughter, and he had given her a key and permission to stay at his apartment if Sal ever started using again. He had promised her she would be safe. Tommy walked in on the end of the fight, and Carmen had already been stabbed.

He learned later that Sal and his friend had entered through the fire escape window, and after Sal stabbed Carmen that was the same way they both left. Tommy was left with a bleeding nearly dead victim and a son that he knew he was going to lose, so he decided to take the fall for Sal. He finished his story and wept into his arms. Sonny put his hands on Tommy's shoulders and silently walked out to the living room.

Sonny called Mike on his cell and told him everything. Mike cursed as he told Sonny he was going to come over and re-open the case. As much as it burned him, he knew Sonny was right, and he could not let Tommy take the fall for his son. Sonny was relived. Mike had proven he was his father's son and a good cop.

Tommy came over to Sonny and wept in his arms. Sonny patted him on the back and led him over to the couch, where Tommy leaned back and stared at the ceiling as tears continued to stream down his tired eyes.

As Sonny looked over at Tommy, he felt a tremendous relief. He realized for the first time since retiring that he could no longer be a real cop. He finally accepted it. Right behind that thought was the knowledge that there was still good that he could do in the world.

Sonny was just about to let himself sink deeper into the couch when he heard a shuffling noise coming from the kitchen. Tommy was still absorbed in his grief, so Sonny decided to leave him on the couch while he investigated the cause of the noise. Just as he walked into the kitchen he stopped, as he was face to face with a thin and greasy looking man dressed in blue jeans and a stained t-shirt.

The man was halfway through the window, and in his left hand he held a revolver. As soon as he saw Sonny, he pushed himself through the rest of the window and pointed the gun at Sonny's chest.

Sonny felt his stomach drop. Without thinking he reached for his gun, only to realize he had left it on the nightstand in his apartment. He didn't think he would need it. At first, he thought it was just a robbery, but as the man moved a little closer he realized it was Sal.

He was at least thirty pounds lighter than the last time Sonny had seen him, and his eyes were a desperate shade of black, but it was Sal. He quickly looked at Sal's hands and could see he was wearing a large ring on the same hand carrying the gun. Sonny had no time to connect this detail to what he knew to be the truth, but somehow his cop's brain managed to take note of this small detail.

Sonny could see Sal's hand was shaking and that the hammer on the revolver was already cocked. The slightest bit if pressure or a nervous twitch of a finger would cause the gun to explode in the direction of his chest.

"Sit. I don't know what you are doing here Sonny, but this my father's apartment, and he's locked up, so now it's mine. Now you just sit there while I get some of my things and this will go smoothly. But if you make a move, I'll kill you."

Sonny put his hands flat on the table. He had to figure out a way to get the gun away from Sal. If Sal left the room or turned his back he could move in and try to get the gun, but right now the gun was still pointed at his chest and he was too close to try anything.

"I know you ratted me out to the cops. That fat-ass detective came and interviewed me, but I fooled that son-of a-bitch good. He couldn't get nothin on me. Well, what else should I have expected from another cop? You all stick together, all the time. You are a lousy bunch of...."

Sal's last sentence was cut off by a loud and wet thump, as Tommy hit Sal on the back of the head with a large plumber's wrench. Sal didn't see Tommy sitting in the living room, but Tommy heard the entire conversation. As he hit Sal the gun went off and then Sal fell to the ground. The shot sounded like a cannon in the small kitchen, and Sonny unconsciously gripped the sides of the table. There was no pain, only a dull echo in his ears and then a steady ringing.

Sonny thought he must be shot. It was too close-there was no way the shot could have missed. He was just in shock, but in seconds the searing and terrifying hot pain would come. He could not bring himself to take his hands from the sides of the table. He felt that if he kept them there, this could not be real and that he would be safe. Tommy was now standing over Sal's limp body, and he slowly removed the gun from Sal's hand and gently placed it on the table with the wrench in front of Sonny.

Then he walked over to Sonny and put his hand on his shoulder. Finally, Sonny released his grip on the table and felt his body and his face and realized with relief he had no extra holes that did not belong there.

He turned behind him and could see a bullet hole in the wall about six inches to the right of his head. He let out a loud gasp and felt his body slump over in the chair. His hands began to shake, and he had to grip them together in a tight ball to keep them from trembling.

Tommy looked down at him with determination.

"I could not let the boy do it. He would have killed you Sonny, and you always helped me. Tonight, and all those times he got into trouble. You were always there. You saved my life tonight, so I owed you the same. But no worries, now we are even."

He stuck out his hand towards Sonny. Wordlessly and with some awe Sonny shook his hand. At that moment there was a loud banging at the door, and Sonny realized it was the cop from downstairs. Sonny knew he must have heard the shot. As he gathered the wrench and the gun and made his way to the door to let the uniform in, he turned to Tommy with a wide smile.

"Tommy, not to sound too sappy or clichéd, but I think this is the beginning of a beautiful friendship."

Just a Dream

(A John Moss Mystery)

Jim Guigli

John Moss had a strange dream one night in Illinois. Not about Viet Nam. His younger sister, Karen, stepped from the dark to face him. She seemed so real he tried to touch her. She smiled, turned, and vanished.

A week later, Karen's San Francisco roommate, Sandy, called John looking for Karen. She said Karen was missing.

Now he was afraid the dream was Karen saying goodbye.

*****

Sandy contacted the SF police after three days, insisting that something was wrong. They had paid for summer classes together, but Karen didn't show, and the restaurant manager at Karen's part-time waitress job called looking for her.

After a week, Sandy called everyone who knew Karen. After two weeks, John arrived from Illinois to look for her. Sandy could not tell John exactly when or where Karen had disappeared because Sandy had been away for the weekend, and Karen was gone when she returned. Karen's bicycle was missing, too.

For four semesters, September 1974 through June 1976, Karen rode her yellow bicycle between the San Francisco Art Institute on Russian Hill and her warehouse studio in The Mission, the last year wearing a blue vinyl hooded rain slicker, rain or shine. The previous summer she wrote to John saying it had rained on a day they said it had never rained in San Francisco. That's when John found the hooded blue raincoat in a mall and mailed it to her.

When John asked Sandy about a place to stay, she said there was a furnished studio to sublet on her floor at the other end of their warehouse. He saw the building manager and exchanged a cash deposit for a key, dropped his things inside the studio, and drove to the Hall of Justice.

*****

John found the room number and entered a small reception area, where a woman behind a window asked him to sit on a bench while she summoned the detective who would help him. While John sat worrying about his sister, he heard voices and phones ringing beyond the reception area. Detectives and clerks ignored him as they passed on their way in and out of the inner door. Two men stopped near him to discuss a problem.

"Yeah, that place, it's a real shit hole."

John smiled when the man noticed him.

"Excuse my language, sir. I thought you were...I'm sorry."

"It's all right." John was new here, but it probably was a shit hole.

Finally, a man opened the door, leaned out, and said, "Mr. Moss, John Moss?"

"Yes, that's right."

"Good. I'm Detective Ray Madison. Come on in and we'll talk at my desk. You've come here all the way from Illinois?"

"Yes —"

As John was standing up, another detective entered the reception area from the hallway and saw Madison.

"Ray, they found another one — maybe your blue slicker girl."

Madison said, "Hold it, Rich," and nodded toward John.

Rich said, "Oh. I'm sorry."

Madison tried to feign routine, but his eyes lied. "Mr. Moss, would you wait out here while we take care of some business? It'll be just a minute."

John wasn't an optimist. He knew cops and how they talked. Illinois, San Francisco, Biên Hòa — there was a universal language, spoken mainly with the eyes.

Your blue slicker girl — he knew they were talking about Karen.

The door opened, and Ray Madison leaned out. "Mr. Moss? You want to come in now?"

The detective led John through a maze of cluttered desks crowded into a large bullpen. He offered John the chair at the side of his desk and they both sat.

"A few days ago, a cop friend from Illinois called and said you'd be here for your sister, and I should give you some time. I'm not Missing Persons, but your sister's disappearance was suspicious from the get-go. Nothing said she was a runaway or space-case."

"That cop, he was in the service with me. You're homicide?"

"Yes."

"Is it certain?"

"The detective you saw in the reception area, Richard, he's trying to confirm the victim's identity, but it might be your sister. I'm very sorry."

"I wasn't optimistic after she'd been missing so long. Karen wasn't a flake who would run off or dive into drugs."

"Yes. You find a place to stay?"

"In her building, a sublet."

"Phone?"

"Not yet. I'll call you when I have a number."

"Here's my card, Mr. Moss. Give us a little time to be sure. We might know tomorrow afternoon. Thank you for flying out here."

"I drove. I thought I'd need my car."

"Yes. Again, I am sorry."

"Thank you."

*****

John returned to the warehouse and asked Sandy about a phone.

"You can use our number for now. If there's a call, I'll come get you, or leave a message under your door."

John left Sandy's number for Ray Madison, then called the phone company.

Sandy didn't appear any more stressed than when John had first met her. Maybe Sandy hadn't heard yet, but it wouldn't be long before the radio would mention a body found, another young female — if they could make room for it between all the stories about the Bicentennial.

*****

John's small, slice-of-pie-shaped studio lay in the warehouse's northwest corner, near the intersection of Harrison Street and Mariposa Street. With a thirteen-foot ceiling, light from two seven-foot square windows high on the Mariposa-side wall filled the studio. Across Mariposa, a blank, ochre warehouse wall above the sidewalk filled his view. Looking to his left, there was a narrow view of Harrison Street and a railroad yard on its far side.

John looked up at the ceiling, the building's cast concrete roof, and saw where he would sleep. Suspended by chains at one end and fastened to the sheetrock and metal-stud wall at the other, a queen-size wooden platform and mattress hung just above his head. A crude wooden ladder led up.

That first night, though he needed sleep, he woke several times to the noise in the hallway from tenants returning from a night out drinking, and then noise from the railroad yard: one empty box car slamming into another — a jarring noise louder than anything he'd heard since the war.

*****

He planned to have breakfast in the morning where Karen had worked, and then drive her likely route to the Art Institute. When he approached his car, diamonds of tempered glass sparkled in the sun on the pavement and covered the driver's seat. Now he needed a new side window. Welcome to San Francisco.

John drove east down 16th Street to Karen's restaurant. Set on the waterfront, its sprawling deck outside offered him a postcard view of San Francisco Bay. He ate a decent Denver omelet, home fries, and thick buttered toast at a table made from an old wooden cable spool turned on its side.

After his coffee, John nodded to the waitress for his check. When the waitress arrived, John identified himself and asked for the manager. They both said Karen was a hard worker, reliable, and everyone liked her. Until, without notice, she didn't show up for work.

John left a large tip and Sandy's phone number in case they heard anything.

Returning along 16th Street, John noticed many trash heaps between one- and two-story industrial buildings, along with long-haired men with dirty faces picking through the piles.

The drive from the warehouse to the Art Institute was better, but John still saw panhandlers with sleeping bags on some sidewalks. Climbing Hyde Street, his tires squirmed back and forth on the iron cable car tracks set between History's rounded bricks. It was easier rolling down the flat bricks of twisty Lombard Street. Russian Hill near the Art Institute was beautiful. He could see how Karen would have been happy going to school here.

After finding a place to park on Leavenworth, John walked down Chestnut Street to the Art Institute entrance. The steep street strained his bad knee.

The Art Institute's raw concrete walls supported red clay tile roofs set at different angles and elevations. He stepped through the arched entrance into a courtyard surrounding a fountain encircled by a tile bench. He sat on the bench to rest his knee and watched people pass through the courtyard. In time, he found some students and a few teachers who knew Karen. They all liked Karen but hadn't seen her for weeks. One teacher warned that the Art Institute was very free and informal. "If you don't show up for class here, no one will look for you."

*****

Back in his sublet, John brewed some coffee and looked out his windows. Down on Mariposa, he saw a young woman sitting in the middle of the street, her head rolling around while she talked to the sky. John was about to go down to her when two young people arrived and talked to her. Whatever they said, she refused, shaking her head. Then she climbed into the bed of a pickup truck parked nearby and went to sleep. At least she was out of the street.

That night, his war dream returned. In the dream, as in his real Army service, John was a new intelligence officer working with a long-range reconnaissance patrol team. The dream tortured him in Illinois, long after he was safely out of Viet Nam and the Army. It had gradually faded from his nights and almost disappeared last year. He blamed its return on the new stress of losing his sister. After enduring the dream, he slept without further interruptions.

*****

The next morning, Sandy knocked on John's door. "Detective Madison is on the phone."

"Mr. Moss, it's a homicide case now. Assigned to me. The body we found — you won't have to identify her. We're sure it's your sister. I am sorry."

"Thank you. I hoped at first...but now, I'm not surprised. How are you sure?"

"Fingerprints. There were ample print samples in her studio. Soon we'll have dental records, too. She and her roommate used the same dentist.

"How? Please."

"It appears it happened a few days before her roommate reported her missing. Two weeks of decomposition destroyed some evidence. Small comfort, but, best we can tell, no sexual assault. But it was a violent attack, probably while she was on her bicycle. Broken bones suggest a fall. Knocked to the ground, beaten, then strangled. Hands, no ligature. Also burned. One hand was in direct flame for a time. Not our typical mugging."

After his stomach settled, John said, "Match any of your knowns?"

"No. They found her in an area used by transients and street people, an empty lot between 16th and 17th Street, near the freeway."

John realized he'd probably driven by her.

"A lot of trash there. The bicycle was bent up, stripped of some parts, and left hidden in weeds. She was under a mattress, half-clothed, no blue rain slicker. Some guy wanted the mattress and uncovered her."

"It feels like it's my fault. The last time I talked to her, she was happy, loved school, no hint of trouble."

"Mr. Moss, my Illinois cop said you know police work."

"It's John, please. What I know I learned in the Army in Viet Nam, in the Phoenix Program. For three years my Vietnamese counterparts and I were doing basic police work. I worked villages near the Cambodian border, interviewing witnesses, developing informants.

And I handled VC defectors."

"Why didn't you join a department when you got home?"

"I had our parents' house and my savings, along with the disability payments from the knee that never healed. I did work some, now and then. Someone would have a problem that didn't interest the local law enforcement enough, and I would help. They paid sometimes."

"PI license?"

"No. I thought about it."

"Well, if you hear anything or have any theories, I'll listen. Call me Ray."

"Thank you, Ray."

*****

John gave Sandy the bad news.

"I'm not surprised. I knew she wouldn't run away. But I still can't believe it. I expect her to walk through the door any minute. Everyone says that. Don't they?" Her eyes were tearing. Her voice cracked. "How do we deal with this?"

"Yes."

*****

That evening, John thought about what he'd told Ray Madison about his Army service.

What John didn't tell Madison was that he'd gone through Fort Bragg after OCS, the full slate of Special Forces courses, concentrating on intelligence. Then they sent him to Viet Nam to work for SOG. He worked with long-range reconnaissance teams near the Laos border, but on the forbidden far side, monitoring the Ho Chi Minh trail. He'd volunteered for the work, but later he wanted out.

The recon teams, a few American Special Forces enlisted men and Montagnard mercenaries, were special to John. A lieutenant then, John was older than the other team members. His few patrols in enemy territory both excited and terrified him. Because Laos was officially off-limits, the team members wore sterile uniforms and carried no identification or personal items. Were they caught, the U.S. government would deny their existence. Return to base, or rescue, depended on helicopter-friendly weather. Yet his younger team members were always alert, confident, and cheerful, as if the danger was manageable and there were no problems they could not solve. He often felt unworthy in their presence.

On his fourth and last patrol, an NVA hunter-killer team almost caught them. John did his job. They survived. The unit commander told John they had recommended him for a Bronze Star. John deflected the praise, saying the Army had trained him well, and then asked for a transfer. It would have been easy to say his knee wound forced the transfer — he could no longer hump an eighty-pound pack. With a bad knee, he could have stayed with the teams but remained back at base doing his intel work. Instead, he moved to the Phoenix Program.

*****

Late that night at the warehouse, John woke to someone screaming. It wasn't a cry for help, but a loud, high-pitched, intense argument, full of aggression and anger, fought out between two parts of the same person. The noise had started on Harrison, then continued up Mariposa. John sat up in his sleeping loft. Across Mariposa he could see the sidewalk along the blank warehouse wall, but the screamer had already disappeared around the corner onto Alabama Street, the volume of his screaming diminishing as he moved north. John tried to go back to sleep. What's next? Would he ever get a complete night's sleep?

*****

After they connected his phone, John called Ray Madison with his new number.

"Hey John, we got a guy, someone arrested for something else a few weeks ago. They finally told us he had your sister's wallet and ID. Said he found it in the street. That appears to be his only connection to her. He has a record of assaults, some sexual. The prosecutor wants to prepare a case if we can get more evidence. Perp says he didn't do it."

"What do you think?"

"I don't know. Your sister didn't have a boyfriend or enemies — my money's on a stranger. We have open cases on young women like your sister, six in the last few years. There is no pattern except for the victims being found near these transient camps."

"The number of transients here surprised me."

"We have too many potential perps on our streets. Many of our ex-cons wind up living on the street. To some extent, they are predictable, and we know who they are. The scary part is all the insane lulus we have on the street. It's a chicken-egg problem. Either they were nuts before they used drugs, or they went nuts because they used drugs. Either way, they're nut-jobs on drugs. Without a sexual assault, my instinct points to a nut-job."

"Then you'll grind it out, day-to-day. Police work."

"You do know, John."

*****

Waiting wasn't something John liked, but it was part of police work. While the police did what they could, John needed to do what he could. Even though he'd be working on his sister's murder, keeping busy would help him stay sane. He would start by re-interviewing the people he first questioned, and then the others he had seen while driving. John went downtown and purchased a Polaroid SX-70 with a case of film, and then a portable typewriter and paper to document his interviews. Interviewing and photographing the people was what he'd done in Viet Nam.

With all these people living on the street, one of them must have seen something. John had a photo he showed each subject while he asked the same questions. Sandy had taken the photo, Karen in her blue rain slicker standing next to her yellow bicycle.

When he showed them Karen's photo, the ones who recognized her usually smiled. A few seemed to recognize her but denied ever seeing her. One addled, near-mute old man put his finger on the blue rain slicker in the photo, but shook his head *NO* when asked about the coat. These few deniers looked around like they were afraid of someone watching them.

When people were helpful, John gave them Polaroid portraits and a few dollars. Many of them enjoyed watching their image come to life as the Polaroid developed. John took his notes and photos back to his sublet to type a dossier for his file, under whatever name they'd offered.

John did his interview work for two weeks while he waited for the police to find something he hadn't. Warehouse residents, drunks in the street, colliding box cars, and three more visits from the screamer interrupted John's sleep. Each time, the screamer turned the corner onto Alabama Street before John could see him. The man never stopped screaming. Lungs of a buffalo, John thought. On the screamer's last visit, John didn't sit up to see. He had lost any desire to see the screamer. The screamer was just another druggie with a fried brain.

*****

While Sandy helped John pack up some of Karen's things, he asked her again if there could have been anyone who argued with Karen or paid her too much attention.

"No... wait. There's this guy — I don't know his real name, but he wants people to call him Lucifer — he and Karen argued once. Lucifer took her bicycle. He returned it when she called him on it, but Karen was really pissed."

"Where can I find him?"

"Look up on the roof, in the garden. Lucifer used to crash there until we finally had a meeting about it, and the manager told him he had to leave. I forgot about him until I saw him in the building again this morning. He's scruffy, and has a big knife strapped to the front of his leg, where you can't miss it. People are afraid of him."

*****

John returned to his studio for his camera and hurried to the staircase. The stairs opened to the roof right over John's sublet. He didn't see anyone, but there was some structure on the roof at the far end.

Approaching quietly, John saw an assemblage of boxes, trellis, and potted plants — the garden. A wooden bench extended beyond a vine-covered trellis. Snoring and two feet in army boots stretched out on the bench said someone was at home. Though John had not yet found Jesus, he had found Lucifer. Flat on his back, he was scruffy, and the knife and sheath out front completed Sandy's description.

When John saw the knife, he knew Lucifer, the type. A phony.

Leather laces wrapped the knife and leather sheath around his right leg. A metal skull topped the knife's fat, leather-wrapped hilt. John bet the blade, although wide, was just under four inches long. Lucifer wanted to look scary to the young artists but didn't want to be hassled by the cops. A single-edge blade under four inches long in plain sight would pass as a legal tool.

John set his camera down and selected a potted plant. He stepped closer and put his knee into Lucifer's gut, then dumped the plant and its soil onto Lucifer's face. While Lucifer tried to wake and breathe through dirt, John snatched the knife from its sheath and pressed the tip of the three-and-a-half-inch-long blade into Lucifer's Adam's apple. Lucifer froze.

"What?"

"So, Luci, you like to scare people?"

"Who're you?"

"I hear you fought with my sister. You took her bicycle."

"Karen? You're her brother?"

"Less than before, because she's dead now. You killed her."

"Noooo! I didn't know. I been in L.A. for months. I just hitched back today." Sweat was forming streams and rivers that cut through the dirt on his face.

"Tell me."

"The knife?"

John backed the knife away but held it close, where Lucifer could see it.

"Been in L.A. County lockup until two days ago." He gave John his case number. "Paper's in my pocket."

"What happened in L.A.?"

"I was just tryin' to borry a six-pack from this mom-n-pop. I was good for it, but the man wasn't havin' it. Little Chinese guy. We wrassled, and I hit my head on somethin', woke up in the slammer with a felony-assault ticket. No O.R., no bail money, at least a month 'til my trial date. Just before my trial, I luck out. Somebody kills the little guy robbin' his store. No more witness — time served. Can I go now?"

John grimaced with disgust. "Wait. Don't move."

John lifted a watering pail and dumped it over Lucifer's face.

While Lucifer sputtered and spit, John opened his camera and took pictures for his files, both mug shots and a full-body showing the empty sheath laced to his leg.

"What about my knife?"

"Watch." John stepped to a plumbing vent stack and dropped the knife in. It clanked on the way down.

"Why?"

"To save you, Luci. If I saw you with a knife again, I'd have to take it. And if I saw it strapped to your leg, you might lose the leg."

"I wanna go."

"Good. The people here say they don't want to see you anymore. Don't come back."

*****

The days passed and blurred together for John, but his gut still twisted when he thought about his sister. Their father had fallen ill and died while John was in Viet Nam, their mother soon after he returned. John felt like he was Karen's parent. Now he was the last of the family.

In building his files, he'd encountered so many drug-damaged people. They made John think of Ray Madison's chicken-egg problem. He thought about all the sacrifice by good people in Viet Nam, to come home to this. He could only wonder what the nation's founders would think, today, the fourth of July, if they could see what had become of their work at the Bicentennial. Was it just a dream?

John took his file of street people interviews and photos down to the Hall of Justice and gave them to Ray Madison. "These might fill a few holes in your files. I'm returning to Illinois, at least until a trial. My sublet owner is due back, and I don't know what else I can do to help. I'm leaving it to the S.F.P.D., and then maybe a jury, to decide if you have Karen's killer."

"Thanks for the file, John. We'll do our best, and hope that will work. The Coroner's finished now. You can arrange for your sister's remains. If I don't see you again before you leave, take care. Keep in touch."

That evening, John climbed the ladder to his sleeping loft early. He wanted a good night's rest before starting his drive back home in the morning.

By this time he was almost used to the night noises in the warehouse and surrounding area. He fell into a dream-free deep sleep for several hours. Near four, his Laos dream returned.

The dream was always the same. The team had set up for the night in thick brush under a rock overhang, and John had the watch for the last two hours before they would wake.

Earlier in that day's patrolling, the team leader had selected this site for their overnight. As the light faded in the late afternoon, John had watched their Montagnard point man lead them back and forth, sometimes doubling back on their own trail, while the tail-end team member carefully cleaned their back-trail, removing any evidence of their presence, all to conceal the path to their overnight location. In the past, this would have been enough to keep them safe, but recently intel said the North Vietnamese had formed special sapper teams to track and capture or kill the American patrols. One complete team had vanished.

Besides staying awake when everyone else was asleep, John's task was to listen for any movement in the darkness and be ready to respond. Their location suited their needs because the only area that would allow attackers a direct path to the team was a space to the front between large boulders.

John set his pack against a small tree trunk and sat leaning against it. With his CAR-15 short rifle across his lap and spare magazines stacked at one side, John placed at his other side the clacker to the Claymore mines they had daisy-chained together to defend the boulder gap.

There was only a sliver of moon that night. John kept moving his eyes, trying to catch any change in what little he could see. He heard a slight rustling in the dry leaves that covered the ground. This could be anything: small animals, snakes, leeches. Even the leeches made noise, slowly advancing across the ground toward the smell of fresh meat. An hour passed.

Then John's eye caught a change in the darkness between the boulders. In a moment, he was sure. A shape advanced in concert with some leaf rustling. John froze, paralyzed with fear. No team member was so close that John could reach out and wake him. Saving or losing the team would be up to John alone. He rotated his rifle's selector from SAFE to AUTO.

While John was trying to decide which to use first, his rifle or the clacker, a large man stood up in the boulder gap. John could see him clearly. He was staring at John. Others stood behind him. It was the NVA hunter-killer team. The man looked pleased. He started laughing, a long, horrible, taunting laugh.

John heard some of his team members move, but they would be too late. The laughing changed to screaming when John emptied his first magazine, all red tracers, into the man and those beyond, then squeezed the clacker. The seven hundred pellets from each Claymore hit the NVA team. Some bounced back off the boulders. The un-godly screaming from the shredded NVA team was so loud John would hear it for years in his dreams. His own screams were almost as loud.

John and his now-awake team members emptied more magazines full-auto toward their attackers. They would stop only after there was no sign of life from the NVA hunter-killer team. They quickly checked each other for wounds and gathered their equipment. John's knee was hurting and bleeding from Claymore pellets bouncing back off the rocks, but, after some morphine, it wouldn't stiffen for a while.

After moving through the dark to a pre-designated landing zone, they waited for morning and helicopter evacuation. That's where the incident ended. But in the dream, John always woke during the attack, sweating and shaking, with the big man staring, laughing, and John screaming.

This last night in San Francisco, John again fought the dream, trying to stop it before the NVA team appeared. He knew it was just a dream, but he couldn't wake himself. He always knew what would happen in the dream, at each step before it happened. When the big NVA leader stood to taunt the team, John cringed, anticipating the laughing, and then screaming, but this time another sound did what John could not do. It stopped the dream.

John heard the screamer coming down Harrison Street. The full-volume, demented rant had overwritten John's Laos dream. Instead of sitting up in bed to look for the screamer, John covered his ears with a pillow. Thankful the dream had stopped, he rolled over to go back to sleep.

The screamer turned the corner into the dark canyon of Mariposa Street between the two warehouses, his random shrieks echoing off the walls. Moving up the sidewalk across Mariposa, the screamer shook his head and arms, punching the air with his right fist, screaming epithets and threats, while taking long strides uphill toward Alabama street. With each stride and punch, the tall man's long hair and flowing rags moved like kelp in ocean waves, and then re-conformed to cling to his body. Timed to each stride, he clicked the butane lighter in his left hand to shoot a two-foot-long orange flame straight up, past his filthy, contorted face, into the night above his head. The pulsing light from the flame painted his silhouette across the ochre warehouse wall behind him and reflected off the shiny blue vinyl rain slicker riding his shoulders.

The Florida Keys

John M. Floyd

Miami police officers Mason and Biggs stood at the edge of the beach behind the Fontainebleau Hilton, their suit jackets unbuttoned and their polished shoes buried up to the laces in the white sand. The desk clerk beside them looked around a moment, squinting and sweating in the noonday sun, then pointed to a bikinied woman on a lounge chair. Mason thanked him, and the clerk hurried back toward the hotel.

Biggs looked east, out over the vast blue Atlantic. "So this is how the other half lives," he said. Fifty feet away, the surf chased giggling children inland before receding again. Palm fronds rattled in the sea breeze.

Officer Mason didn't reply. He closed his eyes to the glare, listened to the kids's laughter, sniffed the sweet and memory-laden odor of sunscreen. Behind them, somebody splashed into the same pool that had appeared in one of the opening scenes of *Goldfinger*, more than fifty years ago. The thought made him feel old.

The two men exchanged a glance, then trudged across the sand to the lady the desk clerk had identified. Out of long habit they flashed their IDs and introduced themselves.

Roxanne Key was what Mason's wife would have called "voluptuous." That, he thought, would be an understatement. As if reading his mind, she tilted her head and studied him over the top of her sunshades. Her teased red hair looked as dry and stiff as cotton candy.

"You filed a complaint this morning?" Mason asked her.

"You bet I did. My ex-husband's trying to kill me."

Mason produced a notepad and flipped it open. "Dennis Key?"

"Old Skinny Denny," she agreed. "Yesterday he threatened me, last night he shot at me."

"Want to tell us about it?"

She sat up, squished sunblock into her palm, and slathered it onto her flat stomach with vigor. Her tiny swimsuit top managed to stay in place, but just barely. "I told you. He wants me either gone or dead. Or both, I guess."

"What exactly..." Biggs said, and cleared his throat. He seemed to be having trouble keeping his eyes on her face. "What exactly has he done?"

"For one thing, he pulled a gun on me, here at the hotel."

"When was this?" Mason asked.

"Late yesterday afternoon, six or so. I was laying here minding my own business, and all of a sudden this big shadow falls over me. He was standing right there, between me and the ocean." She pointed with her tube of sunscreen, and a quarter-sized glob squirted out onto the sand. "Dammit," she added.

"And what did he say?"

"Dennis? He didn't say nothing. He just aimed a gun at me."

Mason frowned. "Right here, on a public beach?"

"In front of God and everybody. Dennis wasn't never the smartest light in the chandelier." Roxanne Key pushed her sunglasses higher on her nose and gave Mason a long look. Every finger, he noticed, was adorned with at least one ring. "Ain't you boys hot, in suits and ties?"

"We're used to it," he said.

"You can pull your coats off, if you want to. Don't matter to me."

"We're fine, Ms. Key." Mason tapped his notepad with a fingernail. "Did you see anybody who could confirm this?"

"Confirm what?"

"The fact that your husband pointed a gun at you. You said 'in front of everybody.' You know of anyone else who saw him do it?"

She shrugged. "I wasn't exactly looking."

"What kind of gun was it?" Biggs asked.

"Revolver. That, I was looking at." Roxanne leaned back in her chair, picked up a cocktail glass from the little table beside the chair, drained it, and plunked it down again. "A thirty-eight, I think."

"You said the sun was in your eyes—"

"I said I was in his shadow."

"But you're positive it was him."

"It was him all right. I should know. He lives near here, by the way."

"And where do you live?"

"New Orleans, now. I'm a dancer." With a raised eyebrow she added, "A great dancer."

"I'm sure you are," Mason said. He glanced at Biggs, who blushed a little. "What happened then? After Mr. Key threatened you."

"He didn't actually threaten me."

"You don't consider a pointed gun to be threatening?"

"What I meant was, he didn't say nothing. I told you that."

"What did he do then?"

"He left." She spotted a distant waiter, waved, and shouted for another drink. He ignored her.

"And what about last night?"

"Last night I was almost killed, that's what. I was walking out of a nightclub, alone, and since trying to scare me off didn't work, he tried to murder me."

"Your husband?"

"Ex. Ain't that who we're talking about?"

"Anyone else see this?" Biggs asked.

"I said I was alone, didn't I? And it was late."

"What happened, exactly?"

"He shot at me." She raised a forefinger, shut her left eye, sighted past a ring the size of a doorknob, and squeezed an imaginary trigger.

"Shot at you?" Mason said.

"Twice. Missed me, though—Dennis never could do nothing right." She seemed to think that over. "Guess I'm lucky he can't, huh?"

"What happened then?"

"He turned around and run off."

Mason stayed quiet a moment, watching her fiddle with her earrings, which looked as big and heavy as billiard balls. He was beginning to wish he *had* taken off his suit jacket. Breeze or not, it had to be a hundred degrees out here.

"And you're absolutely sure it was Dennis Key?"

"I'm sure. Same gun, too—I seen it. I even seen two shell casings on the ground afterward."

"You pick them up?"

"No. But they was laying there in the street."

"No one heard the shots?"

"I doubt it. They was just spits, POOF, POOF, you know?"

"A silencer, you mean?" Mason asked.

She nodded. "Like this big"—she held her palms up, about a foot apart—"on the end of the gun."

"You're sure it was the same weapon?"

Another nod. A good thing, Mason thought; if she shook her head her earrings would probably knock her unconscious.

"How can you be positive?" he asked. "That it was the same gun, I mean."

"Because he was standing under a streetlight, the stupid idiot."

"I see." Mason scribbled a note in his book.

A minute passed. Gulls mewled overhead, the surf whooshed and whispered, someone laughed aloud from the direction of the poolside bar. In the silence, Roxanne Key absently adjusted her swimsuit top. Officer Biggs watched this with great intensity. Probably looking for clues, Mason thought. He almost smiled, but didn't; this was too crazy to be funny.

Mason focused again on Roxanne and the task at hand. "Can you think of any reason, Ms. Key, why your ex-husband might want to harm you? *Or* scare you off?"

She snorted. "Sure I can."

"What might that be?"

"Because he wants to keep our daughter for his own self." Roxanne picked up her empty glass and rattled her ice a moment, her face hardening.

"Your daughter?"

"Jacqueline. Dennis was granted custody a year ago. I want her back." She paused, as if pondering that. "And I'll get her back, too. A little girl's place is with her mama. Right?"

Mason didn't bother to answer that.

The questioning continued for several more minutes, but there was no more to be learned. Mason had already decided that if he were married to Roxanne Key, he'd probably try to kill her too. He thanked her, snapped his notepad shut, and told her they'd keep in touch.

"Just get me a waiter," she growled, as they left.

"I'll send one right over," Mason said.

They walked straight to their car.

*****

An hour later they located Dennis Key. He was an auto mechanic, and apparently off on Saturdays. When officers Mason and Biggs arrived at his home address, Key and a curly-haired little girl were sitting in cane-backed rockers and shelling butterbeans on the porch of a neat cottage on a two-lane road west of the city. An old pickup sat in the driveway looking tired, and a small vegetable garden was visible in the side yard. Palmettos and scrub growth bordered the well-kept lawn.

Both cops climbed out of their car and shrugged into their suit coats. Mason stood there a moment, looking everything over. No ocean breeze here, but somehow it still didn't seem as steamy as it had been at the beach. He took in the smell of the pineforest across the road and the watermelon-like scent of freshly cut grass.

He spotted a hawk perched high in the branches of a water oak. It appeared to be watching a pair of squirrels playing in the side yard of Key's home—but made no move toward them. They were a long way off, and fast, and had plenty of cover nearby. The hawk probably understood that the effort would be a waste of time. Mason knew the feeling.

"You okay, Chuck?" Biggs asked him.

"Just thinking," Mason said.

Both the man and the little girl stood up to greet the policemen. Dennis Key looked curious, Mason thought, but not worried. The child was introduced as his daughter Jacqueline. He explained that they hadn't seen or spoken to his ex-wife in some time, but that they would be doing both soon: Dennis had been told that Roxanne had flown in for a custody hearing on Monday.

"Can you account for your whereabouts yesterday afternoon, Mr. Key?" Mason asked. "And last night?"

"I was at work till five-fifteen or so, and right here from five-thirty on."

"Any witnesses to that?"

"My boss, at work. After that, well, Jackie had two of her school friends come over about that time, for supper and a Friday night sleepover. She and I drove 'em both home this morning, after breakfast." He paused, watching the cops' faces, then seemed to understand where this was headed. "What did Roxanne tell you?"

Mason shook his head. "It doesn't really matter, if you can prove you were where you said you were."

"You can find my boss at my workplace, and I'll give you the girls' names, and their parents'. And I paid the pizza delivery guy around six. There should be a record of that."

Mason handed his notebook and pen to Dennis, who jotted down the information and handed them back.

"Thanks. We'll check it out."

Dennis Key stared off into the hazy distance for a moment, then said, "She's a piece of work, Roxanne. I suppose you know that, if you spoke to her."

Neither officer made a reply. A small plane droned overhead. Somewhere in the marshes behind the house, a bird screamed. Mason glanced up to check on his hawk, but it was gone.

"She's about to remarry," Dennis said, as if to himself. "Some big shot from New Orleans." He looked up at them. "She's a dancer there, in the Quarter."

"What kind of dancer?" Biggs asked.

"Guess," Dennis said, rolling his eyes.

Mason put his notebook away. He could still feel the sand in his shoes. "One more question, Mr. Key. Do you own a gun?"

"Yep. Thirty-eight caliber revolver, Smith and Wesson—it was a gift from Roxanne, years ago. I think it's in my bedroom closet."

"I'll like to take a look."

Dennis blinked. "Don't you need a search warrant for that?"

Biggs gave Mason a look that said *Damn right we do.*

Mason shrugged. "I can get one, if you want."

"No need," Dennis said. "Follow me."

All of them trooped inside. The rooms were sparsely furnished but clean and tidy. The pistol, it turned out, was unloaded and still in its original box. No boxes of cartridges were in sight. After inspecting the gun, Mason knew it hadn't been fired recently—in fact he doubted it ever had been. Dennis Key confirmed that.

They had returned to the porch when little Jacqueline spoke up.

"Are you going to make me leave my daddy?" she asked.

Both officers looked at each other. Dennis seemed embarrassed. The child's eyes were wide and pleading.

After a long pause Mason leaned over to face Jacqueline, his hands propped on his knees. "From what we've seen and heard, young lady... I don't think you have anything to worry about." He looked up at Dennis Key. "You either."

As they returned to their cruiser, Biggs asked, "What's up with you, anyway? Did you get appointed judge, when I wasn't paying attention?"

"You're right about not paying attention," Mason said.

Biggs made a face. "Sorry—guess I've been a little preoccupied, lately."

"What you've been, is on your cell phone all the way over here."

"Gimme a break, okay? You got two sons. This wedding of our daughter's is going to put me in the poorhouse—"

"I'm just saying, while you've been yakking with your wife, I've been thinking." Mason paused with his hand on the driver's-side door and looked at his partner over the top of the car. "Her story stinks, Biggs. You realize that, right?"

"That business about silencers and shell casings, you mean?" Both of them knew—almost everyone knew, these days—that revolvers didn't work well with silencers, and also couldn't automatically eject spent rounds. Roxanne Key had probably watched just enough TV to get the facts wrong.

"That's part of it," Mason said. "And I figure she described the gun to us in detail because she knows Dennis owns one like that."

"She wants to incriminate him, you mean?"

"That's right. So she can get the daughter."

"Makes sense," Biggs said. "But what if she was just mistaken, about the gun?"

"She wasn't mistaken. Roxanne Key was lying from the start. I knew it as soon as she told us her ex-husband had visited her, on the beach behind the hotel."

"How do you figure that?" Biggs asked.

Mason climbed into the car and shut the door. When they were buckled in and the A/C was blowing full blast, he looked at Biggs and said, "Think about it. Dennis Key couldn't have been positioned where she said he was, at the beach. Not in late afternoon."

"Why not?"

"Because this is Miami, and the sun sets in the west, not over the Atlantic. She couldn't have been in his shadow if he was standing between her and the ocean."

Biggs thought that over, then nodded. "And if she lies once..."

"She'll lie again."

Mason backed out and pointed the cruiser toward town. Little Jacqueline waved at them from the porch, and Biggs smiled at her as they pulled away. "Think anything Roxanne told us was true?" he asked.

"Maybe one thing."

"What's that?"

For the first time today, Mason grinned. "I bet she's a great dancer."

Sweet Dreams Are Made of This

Kevin R. Tipple

"Sheriff?"

The FM radio, turned low, constantly fought with the annoying background static of the patrol car radio. But the voice of the day dispatcher, Sue Ellen, broke through.

"Max? Are you still in range?"

Sheriff Preston sighed. Sue Ellen being the sister of the town mayor, Jack Tailor, should have meant a quick approval of the repeated budgetary requests for new radios. But every year, for the last five years, it had come back as declined.

He turned off the FM, picked up the mic and said, "Go ahead, Sue Ellen."

"You're going to love this. Miss Graves over at the high school just called in and told me to tell you it's been exactly thirty-three minutes since she called the first time. So now she wants to know *exactly* when you'll be there."

Preston bit his bottom lip, suppressed a curse, and shook his head. Rachael Graves was a walking, talking, abomination in human form. Plain and simple. In fact, Preston was sure she'd be doing the world a favor if she could find the open pit to Hell that she'd crawled out of, and simply crawl back down into it again. Every week she managed to come up with yet another hoop for him to jump through, and there was nothing he could do to avoid the damn things.

Not that he could say any of that over the radio for everyone in the county to hear on their scanners.

Sue Ellen, having all the brains and the only working moral compass in her family, waited for him to respond.

He thumbed the button on the microphone. "I am headed there now,

Dispatch. ETA unknown, but believed to be around 20 to 25 minutes from now."

Sue Ellen came back with a giggle in her voice. "Those about to die, I salute you," and the radio went back to its usual hissing and spiting. It was the weather that screwed up the reception. Even though it was coming up to the evening, the heat was oppressive and just hung in the air, as antagonistic and provoking as a vagrant waiting to be moved on.

Preston put the 2012 Dodge Charger into drive, pressured the accelerator and started down Main Street, putting the reds and blues on so he could run through the red stoplights at each end. From there he picked up the two-lane Farm Market Road 790 that went by the old Thompson place south of town and the nearby almost-abandoned church. Thompson had built that church back in the 1950s in an effort to save his immortal soul. If even half the legendary exploits that Preston had heard about as a child were true, then no church on God's green earth could ever have had the power to save him. About five minutes later he turned onto the small visitor parking lot at the new high school.

Old Dooley High, home of the Fighting Bobcats—where Preston had toiled for four years in hot classrooms and on hotter athletic fields—was long gone, with nothing on the land to mark its passing. The new high school had the same name but none of the history, having been built a mile away from the old school, on the site where the overflow prison was supposed to have been. Looking at the new school complex, you could tell it had been built by the same contractors, using pretty much the same plans. Even from a distance as you approached it from either direction the three-storied, grey concrete and metal windowed monstrosity gave off an atmosphere of a high security prison building rather than a welcoming place of education. To put it bluntly, it had none of the charm or history of the original old Dooley High brick built buildings.

Preston turned off the engine and picked up the mic.

"Dispatch, this is Sheriff Preston."

"Go ahead."

He could hear the sunshine in her voice, which made him feel all the more depressed about his up-coming meeting with Miss Rachael Graves. "If you would kindly call ahead and let both Reception and Miss Graves know that I've arrived?"

"Consider it done. And don't forget to pack some garlic, just in case the sun goes down while you're still with her."

"And I thought it was just the kids who believed in vampire head teachers. I'll give you a call when I'm back on the road again."

Preston clipped the mic back on the dashboard, undid his seatbelt and turned slightly in the driver's seat. Bracing himself, he touched the toe of a dusty brown boot against the inside of the driver's door and pushed hard.

Six months earlier the Dodge had been involved in a confrontation with the McKenzie brothers, who had started brewing methamphetamine again. They had rammed their pickup into the side of the Dodge, just before their farmhouse had gone up in a massive chemical explosion. Where was the Hand of Darwin when you needed it to truncate an evolutionary line?

With a squeal, the recalcitrant door opened and allowed him to get out of the patrol car. Just like new communications equipment, they needed new patrol cars, and more of them, since one of the existing three was almost always in the shop. That, too, was going to have to wait until next year, if not longer.

Reaching down, he pulled out the secure weapons box from under the driver's seat, unlocked it and put his SIG P320 inside for safe keeping. The brilliant powers that be that run things at the State level had taken away a peace officer's legal right to carry guns on school campuses unless responding to an actual active shooter. Of course, that assumed nothing went sideways while the unarmed officer was on campus.

Pushing the door shut and trying to get his poker face on, he started the long walk to the main entrance — the late afternoon Texas sun glared off the side of the building, and reflected up from the paved sidewalk.

He hated these calls and he could feel himself starting to tense up before he'd even made it through the main entrance. They just wasted his time and the department's meager resources.

The whole point of him finally coming back home had been to avoid the big city hypocrisy and bureaucratic nonsense. He wanted to recapture the freedom he'd known as a boy. The space to breathe, and to rekindle the desire to help those who truly needed help. That was why he'd become a cop in the first place. That, and to try and get a part of him back that he'd so carelessly thrown away years ago when he'd left home without telling anyone. His family and hometown friends were mostly long gone, as was pretty much his town and everything he had grown up with. Nothing was like he remembered. Even the old Miller General Store where he used to buy comics and, as he got older, cheap paperbacks with lurid covers that hinted at forbidden delights within was empty and deserted — now just a shooting gallery for junkies and winos. Times had changed, and certainly not for the better, he thought as he pressed the door buzzer and waited for somebody to let him in.

Classes had ended at four and forty-five minutes later there wasn't a student in sight. No kids loitered around the building making plans — illicit or otherwise — for before or after the football game tonight. Freed from their daily confinement, the kids had fled to parts unknown, and he couldn't blame them since he would have run away as fast as he could every day, too.

Moments later the door lock buzzed like a pissed off hornet and Sheriff Preston walked inside.

Just like it had last month during the fake bomb threat, the place smelled antiseptic and sterile. Back when he was in school, a school smelled like a school. He wasn't sure what this place smelled like, but it wasn't a school.

The steel tips on the soles and heels of his boots made small ticking noises as he walked down the short white-tiled hall to the front office. Having left his sidearm safely locked in the patrol car, he was ready with his driver's license, which prim and proper Noreen Johnson, the late shift Receptionist, scanned into the sex offender database. Without looking up, Noreen said, "She's been expecting you." Then she looked back at the computer screen while he put his driving license back into his wallet.

Both silently waited for clearance to be returned before he would be allowed to venture further into the building on his call. His silver badge made no difference when it came to State rules. Very little did these days.

After a couple of minutes the computers over in Austin all agreed that he wasn't a pervert. Or, at least, not a registered pervert — though his ex-wife probably still felt he was one. He was sure she was really a succubus, so that most likely made them even.

Noreen tapped the keyboard, clicked the mouse several times, then tore off the resulting print off. She pushed it under the protective barrier and he picked up the white stick-on badge. It had his name and date of birth on it for all to see, along with his horrible driver's license picture.

Once he had it affixed properly on his shirt, he made his way through the functional labyrinth to Miss. Graves's classroom.

Unlike the overly cheery classrooms of his youth with posters and colorful pictures everywhere, Miss. Graves's classroom was more of the same sterile environment he had seen throughout the building. A poster listing at least twenty rules hung above her corner desk in a room devoid of color. The automatic blinds were down and locked, preventing the sun or any outside distraction to penetrate the austere surroundings. The woman herself sat primly behind her desk in a long sleeved, high-collar blue dress that would be stifling outside in the last of September heat. It would have also been perfect for a Sunday at church one hundred years ago. He figured she was in her mid-forties, but with her once-brown hair pulled severely back into a bun, steel grey eyes and no make-up, she looked older than she really was.

She refused to acknowledge his presence and purposely made him wait near her desk as if he was some misbehaving child. Not that he would have interrupted her anyway until she was finished. After a few seconds of scrutinizing a paper, she made a quick red mark on it— probably an F-minus—before looking up at him.

"Finally, Sheriff. I was wondering when you'd get here."

God, how he wanted to kill her.

"I got here as soon as I could, Miss. Graves."

"I'm sure you didn't, Sheriff Preston, considering how you voted in the last election."

The truth was, he hadn't hurried that much other than busting through those horribly timed and needless stoplights on Main Street. The new law was stupid and yet another example of things being passed in the guise of solving crime, but in reality he knew they never worked. Opening up voting records for scrutinizing by all a year ago certainly hadn't helped things, though it had made most folks vote when the election rolled around last November. Also made it harder for many to do what was right now that everyone knew how everybody else voted, thanks to the records being published in the local weekly paper.

He wasn't sure, but it looked like she was sneering at him. "You remember the recent incident involving James Wilson?"

She reached down and opened one of her desk drawers. With what looked like overly exaggerated distain, she took out five paperback books, arranged them in a pile on top of her desk, and closed the drawer.

"Do you know what these are, Sheriff?"

"No, ma'am, I do not."

"They are publications that have a damning and seditious effect on young minds, and as such they have no place in this, or any other place of learning." Then, with two fingers she plucked the top one from the pile and tossed it at Preston. It landed hard, flipped and skidded against his feet. Not the way to treat a book at all. Unguarded for a moment, his emotional glare at the schoolteacher stopped her from throwing any more at him.

She looked down at the remaining pile on her desk. "These books are why the Wilson boy did what he did. These are what corrupted his mind and encouraged him to shoot both of his parents. He gave these books to Peter Stevens to look after the night before he went on his killing spree. Personally I think you should arrest the Stevens boy as an accessory to the murders, but I'm also going to deal with him myself. The Wilson boy is your problem, and good riddance to that trash."

Preston knew that it wasn't any of the books that had caused Jimmy Wilson to finally snap. It was probably the fact that old man Wilson had regularly abused both Jimmy and his sister, Megan —both mentally and physically for years — that was the root cause of it all. The fact that their mother had done nothing to stop the abuse and had, so gossip said, even aided her husband on more than one occasion, did nothing to help break the systematic cycle. Put Graves into the mix and the kids didn't stand a chance.

The real cause might never be known, but as far as Miss Graves was concerned, it was all the fault of the books.

Preston felt the pain radiate across his back as he bent and picked the paperback off the floor. How much of it was his back and how much of it was the burdens of his job he didn't know. He tried to smooth the cover then added it to the other 4 and picked them off her desk.

As he turned to leave, he gave a quick look back, catching the bitter and judgmental spinster smiling contentedly. She was not a teacher. She was as evil as the deliberate misinterpretation of House Bill 3979, and there was not a damn thing he could do about the State's list of 'banned' books, or her.

As he reached the door, behind him she said, "I trust you know what to do, Sheriff, and that you will do the right thing. After all, you are sworn to uphold the law."

"Yes, ma'am, sadly I am." As he closed the door behind him, he didn't add that he felt that the law was one of many stupid laws which had been forcibly passed in the last year or so because of media induced hysteria. He was powerless to prevent such rampant bigotry and stupidity in the cause of Politics.

Noreen, still at her Receptionist post, glanced briefly at the 5 paperbacks he was carrying as he signed out.

"You taking home some reading, Sheriff?"

"Yeah, you could say that."

"Good for you. Reading expands the mind, I always say."

Back at the Dodge he climbed in, then carefully laid out all five paperbacks on the passenger seat. The covers were creased, spines worn and one had a yellow colored label seemingly placed to obscure part of a title. All had been repeatedly read, then passed on—maybe in an effort to understand why the 'adults' said they shouldn't read them. Replace 'shouldn't' with 'couldn't' and then burn them to be on the safe side.

He took the SIG from the lock box and clipped it back onto his belt, buckled up and then drove out of the Dooley High parking lot.

Picking up FM 790 again, he drove as if in a trance, lost in his thoughts and memories, until he decided to pull up alongside the old Thompson church. Despite the setting sun, the heat was still oppressive, and if anything it seemed more so as he stepped into the church itself.

Settling on one of the dark wood pews towards the front, he allowed his thoughts to take control once more. It had been a battered and dog-eared copy of *To Kill A Mocking Bird* that he'd found in a draw of his father's nightstand. He'd sneak into his parents' bedroom, 'borrow' the copy, and return it an hour or so later, having read a chapter or two. That book had awakened within him a love of reading and the written word, and their collection of jazz and blues records had also opened up a whole new world to the young Max Preston.

Now on the wrong side of fifty—born April '68, he was, according to Rachael Grave, "a product of the Summer of Lust"—it mentally hurt him to witness the bonfires and hysterical, ill-informed protests, seemingly manipulated by those who made it their policy to stand on the sidelines and observe their induced chaos. If anything was the work of the Devil....

He checked his watch. 8.10pm. His right hand went to the butt of his holstered SIG. Rachael Graves would no doubt have left Dooley High for the day by now. Still, there was always tomorrow.

Back in the Dodge he looked at the five battered paperbacks still on the passenger seat. Miss Graves could wait for another day. Time to go home and do some reading.

A Goldy Opportunity

Maddi Davidson

"Put the cash in the bag," Davy said. Since he wore a gorilla costume, the request came out as "Pud-da-ash-n-da-agg." Nevertheless, the balding, bespectacled clerk at Olaf's Liquor Store understood. He pulled a handful of bills from the till and dropped them into my proffered sack, his eyes never leaving the gun in Davy's hand.

Clarke, in the guise of the front half of a mangy horse—even though a horse's rear end might have been more appropriate—grabbed a bottle of whiskey off a shelf and we beat feet and hooves out the door. We ran three blocks through the cold air of an October night, autumn leaves whirling about, to where Clarke had left his ten-year-old Chevy Nova, a rust bucket on wheels.

I easily outpaced the others, but Davy called shotgun from a half a block behind me, so I when I reached the car, I dove into the back seat. Clarke and Davy jumped in the front and tore off their disguises. Clarke turned the key while I struggled with my gopher outfit, taken like the prop gun and other costumes from our high school drama club storeroom.

"My zipper's stuck!" I yelled.

"Get down! We're leaving!" Davy replied.

I did, but we didn't. The engine wouldn't turn over. Clarke pumped the pedal and tried the key again. The car responded with a series of rapid clicks. Sirens wailed in the distance.

"Battery's out of juice. Time to boogie on foot," Clarke said.

"My zipper's still stuck."

"We have to go, Bobby! Now!" Davy jumped out of the car, opened the back door, and dragged me off the seat. I saw Clarke already high-tailing it, whiskey bottle in hand.

Halfway along the block, Davy directed us into a narrow alley. "Climb in," he said to me, pointing at a battered aluminum trash can. "You're too conspicuous. We'll carry you until we get near the U."

We dumped out the rancid garbage and I clambered in. The whiskey bottle followed. Moments later, Davy and Clarke, each holding a handle, were huffing and puffing. A junior in high school, I hadn't hit my growth spurt yet and weighed a mere 137 pounds, but neither of my companions, high school seniors, had ever bench pressed more than a 12-oz can of beer.

The pervasive stench of sour milk made me nauseous. "Let me out! I need fresh air," I bellowed.

"Shut the hell up!" they responded in unison.

We turned a corner and the traffic noise grew louder.

I heard a baritone voice ring out. "Hey, what are you kids doing?"

"Uh, we're taking out the trash," Clarke replied.

"On a Saturday night?"

"It's a fraternity hazing thing," Davy added. "We're new pledges."

"Stupid frats," came the reply.

A few moments later we crossed what sounded like a busy street. Clarke tripped over the curb on the far side and we all toppled over.

My memory is a bit spotty, but I recall lying on my back with my head throbbing, gazing at a looming red wall reaching to the dark sky. I lay at the base of The Brick House, also known as the University of Minnesota's Memorial Stadium.

I rolled over and pushed myself to my feet, waving like a willow in a stiff breeze.

"You okay?" Clarke asked.

"Bit dizzy," I mumbled.

"We don't have time for this." Davy grabbed me and pushed me back against the brick wall for support. He said something about the cops looking for three guys and we should go our separate ways.

"Okay," I replied, hoping my world would stop spinning.

Clarke mentioned dividing the cash.

"Okay," I said again.

Belatedly, I realized Davy and Clarke were insisting I produce the dough.

"I don't have it." At least, I didn't think I did.

"You had the bag in the store," Clarke said. "Davy, look in the trash can. Bobby, check your pockets."

I put my paws where pants pockets should be. Nothing. I closed my eyes, hoping the vertigo would pass and heard Davy reporting the cash was not in the can. I had a vague recollection of placing the paper bag on the floor in the back seat. Damn.

"Do you know that Gophers don't have pockets?" I said. "They have pouches."

"Check your GD pouch, then," Clarke responded.

I snickered. "Gopher's pouches are in their cheeks," I waggled my rear end. "Not these. The ones by the nose."

In my defense, I'd sought a bit of Dutch courage before the heist, draining a couple, maybe three, Hamm's beers on an empty stomach.

"I bet he left the cash in the car," Davy said. "I'll hustle back and get the bag. You stay here with Goofball."

Although Davy and Clarke had pulled off several small crimes, this was my first time. I could tell they rued having persuaded me to join in. Even now, years later, I don't know why I agreed.

I slid down the wall to a sitting position.

Clarke removed the cap on the whiskey bottle, took a swig, and spit the stuff out. "Jee-zus, this tastes like cough syrup. Want some?"

I shook my head. Big mistake. When the dizziness subsided, I realized two Minnesota coeds were standing over me.

"Hi, beautifuls," I said.

"What's the matter with Goldy Gopher?" said a vision of loveliness, mistaking me for the University of Minnesota mascot. She had long bare legs leading to a miniskirt—how do girls in short skirts not freeze their – ah – assets off? Above were all the right curves and, low and behold, long, chocolate hair—brunettes were a rarity in this land of Scandinavians, dontcha know. I wondered for a moment if I were hallucinating.

"He's blitzed," Clarke responded, no doubt thinking that would cover any strange behavior I might exhibit.

"Poor thing! Such a tough loss to Michigan, but I think you looked good, Goldy," the girl said. "I loved your dance moves with the marching band. By the way, I'm Gail." She nodded at her companion, a short, tubby blond. "This is Diane."

Behind the costume's buck-toothed grin, I leered.

My next fuzzy recollection is being sprawled on a lumpy sofa while around me college students were dancing, drinking, smoking, and making out. Clarke told me later he became concerned when Davy didn't return and left to check on him. A U.S. Marine wouldn't leave a man behind, but then, Clarke could not be considered military material, nor even high school material. His poor attendance and even worse academic performance guaranteed he wouldn't graduate without repeating a year.

Gail had dragged me to an open kegger hosted by Epsilon Delta fraternity—I never gave a second thought about what happened to Diane. Gail cuddled under my right arm, stroking my chest, ears, and nose, and cooing about my soft paws. She had to yell in my ear to be heard over the pounding, big brass music of Chicago. From time to time someone would offer me a brewski. Equipped with but a tiny breathing hole in my costume, I couldn't indulge. Gail, however, eager to quench her thirst, soon became schnockered. She kissed me, or rather the gopher mask, more than a few times.

With "Feeling Stronger Every Day," blasting through the speakers, two of the frat brothers asked Gail and me to move. They wanted to carry the couch to another room, freeing up more space for dancing. I struggled to a vertical position and almost keeled over.

"C'mon Goldy," one of guys said. "I'll help you to your room."

My room? Goldy, an Ep-Delt?

The brothers half-carried me up a flight of stairs and into a decent-sized room with clothes strewn on the floor. The matching desks, pushed together with a small refrigerator underneath, were covered with open bottles of booze. Empty beer cans crowded a set of shelves, with few books to be seen.

I collapsed on one of the beds.

If I could get the damn head off, I could down a beer, or two, and take a nap.

Gail, who had followed us, stood looking at me.

"Don't take off your costume," she said. "I've never made love to a gopher before." She began gyrating to the beat of the music thumping through the walls. Undoing the back zipper of her skirt, she let the garment fall to the floor, revealing a black thong. Crossing her arms at her waist, she did the maneuver only girls can do: pulling her sweater up by the front and over her head to reveal a black bra.

At least, I think she did. In any event, the memory, real or imagined, is a pleasurable one.

The door burst open, destroying my fantasy. A young man my size stepped into the room.

"What's going on here?"

Gail squeaked, and grabbed her sweater, clutching it to her chest.

The student pointed at me. "You're an imposter! I'm the real Goldy Gopher!"

Did I imagine he had buck teeth? He started toward me and I raised my paws in a placating gesture. "Jeez, man. Stay cool."

The odds of taking him in a fight were good. I'd won a few bouts with my fists and numerous wrestling matches at the much lighter weight of 103 pounds. Lurching to my feet I nearly fell over. Shit. Change in plans: better to run than fight.

I staggered to the window, which was half open to accommodate a cage housing a small rodent. Removing the cage, I tossed it aside, eliciting a loud protest from the other Goldy and another squeak from Gail, not to mention a squeal from the captive rodent. Half diving and half tumbling out the window, I landed in the evergreen bushes ringing the frat house. After fighting my way out of the bushes, I took off at a half-run without glancing back to see if anyone had been stupid or drunk enough to jump out after me.

Weaving my way across the unfamiliar campus, I ran into a pack of streakers and knocked one poor guy off his feet—I bet *that* hurt. Eighty to a hundred naked men and women were running through the quad, droves of students cheering them on. Of course I stopped to watch. Observing the spectacle far surpassed ogling the dog-eared *Playboy* magazines that Clarke purloined from his older brother. I would have followed the procession, but I still felt light-headed. So much so that I dropped onto one knee.

"You okay, pal?" said a distance voice. "Let me help you."

Someone started messing with my neck and, low and behold, succeeded in zipping the gopher head off. With an influx of fresh, cool air, I felt much, much better. My Good Samaritan lifted his camera and took a flash picture.

"Thanks, Goldy. This will be a photo for the *Daily*."

Before I could protest, he took off.

With the head off, I secured a better grip on the body zipper and slipped out of the costume. I found my way back to the Brick House, but saw no signs of Clarke, Davy, or a dilapidated Nova. Hopping a bus for home. I reached my neighborhood past midnight. This wasn't a problem since Dad worked the night shift and Mom hadn't been home for twelve years. No one ever cared about where I went or what I did. Except that night. Two cops were waiting for me as I strolled up to my front door with the rolled-up gopher costume tucked under my arm.

Police responding to the robbery at Olaf's had noticed Clarke's car; he'd parked in front of a fire hydrant, the dumbass. When the cops spotted the discarded costumes and a few bills hanging out of a paper bag, our fates were sealed. The police waited in an unmarked vehicle for the miscreants to return for the money.

Davy and Clarke had been carted off to jail and confessed all, including my participation. So much for honor among thieves. Not yet eighteen, I avoided joining my older partners in crime and spent the night in juvenile detention, dreaming of what might have happened with Gail had not the real Goldy showed up.

Our ill-fated caper was embarrassing in many ways, including the meagre haul—Olaf's clerks were trained to hide the larger denomination bills under the cash tray. Our total heist amounted to less than one hundred dollars, enough to buy each of us a few 6-packs of beer, but not much more.

Since I had no priors, the cops released me with a warning. However, a report of the streaking incident ran in the next issue of the *Daily*, the Minnesota student newspaper. Included were several photos, including "Goldy enjoying the show" and "Goldy disrobing to join the chase."

The apoplectic UM administration demanded Goldy be punished for violating the mascot code of conduct. The photo of me kneeling did not match any of the students who acted as Goldy, but in time the investigation led to my doorstep. With the revelation of my guilt, I gained a certain notoriety among both my high school classmates— "Way to go, Bobby!"—and UM officials—"Stay off our campus."

Awakened to the attractions of college girls, the wrath of my father, and the dismal conditions of juvenile detention, I began to apply myself academically. After completing high school and two years at a junior college, I enrolled at the University of Minnesota—evidently, the admissions office did not connect me with the three-year-old streaking incident. I joined the UM Spirit Squad and, having grown a few inches since high school, had the opportunity to dress as Goldy for numerous sporting events. Gail had long since graduated, but I discovered quite a few girls were hot for gophers, and not just for their oversized teeth.

Davy and Clarke didn't fare as well: neither graduated high school nor secured a decent job. I ran into Clarke one summer and found him a pitiful shell of his prior third-rate self.

The adage states, "crime doesn't pay." However, my experience proves that crime can hand you a Goldy opportunity. If it does, go for it.

Fort Kent Public

Michael Grimala

The Auburndale Public Library was a modern building, all windows and natural sunlight, but there still remained crevices that provided adequate shade. That's where I usually set up, at the far end of the row of study desks against the back wall. A semi-private area where it wasn't so bright.

It also allowed a wide view of the rest of the floor. Auburndale was a small town, but its well-stocked, one-story library served as a point of pride. Not many people seemed to realize it, but the ones who came every day, like me—the regulars—they knew what they had.

And yet, I didn't notice her come in. I should have. I knew the place like the back of my hand, and she was no common occurrence. I have no idea how long she had been there in the aisles, operating under my radar, before she finally caught my eye by pulling up a chair under the giant picture window that took up nearly the entire wall. She thumbed through a book for a moment, then stood and slung a purse low over her hip. She pushed in her chair, careful to do it quietly, and walked out through the reception area.

As she went through the front doors, she looked back over her shoulder at me. Or in my general direction. I couldn't quite tell. Then she was gone into the daylight.

I could have stayed at my desk and continued reading, like any other day, but after recovering from the strange woman's stunning exit I noticed she had left a large hardcover book on the vacated table.

The book couldn't have been more boring. A World Encyclopedia volume, apparently from the seventies. Eager to do a good deed even in her absence, I hoisted the heavy thing and lugged it back to the reference section.

The library had two sets of encyclopedias, and they were both Britannica. And they were all in place. Every volume, shelves full. That left nowhere to put her shabby World Encyclopedia.

I brought it to the front desk and set it down for the clerk.

"I don't know where this goes."

"Reference section," the college-aged boy said, barely looking up.

"I tried there. You've got a different set of encyclopedias on the shelves. Maybe this belongs to an old set you keep somewhere else in the library?"

"The only encyclopedias we carry are out there. If we had any extras we would have sold them. They don't exactly get much use these days, you know? Not much need for a backup."

"So where did this come from?"

The clerk let out a slight huff and cracked open the front cover.

"It looks like this guy belongs to the Providence Public Library. Main branch." He raised an eyebrow. "Why'd you bring it all the way here?"

"My mistake." I gathered the book and left.

It stayed on my kitchen counter overnight as I pretended not to think about it, or her. But with internet access and cable television long gone from my apartment (too expensive for a man six months between jobs), there remained little else to occupy my mind. My options were to read a book or wonder about the encyclopedia woman.

In the morning I drove to Providence. It's extraordinary the lengths you'll go to when you don't have anywhere to be.

The Providence main branch stood three stories high, and a quick stop at the layout placard put the reference section on the top floor. I trudged up the open stairs and found the correct, matching encyclopedia set displayed on a low shelf in the reference section. Sure enough, there was a hole where the Ma-Mt volume belonged. I crouched down and slid the book in its place and felt satisfaction in doing so.

When I stood, her face appeared over the horizon of the stairwell. As she ascended the steps, her shoulders came into view, then her yellow dress, then her legs, and finally her white shoes.

The entire floor, empty except for the two of us.

"Excuse me, sir," she said, "did you just return my book for me?"

"I think so. If someone wants to study Mars, Mickey Mantle or Missouri, I think they're okay now."

She smiled but didn't laugh. The smile was just as good, as far as I was concerned.

"That was very nice of you. Are you a library cop?"

"That's a real thing," I said. "Library cops take their jobs very seriously. And you shouldn't say anything else until your library lawyer gets here."

No smile, but she continued to move closer.

"Did I leave it in Auburndale?" she said.

"Yeah, my home library."

"And you came all this way. To do something good for me."

Having run out of things to say, I turned up my palms.

"Listen, thank you so much," she said, pulling a slip of paper from her purse. "I've got to run. But here's a number where you can reach me."

She lifted a pen from a nearby counter and jotted while I stood there trying not to shake. She folded the paper and wrapped my fingers around it for me.

"Thursday afternoon," she said. And before I could respond she bounded down the stairs. She didn't look back this time, but I didn't want her to—I didn't think I could survive that.

I rubbed the paper between my fingers to make sure it was real, then unfolded it to find a strange jumble of digits that in no way resembled a phone number.

A bead of sweat rolled down my forehead and splashed onto the brown carpet. I couldn't blame her—she wanted to thank me for my "good deed," but she didn't actually want to see me again, so that was her way of exiting the situation gracefully. No harm, no foul.

I stayed on the third floor for a few minutes to collect myself, then made my way down. As I passed the non-fiction section on the second floor, the aisle markers gave it away. Her digits weren't so random after all.

On the first floor I plunked myself down at one of the computer stations and accessed the library's online catalog. I clicked on the search bar and carefully typed in her number—a Dewey decimal number, now so obvious—and it returned one hit: "An Illustrated History of Magic in Europe and North America," some type of reference guide for stage magicians published around the turn of the twentieth century. I had no idea what significance it carried.

The book was not currently in stock at Providence Public.

It took another twenty minutes of wider library searches before I found the only place in all of New England that seemed to carry that title. A satellite branch of the Worcester Public Library, a good ninety-minute drive from where I stood.

Two days later I skipped my Thursday book circle at the Auburndale library (I also belonged to Monday and Sunday groups) and made the trek to Worcester. I found the satellite branch in a state of disrepair; the faux-Roman columns in front of the building were crumbling, leaving clumps of plaster scattered across the steps. The parking lot was empty. The entire city block appeared to be empty.

It was a small space, and maybe the most cluttered confines I'd ever seen for a library. The pleasant woman behind the checkout desk picked up her head and waved at me, probably just glad to have company.

I maneuvered through the stacks, looking for the section that contained my book. I turned left down a small corridor of shelves, and when I reached the end she was there, just around the corner, waiting for me.

She stood just outside the aisle, reading through a grey hardcover book: "An Illustrated History of Magic in Europe and North America."

"Did you come here because you're a good guy, too?" she said.

"You may have overstated my innate goodness the other day."

She turned the book to me and placed it in my hands.

"Did you know this was printed more than a hundred and twenty years ago?"

"I did," I said.

"And did you know that this is a first edition?"

"No, but it wouldn't surprise me. I don't think this library has acquired anything new since all those people were getting murdered on the Orient Express."

"There's only one murder on the Orient Express."

"That explains the title, then."

We talked in hushed tones for a while. Her name was Elizabeth, she said, and she came from California. She was a student, or had been, and was now wandering the east coast on summer break. She didn't strike me as the student type, but then again people often mistook me for a professor during my college days, so what did I know about style?

"What do you do for work?" she said.

"I'm unemployed." Might as well rip off that Band-Aid right away.

"That makes sense then. Why you would spend so much time in places like this, I mean."

"Why the big game?" I said. "Is this some kind of human experiment? Am I a hamster in a maze?"

"No, nothing like that. I just want to like someone before I meet them. It's easier that way."

I tried to think of something witty to say, but before that happened she put one arm around my shoulder, then the other. She clasped her hands behind my neck and brought her body close to mine, until the book was pressed between us. For the first time in decades, "An Illustrated History of Magic in Europe and North America" was getting some action.

"Do you like Evelyn Clay?" Elizabeth said.

"I do. A lot. How did you know that?"

"Just a guess. Is she your favorite author?"

"She is," I said. It wasn't exactly true, but she was close enough.

"Do something for me," Elizabeth said. "Take this book."

"The magic book?"

She nodded, once.

"I don't have a card for this place," I said. "I live a hundred miles away. I only came here for..." I trailed off.

"I don't mean check it out. I mean take it."

"As in, steal it?"

"No, not 'steal it.' Abscond with it, maybe."

I'm not going to lie, the idea intrigued me. I don't know why. Not just because of the way she traced her finger along the nape of my neck at that moment. I wish I could say it was.

"It's an old library," she continued. "No one has checked out this book in years. No one even realizes it's here. And it's worth money."

"How much?" The question was crass, and it sounded ugly as I said it. The money wasn't the point.

"In good condition, it would sell for three-thousand dollars. This copy doesn't have its dust jacket, though, so maybe five or six hundred. You wouldn't believe how many libraries carry valuable books like this without even realizing it."

I already knew I was going to do it. I had only stolen once before in my life—I helped myself to a fifty-dollar gift card off my boss's desk one night after hours—and the potential reward for that long-ago indiscretion wasn't nearly as great as the opportunity Elizabeth had put in front of me.

"How?" I said.

Elizabeth's lip curled up in a smile.

"You just walk right out the front door with it."

"What? Are you serious?"

"I'm completely serious. This place? No problem."

"They've got detectors at the door," I said. "The alarm will go off. I've seen it before." I spent a lot of time in libraries, and people stole books. Or tried to. Mostly kids. And they got caught. Modern technology allowed libraries to put a chip in the bindings of books that would set off the detector unless it was deactivated by the checkout clerk. That was a standard security measure. Even a run-down place like this would have a system.

"Trust me," Elizabeth said. And I did.

I tucked the book under my arm, in plain sight, and we walked toward the door. The lady at the desk barely glanced as we passed. Without breaking stride, we stepped across the threshold of the security gate.

The alarm sounded so loudly, it's a surprise the fire department didn't show up.

"Excuse me!" the clerk shouted over the noise. "That book—is that one of ours?"

I looked to Elizabeth and she shot me a shrugged expression that said *I'm really sorry, but you're on your own.*

I turned back to the clerk and feigned confusion.

"Oh, shoot. I forgot I was even carrying it. I've been flipping through it for half an hour. My mistake."

"Mhm," the clerk said. She reached under the desk and turned off the alarm. I walked back to the checkout counter. Sheepish doesn't begin to describe it. Elizabeth continued outside, either to wait for me or to leave me behind forever.

"Would you like me to put it back?" I said.

"That's okay," the clerk said. "Just leave it and I'll take care of it." I placed the book on the desk. "Are you a member? Would you like to register?"

"No, thank you. I'm not from around here, so I'm afraid it wouldn't do me much good."

"Well I'm sorry to hear that," she said as she snatched the book and stuck it in a mobile bin behind her.

Elizabeth did wait for me. She leaned against my car as I made my defeated way down the steps and through the parking lot.

"'Trust me,'" I said in my most mocking tone, but really I was ecstatic she hadn't left. "Turns out the mysterious library woman is no master thief."

"Do you still trust me?"

"About as much as I trust this place to collect a late fee from Whitey Bulger."

I got in the car and she slid into the passenger seat without waiting for an invitation.

A book dropped onto my lap.

It was face down. I turned it over. A copy of "The Morning Carnival," by Evelyn Clay. I knew it was a first edition without even inspecting it. Her debut novel, written in the forties, only had one printing.

Rare.

Valuable.

"Did you set me up?" I said.

"It's more believable if you actually think you've been caught red-handed."

"So both books set off the alarm. I return the dummy book, you slip out with the real prize."

"Do you like it?"

"I like it," I said, turning over the Clay in my hands. Honestly, I loved it. "How much is it worth?"

"It doesn't matter. We're not selling it. It's yours to keep."

I thanked her and then it was time to flee the scene.

"Where's your car?" I said.

"I don't have one."

"How did you get here?"

"Just turn out of the lot there."

I did as she said and piloted us through several blocks of the barren city. It felt even more desolate as dusk quickly gave way to night. We stopped at a red light and Elizabeth leaned over to flip on my turn signal. I looked left to discover that her suggested route would lead to the Miss Worcester Motel, a small, dark, dingy place where the parking area lay enclosed behind a barbed-wire fence. The windows were barred.

I raised my eyebrows at Elizabeth.

"It's getting late," she said. "It would be a long drive home for you."

I pulled in and booked a room. I used cash.

In the morning she was gone. I had kind of expected it, and I slept lightly because of it. Still, she had managed to rise without stirring me. Aside from my clothes strewn about the floor, there was no sign Elizabeth had even been there.

A woman who could enter and exit without making a ripple.

At least she left a note on the nightstand. Still lying down, I reached over to grab it and reclined back against the ice-cold headboard. It wasn't a note, but a card from the Worcester library's old-fashioned card catalog. The entry for "The Morning Carnival." Elizabeth had pocketed that as well, and for a small library like that, the card might have been the only evidence they had ever carried the book in the first place. It was mine now, free and clear.

I returned to Auburndale and resumed my daily routine. I displayed "The Morning Carnival" in a prominent spot on my bookshelf at home. It looked proper. For a few weeks, anyway. When I looked at it, I saw Elizabeth. Her yellow dress, her arms around my neck and the Miss Worcester Motel. Then my thoughts always turned to the way she left, without a sound.

Eventually I didn't like thinking about it anymore.

I couldn't take "The Morning Carnival" off the shelf, though, and I had no way of contacting Elizabeth. Every time the Auburndale library's automatic doors swooshed open, I looked up. It was always the senior center's Monday outing, or the Thursday book circle, or a couple of teenagers looking to complete their summer reading assignments. By the time the leaves changed I had given up on ever seeing her again.

But that book stared at me from the shelf. After Halloween I decided to do some research.

I monopolized a computer lab at Auburndale Public for a full week, open to close. I made a list of every library in New England; across the six states there were one-thousand, three hundred and thirty-five physical locations.

I pored over each of their websites—the ones that had websites; some required phone calls—and identified the branches that, in this day and age, lacked online catalogues. There were four.

Barton Public in Vermont was closed for renovations, and Lanesborough Public in Massachusetts was in the process of digitizing. Worcester Public, well, she had already hit that location. That left one: Fort Kent Public, at the very northern tip of Maine.

It was a twelve-hour drive and I didn't mind it one bit. I didn't have anywhere else to be.

For the next ten days, I parked across the street from Fort Kent Public and observed.

On the eleventh day she nudged me awake around nine-thirty. I had dozed off during my stakeout. I was bleary but quickly gained my bearings as she ducked in through the passenger door and joined me.

"You know what would be nice?" I said. "Coffee, a donut, and you telling me why we're at the freaking North Pole."

"Just wait until you see it. It's incredible."

That's it. After all the work I had done to narrow down her potential targets, after all the hours I had put into tracking her across multiple states, I didn't ask any of the questions I really wanted to. And she wasn't offering.

I ferried us across the street to the library and parked close to the entrance. It wouldn't be fair to call the Fort Kent Public Library a building. It was a house. An old-fashioned wooden porch led to the door.

As we made our way inside I couldn't help but notice a road sign indicating that the Canadian border was less than a mile in that direction.

A gruff-looking older man in a dark sweater manned the checkout counter, which was really more of an individual checkout desk. Beyond him, the interior was cramped; stacks and aisles ominously close together, coming together at odd angles to create a byzantine layout.

Everything appeared to be analog, except for the scanner inside the front door. Even Fort Kent had the standard security system.

Elizabeth smiled at the clerk and led me toward the fiction stacks. We left the clerk's view and turned down one of the aisles. With no hesitation Elizabeth pulled down a hardcover book. She gently offered it to me. "The Cold and Crowded Night," by M. John Terry. An American classic I had never read.

"Can you believe it?" Elizabeth said in a low, dry voice. "This place can't have more than a couple thousand books, total, and one of them is a first edition M. John. With a perfect jacket."

"It's worth a lot?"

"In that condition? Six figures, kid. Easy."

It should have sent an electric charge through my body, but it didn't.

"Does this even have a chip in it? Do we have to do the ruse? You could just take it."

"It's a magnetic strip in the spine," she said. "I can take it out, no problem. It'll be good as new. I just can't do it here. It has to be done carefully. I need my tools."

"Why not just check it out and not return it?"

"A sale this big?" Elizabeth said. "If we take it to auction, or even a private buyer, we can't risk having a checked-out book on the records anywhere. Trust me, I know."

"Then pay some kid twenty bucks to do a smash-and-grab for you. There are so many easier ways."

"It's got to be you and me."

She touched the book's cover, running her fingers along the edges.

"Fort Kent Public has had this book since the twenties and it's completely buried here," she said. "It's not doing any good for anyone. Look at that jacket—it might be mint condition. No one has ever read this copy and no one in this town is going to read it. I doubt it's ever been *opened*. But for us, it could change everything. A new life."

Her mind was made up, and so mine was, too.

"Did you take the catalog card?" I said.

"I'll do it now. Grab another book and prepare to get caught."

Elizabeth got up on her toes and kissed me on the cheek before heading to the card drawers.

I walked among the stacks, staying out of view of the clerk. I was cold, exhausted and in need of a shower.

In the next aisle over I pulled down a book with the same dimensions as our prize. "The Edge of Running Water," by William Sloane was going to serve as our dummy book.

I met Elizabeth back at the original spot and without saying a word she slipped "The Cold and Crowded Night" into her purse. I carried the dummy book in plain sight and we made for the door, hand in hand.

The alarm triggered.

"Hey!" the clerk shouted. "Whatcha got there?"

I feigned surprise and confusion.

"I'm sorry, I completely forgot about this. Didn't even realize I was still carrying it."

"You trying to get away with something?" he said. "Bring it here."

"I'll be outside, honey," Elizabeth said. She squeezed my arm and was gone.

I brought the book back to the desk.

"My apologies. I just forgot to put it back."

"You from Fort Kent?"

"Yes sir."

"You got a card?"

"No, I'm afraid not. I'm on vacation and just trying to find a good book to read before it's back to work."

"Egh," he said, pushing a sheet of paper across the counter. "You'll have to fill this out if you want to rent a book."

It was a rudimentary library card application. I filled it out with a fake name and a fake address. The clerk didn't ask for identification or verification, just took my word for it.

"Card will come in the mail. Book's due in two weeks."

He shoved "The Edge of Running Water" into my gut and let me on my way.

I stepped out into the brightening daylight and was not surprised to find the parking lot empty. My car was gone. I didn't even have to pat my front pocket; I knew my keys weren't in there. That little kiss on the cheek.

I walked along the edge of the lot to a small duck pond behind the library. I sat on a bench and rotated my ankles until they cracked.

From my vantage point, the sign was in plain view: Canada, one mile. It was almost too perfect.

I decided to give Elizabeth fifteen minutes to change her mind and come back. When that time elapsed, as expected, I cracked open my book.

The cover—the dust jacket cover—was "The Edge of Running Water," but inside I had a pristine copy of "The Cold and Crowded

Night." I switched the jackets while Elizabeth pilfered the card catalog. If she hadn't noticed by now, she probably wouldn't notice until she stopped to hole up at the Miss Canada Motel, alone.

I affixed a note to the mismatched book/jacket combo, helpfully pointing out the rarity of an M. John Terry first edition (even *sans* jacket), and dropped it in the library's return box. I walked to a nearby bus stop. Three exchanges later I was on a southbound train, alternating between uneasy sleep and a splitting headache.

I supposed the racket could be lucrative—there were libraries out there, unaware of the treasures they possessed—but surely there were easier ways to steal free books, if that was what Elizabeth really wanted. It didn't have to be a two-man operation. I couldn't figure out why she needed me.

When I got home I slept for a couple weeks. Then I took a bus to the Worcester Public Library's satellite branch. I returned "The Morning Carnival" to its spot in the stacks, then put the corresponding card back in the catalog.

After I nestled the card into place I noticed an odd, discolored card directly in front of it. I picked it up and saw familiar handwriting on the back—a note. I didn't read it. I put it back and closed the drawer.

Face the Truth

Robert Petyo

'I know who killed my friend Sally.'

Slumped in the wooden chair just inside his apartment, his eyes half closed, Zak struggled to stay awake. Last night's party at the pizzeria was a rough one, and he planned to sleep all day. He only agreed to meet Kate Robbins because she was a friend of Bonnie's, and, of course, he would do anything Bonnie asked.

'Mr. Conrad?'

He popped his eyes open.

'Maybe my coming here was a mistake.' She stood by the door ignoring his offer of the lounge chair against the other wall. 'Bonnie assured me that you were dependable and would help me.'

That compliment from Bonnie almost cured his hangover. They had been dancing about each other for three months now, and she made him feel like an awkward high schooler who couldn't read her feelings. She was intriguing. She was mysterious. She was passionate. He was obsessed with her, and he never felt that way around a woman before. 'Yes. Of course.' Again, he pointed to the chair. 'Have a seat. Who do you think killed your friend?'

She inspected the chair for bugs, before sitting and facing him, hands in her lap, her eyes wide. 'Harley Jacobs.' She said the name like it was a violent curse.

Rubbing his temple, he leaned back against the wall and sighed. He understood the woman's pain, but nothing could change the facts. 'The police investigated the circumstances of the girl's death. It was ruled an accident.'

'He killed her.'

The violence in her voice startled him away from the wall. 'I'm sorry.

I know it's tough to face the truth sometimes.' He stopped when he saw her violently shaking her head, whipping her shoulder length black hair about.

'Harley Jacobs killed her because she was going to expose him as a fraud. Let me tell you my story.'

Hunching his shoulders, he indicated with a nudging motion of the back of his hand that she should continue.

'Sally and I are both nurses at Allied Star downtown. Have been for five years. Before that we went to school together.'

Zak knew this from what Bonnie told him. He also knew that Allied was about twenty years behind the times and had almost been closed by the State Board of Health, but he didn't interrupt her story.

'Three months ago, we were at a party at the Highlands night club in Pitstone. It was a fundraiser for the children's center that's affiliated with the hospital. I was dancing with my friend when someone passed out on the floor. An older man. I later learned his name was Charles Oleander.' She scanned the apartment and contorted her cheeks as if deciding whether or not to continue. Finally, she said, 'Sally was the first one to the man. He was convulsing and she got him onto his back and tried to keep his airway open. I yelled for somebody to call nine one one and rushed to help her.'

'A heart attack?'

'Right then we didn't know. His pulse was rapid and his breathing labored. It could have been a lot of things. We did what we could to stabilize him and keep him comfortable until the medics arrived.'

'No doctors there? It was a hospital fundraiser.'

Her eyes sloped for a moment before she said, 'Our doctors don't have time for anything as trivial as a fundraiser.'

'What happened when the ambulance arrived?'

'We let the EMTs take over. That is standard procedure. Only they weren't EMTs. It was a cop, a young fireman who looked like he was still in high school, and Harley Jacobs, a trainee. He does little more than drive the truck. But he acted like he was in charge.' She shook her shoulders like she were shivering in the wind. 'We were available for assistance if they needed us, but they ignored us.'

'Did they know you were nurses?'

'We didn't introduce ourselves, if that's what you mean. But they knew. They just pushed us out of the way.' She snorted as if stifling a sneeze. 'They were incompetent. Sally told them that they shouldn't move him until they took his vital signs.'

'And?'

'Harley told her to mind her own business.'

'Did she?'

'Of course not. Not Sally. She started giving them orders. She told them they were risking his life.'

'What did you do?'

She bowed her head. 'I'm not as forward as Sally is. I remained in the background. They got Mr. Oleander on a stretcher and took him out to the ambulance. Sally followed them.'

'Did she get in the ambulance?'

'No. They wouldn't let her.'

'Did the guy live?'

'He was released from the hospital two days later. It was a mild heart attack, aggravated by kidney disease.' She shook her head slightly. 'He has many problems.'

'But the EMTs didn't screw up his treatment?'

'How do you mean?'

'He didn't die because of their actions, right?'

'Correct,' she said reluctantly.

'All's well that ends well.'

She shook her head. 'Sally didn't feel that way.'

'And you think the incident caused bad blood between Jacobs and your friend Sally?'

'I don't think so. I know. Sally went to the Emergency Board at the hospital and complained that Harley had made some basic mistakes on site.'

'And?'

She looked away. 'And two weeks later Sally was dead.'

'A hit and run accident.' He pointed toward a printout of a newspaper article on the floor near his chair. 'They arrested the driver who is awaiting a hearing.'

'Correct.'

'The driver was not Harley Jacobs.'

'That's right.'

When he scrambled out of the chair to grab the printout, his skull screamed and for a few seconds his vision blurred. 'Sally Fontaine was lying in the middle of the street when she was hit.'

'Correct.'

'The police say she was high on weed.'

'Sally didn't use drugs of any kind.'

'That you know of.'

Her lips pumped in and out as she stared at him. 'If you're not going to help me, just say so.' She stood.

He waved the back of his hand again. 'I'm just being straight with you.'

Her thick black eyebrows arched a bit. 'Sally did not use drugs,' she insisted.

'So how did the marijuana get in her system?'

'Ask Harley Jacobs.'

'You think he drugged her?'

'Yes.'

'Planted a butt and left her lying in the street?'

'Yes.'

'I'll talk to him.'

'You will?'

'I'll be straight with you. I don't think you have a case.' He held up his hand when she started to protest. 'You're telling me Jacobs killed her because he resented her going to the board about his screw ups.'

'That's right.'

Again, a chop of his hand. 'Only he didn't screw up. The man lived. Did the Board take any action against him?'

'No.'

'No discipline?'

'No.'

'No stern talking to?'

She pouted again and looked away.

'So Harley Jacobs had no reason to feel threatened. No reason to set up some kind of accident to kill her.'

She clutched her purse like a club.

'I'll ask around, he said. 'But don't get your hopes up.'

'Don't bother.' She spun to leave. 'I'll find someone who believes me.'

*****

'What did you say to Kate?' Bonnie's face always grew scarlet when she was angry, bad enough that Zak once thought she was having a heart attack. Now he found it exciting. Just about everything about Bonnie made him feel like an excited pimple faced teen ager.

And that worried him.

'I told her I'd look into it,' he said.

'That's not what she told me.' Her voice was high pitched and he swore the glass of water on the table before her trembled. 'She was pissed.'

'I told her the truth,' he said as he sipped his soda. 'I don't have high hopes, but I'll give it a shot.'

'You will?'

'Yeah, but I'm just setting her up for the disappointment. I don't think he killed her. The cops looked into it. It was a freakin' car accident.'

'I don't want a half assed job.' She held up a finger. 'I want you to do whatever necessary to prove that Harley Jacobs killed her. Spread the word. Ask a lot of questions.'

She was a woman trying to be a good friend by pressuring him to at least make an effort, and Zak found her loyalty sexy.

There was the teen ager again, he thought. Was he going to ask her to the prom next?

'Do you know Harley Jacobs?' he asked.

'Just barely. Enough to know he's a snob and a prick.'

He winced. 'I guess he'll be fun to talk to.'

'I could give you a million reasons why everybody hates him. He only has the job because his uncle's a big shot at Allied. He's an arrogant sexist who's a thief and a cheater.' She stopped to take a breath. 'Talk to him once and you'll know what kind of prick he is.'

'How about Sally? Did you know she used drugs?'

'I've never known her to use drugs.'

'She was high that night.'

'I don't think so.'

'Did you know Sally real good? Were you best buds?'

She hesitated. 'No.'

'You really don't know if she used drugs or not, do you?'

She didn't respond.

'Give me the name of a real close friend who might know. Other than Kate, that is. She don't like me.'

*****

His contact at the police station got him a look at the police report. They found the driver of the SUV that ran over her while she lay strung out in the middle of the street late on a Friday night. A witness saw the accident and managed to get a partial plate which allowed the police to track the vehicle. Lincoln D'Angelo cooperated and insisted he didn't realize he hit anything more than a pothole. He was on his way home from the late shift at work, and interviews with his co-workers at the plant verified that he was sober when he left, shortly before the time of the accident. He hadn't stopped anywhere. Went directly home. It seemed to be a tragic accident, and though the DA was considering possible charges for leaving an accident scene, the case was nowhere near a priority.

There was no mention of Harley Jacobs in the report.

He went to Allied Star. Even though it was three o'clock, the tiny cafeteria on the second floor of the hospital was packed. After paying the old lady, whose gray hair was shrouded by a plastic cap, for his ham sandwich and a Pepsi, he carried the small paper plate and scanned the room looking for Carlotta Franken. From the front desk on the ground floor he had been sent to her nurse's station on the third floor where he was told she was on a lunch break.

'Can I help you?' the woman in the stiff light blue nurse's uniform asked. She sat at a small table with a black-haired man with a stethoscope twisted around his arm.

Zak had been staring at her for several seconds. 'Are you Carlotta?'

'Who are you?'

He set his tray down on a vacant table next to them. 'My name's Zak Conrad. I'm a private investigator.'

The black-haired man stiffened and grabbed his stethoscope.

'Is there somewhere we can talk?' Zak asked. The cramped cafeteria was awash with distracting chatter.

'About what?'

'About Sally Fontaine.'

'Let's talk right here.'

He winced at a harsh laugh from behind him that slammed into his aching skull. He waited a few seconds for her to change her mind about talking here, then moved slightly so he that he faced the man with her. 'And you are?'

'A friend.' His voice was deep and threatening.

He looked at Carlotta again. 'I'm trying to find out where Sally got the marijuana that was in her system the night she died.'

The man sucked in a breath, but Carlotta showed no reaction. 'That's something the police should be looking into.'

'Did Sally smoke marijuana?'

'She didn't smoke anything.'

'No drugs of any kind?'

For an instant, her pleasant face darkened. 'Absolutely not.' She tapped her wrist. 'You can ask me as many times as you want, but the answer's not going to change. Sally didn't do drugs.'

'You knew her well?'

Sighing, she held up her wrist. 'I only have a few minutes left. I got to get back.'

Zak softened his voice. 'I just needed someone who really knew her to confirm that she didn't use drugs. That would mean someone drugged her and left her passed out in the street.' He hoped that would get her on his side.

The man screeched his chair away from the table. 'I've got to get back,' he told Carlotta. Without a glance toward Zak he hurried off.

'The police are convinced it was an accident,' Carlotta said.

Zak slid into the seat the man had vacated and brought over his plate. 'I'm not the police.'

'Listen, I'd like to help you. I really would. A lot of us think Sally was murdered. But all I could do is confirm that she didn't smoke pot. Never dabbled in any kind of stuff like that. Sally was as straight as they come.'

'Then someone either tricked her into smoking a joint or slipped her something to get it in her system.'

'I guess.'

'I understand she was at a restaurant the night she died.'

She tapped her wrist again, this time checking the slender watch. 'We were at a small party at a pizzeria. Tony's on Fullerton.'

'What kind of party?'

'It was my birthday.'

'Happy birthday.'

'A few of us from work stopped at Tony's.'

'How many people?'

She thought for a moment. 'Seven of us.'

'Could you get me their names?' He pulled out his phone and went to the notepad.

She snatched his phone and worked at the screen. 'Do you really think Sally was murdered?'

'Yes,' he lied.

'Then you should be talking to Harley Jacobs.'

'I will.' Apparently, everybody thought Jacobs was guilty. 'I was told he was unavailable while on duty.' Zak's first stop had been at the ambulance station underneath the hospital. 'Was he at the party?'

She thrust his phone back to him. 'Of course not.'

He glanced at the names she had written and held up the phone. 'Are any of these people users?'

'What? No.'

'You're sure?'

She stood and crumbled her paper plate. 'I've got to get back.'

'Who did she leave the party with?'

'Gordy, I think.' She rushed away, shoving her garbage into an overflowing can near the door.

Someone at that party must have smoked a joint with her in the lot, and if Gordy was the last one to be with her, he was suspect number one.

Zak started to stand but dropped back as the man with the stethoscope wrapped around his arm appeared at the table. 'You want to talk to Miller Stillworth,' he said.

'Who's that?'

'Sally's boyfriend. He would know if she used drugs or not.'

*****

As Zack moved into the wide firehall on Price Street, he was approached by a fireman in baggy pants with wide gray suspenders. 'I'm looking for Miller Stillworth,' he said.

The fireman stopped and planted his hands on his hips. 'What for?'

'Do you know where I could find him?'

'I'm right here,' called a man who was halfway down a short stairway behind a truck. 'What do you want?'

Zak patted his shirt pocket where his ID was, but he didn't pull it out. 'I'm checking into the death of Sally Fontaine.'

'My girl.' He almost stumbled on the last step and took a deep breath as he righted himself.

'Don't bother him about that,' the man in the baggy pants said. 'See how upset he is.'

'It's okay,' Stillworth insisted as he approached. 'I got to deal with it.'

'You had nothing to do with the accident,' baggy pants said.

'I didn't say that he did,' Zak said. He backed a step and gave a beckoning wave, hoping Stillworth would join him outside. 'I'm trying to find out how marijuana got in her system the night she was killed.'

'How would I know that? We never smoked.'

'Never?'

'You calling me a liar?'

'No.' He backed another step, but Stillworth didn't move. 'Did she ever mention a man named Harley Jacobs?'

'You think that bum killed her?'

'I'm just investigating the circumstances.'

'You're looking for Jacobs, aren't you? That bum killed her, didn't he?' He looked at baggy pants. 'I knew it.'

Did everybody in the world think Jacobs killed her? 'Please, can we talk outside?'

Stillworth began puffing slightly like he had just finished a long run. He flexed his fists but made no move to leave the hall. 'We got work to do here, buddy. I don't got to talk to you.'

'Somehow drugs got into her system. If she couldn't handle them, it knocked her out, put her down on the street. That set her up to die in an accident.'

Stillworth sucked in a breath and slammed a fist into his palm. 'Jacobs.'

Baggy pants moved in front of Zack. 'Another time, buddy.'

'Don't you want to help me find who drugged her?'

*****

Zak knocked on the door.

After a few moments a porch light clicked on and there was a muffled voice from inside. 'Who's there?'

'Gordy Westerley?' Zak had gotten the addresses of all the birthday party guests after sweet talking the gum chewing clerk in the hospital personnel office.

'Who's asking?'

'I'm a private investigator looking into the death of Sally Fontaine.' He had his ID in his hand. 'May I come in?'

'I don't know nothing about Sally's accident. I wasn't there.'

'Please, Mr. Westerley. I don't like talking through doors.'

There was a series of clicks and bangs before the door opened a few inches. From the light of the porch Zak saw a thin man in sweat pants with holes in the knees. The man looked toward Zak's ID that he still clutched in his hand. Zak handed it to him. After gaping at it with hooded vacant eyes for several seconds, Westerley returned it and stepped back from the door. Zak entered a small alcove in front of a narrow stairway.

'Why you talking to me?' Westerley asked.

'You were the last person to see Miss Fontaine before the accident.'

'There were a bunch of us at Tony's.'

'But you left with her.'

He thought about that for a few seconds before moving into a small parlor just to the left of the stairs. A reading lamp next to a lounge chair threw a cone of light to the thin carpet. 'Where you hear that?'

'Several people told me that,' he lied. The air seemed thick.

'I walked her to her car. That's all.'

'She was parked in the lot?'

'Sure.'

'As were you?'

'Yep.'

'Was she still in the lot when you left?'

'In her car, yep. I think she was looking at her phone.'

'Did she seem all right?'

'She seemed fine.'

'If she was at her car and she seemed fine, why did she decide to walk home?'

'I have no idea.'

'Why did she pass out and lie in the middle of the street?'

He began to shrivel, his shoulders pressing in, like he didn't want to hear him.

Zak stood. 'Did you give her any drugs?'

'No.'

Too quick of an answer. 'Maybe you shared a hit in the parking lot before you left.'

'No.' His voice was weak.

'Do you smoke pot?'

'What?'

He repeated the question and looked around the room like he was reading the air.

'Medical reasons,' he said quickly, his index finger stroking the side of his neck.

'And you didn't give any to Sally?'

'No.'

Being a good judge of people was vital in his business. 'I think you shared a joint.'

He stiffened, and now two fingers rubbed his neck.

'Since she wasn't a user,' Zak said, 'she decided to walk home after smoking with you. It was only a few blocks.'

'No,' he muttered. 'We didn't.'

'She passed out along the way. Got run over. That makes it your fault.'

'No.' A gasping cry. 'I swear we didn't smoke.'

'Somehow pot got into her system.'

'You'd have to ask her boyfriend Stillworth about that.'

Zak wondered why half the people he interviewed wanted him to talk to Stillworth, and half wanted him to talk to Jacobs.

*****

'How come you didn't know that Sally had a boyfriend?'

'She doesn't.' After a beat as her darting eyes scanned the crowded diner where they met for breakfast, Bonnie added, 'Well, she did. But they broke up.'

'How long ago?'

'I don't know. A few months.'

'Miller Stillworth.'

'Yeah. That was his name. He's a creep.'

'You know him?'

'I know he's a creep.' Another pause. 'I don't know what she saw in him. He was a thug. Beat her up. She dumped him, but I know that he was doing whatever he could to get her back. It's creepy.' She leaned across the table, her face flashing scarlet like a siren. 'You talk to Jacobs yet?'

'Haven't hooked up yet, but I want to see Stillworth again.'

*****

Stillworth hadn't reported for duty and Zak went to city hall where he found that he had a spotty attendance record. Paperwork was underway to have him fired.

'Has anybody tried to contact him today?'

'He doesn't answer his phone and doesn't reply to our messages.' The young woman behind the cluttered desk didn't look at him as she spoke.

'Did anyone go to his home?'

She sifted through papers like she was looking for an escaped mouse. 'No. That's not part of our job.'

Zak went to Stillworth's house, half a double block with a sagging wooden porch and grimy windows. The other unit seemed abandoned as weeds crept onto that side of the porch. When there was no response to his knock, he tried the door. It was locked. He circled the house, moving through a weedy unpaved driveway that separated it from the last house on the block. The backyard was cluttered like a perpetual yard sale. He found an unlocked window on the tiny back stoop and clambered into the house, struggling over a kitchen sink that was cluttered with used paper plates. He rolled onto his side as he dropped onto the linoleum floor.

'Hello,' he called as he stood. He kept calling as he moved through the house.

He found the body in the basement, lying in front of a metal garbage can that was overflowing with rags and bricks.

He called 911 and waited on the front porch.

When a patrol car screeched to a halt in front of the house, he was glad to see Tanya Fetterman get out. She was a friend of Bonnie's. In fact, she had introduced them. He had dealt with her before and found her efficient, knowledgeable, and, most of all, helpful.

'What are you doing here?' she asked him. Her partner got out of the vehicle but stayed near the street.

Zak briefed her on his search for Miller Stillworth.

'You broke in?'

'I heard a noise inside,' he lied. 'The back window was unlocked.'

After a tight-lipped nod, she said, 'I'll buy that. For now. Wait out here.'

He remained on the porch as she walked in, followed shortly by two other policemen who arrived and spoke briefly to the patrolman on the street.

*****

'The dead man wasn't Miller Stillworth.' He sat in the cafe with Bonnie who slurped from a glass of beer.

'Well,' she finally said. 'Don't keep me in suspense.'

'Harley Jacobs.'

'What?' She slapped both hands against her cheeks.

'What was he doing at Miller Stillworth's house?'

'Maybe he knew him. Firemen, ambulance drivers. They work together. I don't know. What do the police think?'

'Still investigating,' he said with a tired shrug as he lifted his coffee cup. His headache was hanging on, so the beer was on hold for now.

'Miller must have lured him to the house and killed him because he killed Sally,' Bonnie said. 'Revenge. I told you he was trying to get her back.'

Zak considered that theory for a few seconds. 'Tanya doesn't seem to think the deaths are connected.'

'Tanya answered the call?'

'Yeah.'

That seemed to disappoint her, and she looked away. 'I think I better get back to work.'

He reached out to grab her wrist, but instead floated his hand in the air.

Bonnie said nothing as she stared at his hand for a few moments before leaving.

He dropped his hand on the table and watched her leave. After leaving some money on the table, he got up to follow her, hovering near the exit, giving her time to get to her car so she wouldn't see him.

He followed her to the police station where she parked in the small visitor's lot to the side of the brick building. He pulled onto Harrison Lane which led to the visitor's lot, but after a brief internal debate, he drove on.

Rather than hang out at the police station, he drove to the tattered Allied Star building that looked look an old decaying castle. He parked in the visitor's lot, and walked to the employee lot on the other side of the building. There he walked inside the iron gate and chatted a few minutes with Harry the security guard who munched on a sandwich, before finding himself a comfortable curb to sit on as he waited.

About a half hour later he jumped up when he saw Bonnie's car come through the entrance. She stopped near him and rolled down her window.

'What's going on?' he asked.

'What are you doing here?'

'You went to see Tanya, didn't you? To push your theory.'

'What are you talking about?'

To avoid a game of twenty questions, he circled the car and got into the passenger's side. 'Miller Stillworth murdered Harley Jacobs because he believed all the people who were accusing him of killing his girlfriend.'

'Ex-girlfriend,' she muttered as she rolled to a parking spot near a small loading dock.

'He was still hoping to get her back, right? He believed your lies about Jacobs' killing her. He called him to his house to confront him. They argued. He killed him, panicked, dumped the body in his basement and took off.'

She clicked off the motor, snapping off the air conditioning. Immediately the car began to heat up. 'He's a creep. Nothing but trouble. I hope the cops find him.'

He watched her face reddening, and not from the heat. His own anger was starting to boil underneath the surface. 'It's too hot.' He opened the door.

But Bonnie didn't move.

He yanked the door shut. 'I guess I'll talk to Tanya. And tell her what I think.'

'What do you think?'

'I know what happened.' He faced her. 'You and your cabal of friends stoked the pot so Stillworth, the creep, would think Jacobs killed his girlfriend. You were hoping he might snap out, and that's exactly what happened. Basically, you put a target on his back.'

'But this isn't your case, is it? There's no reason for you to talk to Tanya.'

'I don't dig being used. You wanted me to snoop around and pick up some dirt on Jacobs. You figured I might hook up with Stillworth at some point, find some stuff to convince him that Jacobs killed her.'

'Stillworth's a creep,' Bonnie said. 'So is Jacobs.'

He couldn't believe what he was hearing. 'You basically set him up to be killed.'

'Of course not.' Her eyes were wide and dark red streaks ran down her cheeks like blood. 'I'm not grieving over his death, but they're both creeps. Stillworth is the one who killed him. How are we responsible for that? We truly believed Jacobs was responsible for Sally's death. That's why I sent Kate to you. To look for evidence. But we certainly weren't looking to have him killed.' She tapped her throat with manicured fingernails like she was having a bogus fainting spell. 'What do you think we are, some kind of secret society of mobsters?'

'Actually, that's exactly what I think.'

A grin flickered and disappeared. 'But it's not your case.'

He opened the door and got out but leaned inside to face her. 'I only wonder how many of you Allied creeps are members of your secret society.' He slammed the door and went to his car.

At least he now knew the truth about Bonnie. This dance was over.

For the Birds

Shannon Hollinger

He's seen the shirt before, on a different corpse. Detective Shane Shaw bites a knuckle as he squats beside the body, fighting the urge to take its hand in his. For a brief moment, he hears the clanking chain of his rusty old bike, smells the aroma of hot dogs roasted over an open flame, feels the rough, splintered slats of his childhood fence as he squeezed through the broken panel into his neighbor's yard to retrieve a baseball lobbed too high.

But that was a long time ago. He shakes his head, sending the memories retreating behind the clicks of the forensic technician's camera and the metallic odor of blood. Swats at a fly trying to kiss his cheek and focuses on examining the body, from its tousled brown hair to the victim's bare feet, the bottoms wrinkled and tinged blue, marbled with livor mortised veins. His gaze takes in the mud smeared on the left pants leg, the strip of pale flesh exposed above the waistband, finally coming to linger on the knife imbedded up to its hilt between the shoulder blades covered by the Hawaiian shirt.

He fights the urge to shiver against the damp chill, a fine mist suspended in the air, hovering like an apparition. And make no mistake, there *are* ghosts concealed within the wintry haze. Not the kind that jump out and say boo, but the kind that wake him from his sleep in the middle of the night, body drenched in sweat and frozen by the same paralysis that struck him over thirty years before.

Shaw rises, knees popping, and glances over his shoulder.

"We good?" The medicolegal investigator gestures with his head at the gurney beside him, waiting to transport the victim to the Medical Examiner's Office.

"Yeah."

"Whatcha thinking?"

Shaw shakes his head. "Too soon to tell."

"Yeah, well, the poor guy's got shit luck, we know that much."

Shaw's eyebrows raise. He gives the man beside him the side eye, waiting for him to continue.

"Guy was on a business trip, wasn't supposed to be home until tomorrow. Must've surprised a robber or something when he came home early, don't you think?"

Glancing around them, Shaw asks, "In the backyard?"

"Maybe he chased the guy outside."

"In my experience, most robbers willing to resort to violence already have a weapon with them. They don't grab a kitchen knife, run out of the house, then circle back to stab the homeowner."

"Then what do you think did happen?"

Shaw watches as a bird lands on a nearby branch, cocking its head as it inspects them with a dark eye holding equal parts interest and wariness, then shrugs, shakes his head again and repeats, "Too soon to tell."

*****

Shaw nods at the uniformed officer as he enters the house. Tall and thin, not short. Red headed, not blonde. His memory's playing tricks on him again.

"You the first responder?" he asks.

"Yeah."

"What can you tell me?"

"Victim's name is Rick Dawson. Neighbor saw the car was back yesterday, knocked on the door, didn't get an answer. Came back today, same thing. Was worried something was wrong, the guy might have fallen and hit his head or something, so he called us requesting a wellness check."

The officer rubs at the back of his neck, wincing. "I took the call. No answer, front door was locked, so I went around back, and, well...there he was."

"What about the back door? Was it locked?"

"Yeah."

"Deadbolt too?" Shaw asks.

Scratching his head, the officer says, "Yeah. Pretty sure it was."

"Then how'd we get in?"

"The vic's sister lives across town. The neighbor told us, had her number. We gave her a call and she drove over, unlocked it for us."

Shaw scribbles on his notepad. "Which neighbor had her number?"

"The one who called for the wellness check."

"And the sister? Where's she now?"

"Had to go pick her kids up from school. Promised she'd come back here as soon as she got them."

Shaw swallows hard, pushing past the lump of memories wedged in his throat. His mom had gone to pick his sister up from soccer that day while he and Jimmy Kraktow from three houses down were in the backyard breaking in his new mitt. The air thick and humid, gnats swarming in clouds, sticking to the sweat on the back of their necks.

A burst of static crackles. The officer grabs the radio on his shoulder, head tilted as he listens to the transmission.

"One last thing," Shaw says, drawing the officer's attention back. "Why'd the neighbor knock in the first place?"

The officer's brows furrow. "Don't know. I forgot to ask."

*****

In the kitchen, Shaw finds mail stacked on the counter, an empty envelope, unstamped, no return address on the top. He shifts through the catalogues and bills but finds no trace of whatever was inside. In the corner, a wood knife block sits, full capacity. There's nothing else on the granite surface except a coffee maker and a twist-off bottle cap.

He imagines the victim's movements. Coming home from a business trip, sorting through his mail, opening a letter. Popping a beer. Making his way farther into the house, settling back into his home, his life, the mysterious paper still clutched in his hand.

The living room appears untouched besides a suit jacket, pockets empty, draped over the back of the couch and the beer, half full, on an end table. Shaw brushes the back of his hand against the bottle. Warm and dry. He pulls on a glove and picks the bottle up. A ring of condensation still lurks beneath. Probably opened the previous night, not before the victim left for his business trip. In the otherwise pristine house, it's the first sign that something is amiss.

He remembers when he first realized something was wrong with Mr. Kirkpatrick. He'd ignored Jimmy, calling his name, asking about the ball, "Shane? Did you find it or not?" Instead, he'd crept forward, knowing in his gut that Mr. Kirkpatrick wasn't resting even though his brain told him that must be the answer to what he was seeing. But the man's hand was curled in the dirt, soil under his nails. Mr. Kirkpatrick never had dirty nails.

He heard Jimmy struggling through the hole in the fence behind him and took another step forward. A pool of blood spread from Mr. Kirkpatrick's head. The side of his face Shaw could see was too pale and tinged grey, with the edges of a wound just barely visible on the forehead. The wrinkles normally crinkled around the edges of his neighbor's warm smile now worked to make his face look slack, like something too big had worn Mr. Kirkpatrick's skin and left it stretched. For the first time the man looked not just older, but old. Really old.

"Is he?" Jimmy asked close to his ear.

"Yeah. I think so."

Jimmy retreated. Shaw thought he'd gone to get help, but the other boy returned only seconds later with a stick. He jabbed it at the body. Shaw snatched it mere inches before it made contact. "Don't." It seemed like an intrusion, an invasion of privacy. But privacy is something the dead are rarely afforded.

Shaw's ankles crack as he climbs the stairs. He finds the victim's shoes in the bedroom, his discarded socks and a dress shirt in an otherwise empty hamper. A carryon suitcase sits on the end of the bed, unzipped, the contents riffled through. In the bathroom a toiletry bag sits beside the sink, an empty wire hanger hanging from the towel rack.

There's a home office in the spare bedroom. Much like his own, it doesn't appear to get much use. A thin layer of dust coats the surface of everything except the closed laptop perched on the corner. He pops the lid, finds that the device requires a fingerprint for access. His gaze roams the walls, taking in the production awards, trade magazines, the plethora of pens and paper pads bearing the name of one drug or another – the detritus of a pharmaceutical rep.

He checks the drawers, finds only office supplies. Tucking the PC under his arm, he turns the light out after him. Nothing seems out of place. It appears as if only the victim had been in the house. Yet there's something important he would have expected to find that's missing. And whatever was in the empty envelope is nowhere to be found.

*****

Shaw nods to the officer stationed beside the door as he closes it behind him. "You say the wellness check was requested by that neighbor?" he asks, pointing to the house on the left.

"Yes, sir."

Shaw nods again and heads to the house on the right. His shoes squeak across the damp grass. His nose twitches, tickled by the scent of laundry softener. A chipmunk darts into a bush beside the house, chirping at him crossly.

There are so many things to ground him to this moment, here in the present. Yet his head is lost in the clouds of the past. It seems like only moments ago that he'd told Jimmy Kraktow to call for help, his mouth dry, his voice choked into a squeak as he stared down at the body, feeling like he'd been the one to do something wrong. It was the first body he'd seen wearing a yellow Hawaiian shirt with a red hibiscus pattern. It had been the first body he'd ever seen, period, and was probably the reason he'd seen so many since.

He climbs the porch, the door opening before he can raise his hand to knock. A middle-aged couple, probably right around his own age as much as it pains him to admit it, huddle on the threshold.

"What happened?" The wife, red-faced, eyes wide, takes a step toward him. "We heard someone was killed? Is it true? Was it Rick? Are we in danger?"

"Honey." Her husband, pale, sweating, grabs her by the arm, his other hand curled in a white knuckled grip on the molding.

She glances over her shoulder at her husband, then launches into another tirade of questions, interrogating Shaw.

"Ma'am." Shaw holds his hand up, shield clasped in his palm, and waits for her to quiet before continuing. "I understand your concern. I'm not at liberty to discuss much at this point, but I would appreciate your assistance in answering a few questions for me, if you will."

Her mouth opens, sharp tongue ready to strike, but her husband preempts her. Wiping sweat off his forehead with the back of his hand, beads of moisture slinging through the air liked windshield wipers in the rain, he stutters, "Of course. Whatever we can do to help."

A bark sounds from somewhere inside the house and the man jumps.

"You have a dog?" Shaw asks.

"No."

"Sounds like it."

"That's the TV," the wife says. She glances nervously back into the house. "Anyways, what did you want to ask? We have to get going soon."

Shaw raises his eyebrows, lets the silence linger between them.

"We have dinner reservations," she adds.

Shaw looks at his watch, sees that it's quarter to four.

"It's in the city. And we need to change. And we're meeting friends for cocktails first."

Shaw opens his mouth to speak but the husband interrupts him. "They canceled, remember, honey." He cuts a nervous glance at Shaw as he rubs his mouth, trying to wipe away the taste of the lie he told to counter his wife's, just in case, Shaw suspects, Shaw were to decide to follow up with the couple they were supposedly meeting to check their alibi.

"Well, we haven't seen anything strange. And we haven't heard anything," the wife says, eyes darting between Shaw and the door. She takes a step closer to the house, backing away.

"And we never really talked to Rick," the husband adds.

"Was there a reason for that?"

"There was some confusion when he first moved in about whose property line some shrubs were on," the husband says at the same time the wife says, "He just wasn't our kind of people."

The husband swallows hard, nodding, a fresh wave of sweat beading his forehead. "She's right. That shrub thing happened at our last house. I forgot."

Another bark sounds from inside the house, this one shriller, more desperate to be heard. Shaw looks from the husband to the wife and back again. The man's grown several shades paler and looks wobbly on his feet. The woman's lips are pressed so tight together, the worried creases surrounding them so deep, they look sutured shut. Shaw nods. "Thank you for your time. I'll be in touch."

He hears them both sigh with relief as he descends down the porch steps. Behind him, the door slams shut, the deadbolt turns, and a chain clinks against the door as it's drawn across and latched. Lovely people.

He catches movement from the corner of his eye, spots the neighbor across the street from the victim's house watching him from the window, creased face peering from beside the front curtain. He changes direction and crosses the road. She, at least, lets him knock before opening the door.

"Ma'am."

"Detective, I presume." He fights the urge to squirm, her manner reminiscent of his third-grade teacher's, a woman who could probably still pin him in place with a stern eye and make him forget the spelling words he'd worked so hard to learn.

"Yes, ma'am."

Her jaw twitches. "I didn't know the man. He was quiet. Kept to himself. Never heard a peep except when a maroon minivan visited. His sister, I think. Let me tell you, those kids carried on worse than a tribe of howler monkeys."

Shaw arches an eyebrow. "When was the last time you heard them?"

"Oh, must have been a few weeks. Why? He didn't die from a headache, did he?" Her teeth clench, audibly grinding together.

Shaw winces at the painful sound of it. At the memory of the raw edges of the wound he'd seen on Mr. Kirkpatrick's head. Wondering if it had hurt, ached, before death stole all feeling away. "Well, we're still waiting for the autopsy results, but I feel it's safe to say that probably wasn't the cause of death."

Her foot taps against the floor. She scratches at her neck, itches her arm, seemingly unable to hold still. "Hmm. Wouldn't have surprised me if it was. But I guess some people are used to that sort of thing. Now, in my day, you could tell the type of parent someone was by how well their children could be seen and not heard. But not anymore. Parents today believe in letting their kids run amok. To express themselves. What a load of baloney."

She catches Shaw looking past her, into her house, and sidesteps to block his view, her eyes narrowing. "Is there anything else?"

"Did you see or hear anything suspicious? Notice any new vehicles in the area?"

"No. Nothing."

"Were you home?"

"I was." She stretches her jaw like a camel yawning. Sniffs. "I can tell you exactly who on this street was and wasn't home last night."

"I don't think that will be necessary quite yet, but thank you."

She nods, her eye twitching.

Shaw averts his gaze from the sore at the corner of her mouth, glances from side to side and leans forward. "Between you and me?" he asks. "What do you think happened?"

Her teeth grind against each other again. "I think he trusted his luck with the wrong kind of person."

*****

Gerald Pickler is clearly lost in his own thoughts. Shaw shifts his attention from Pickler's dazed face and looks around the living room, studying the home of the neighbor who requested the wellness check. The furniture is shabby, the walls long overdue for a fresh coat of paint, the air thick with the mingled odors of the ghosts of meals past, but the place seems tidy enough. He asks a question, but the other man doesn't seem to hear him. He raises his voice and asks again.

"Hmm. What? Sorry." Pickler rubs his palms over his knees. "I was just thinking... today's my birthday. Definitely the worst one ever, and

I've had some doozies. You sure I can't get you something to drink?"

"No, thanks."

"It really isn't a bother."

"I'm good." Shaw shifts his weight, trying to avoid the spring poking at him through the couch cushion.

Pickler clears his throat.

Shaw sees a head of shiny white hair, rosy cheeks, kind, clear, bright blue eyes. A good neighbor, the kind who doesn't mind lending a hand, watching the kids for a struggling single mom, helping a fatherless boy with his bike, pretending he bought doubles of items by mistake, that they'd be helping him out by joining him for dinner.

Except none of that is true. Not now, anyways. He's thinking of someone else, a specter that's slipped out of the fog of memory to haunt him.

The coarse, dark crewcut on the man before him looks sharp and dangerous. His eyes look red, the scleras tearstained. A muscle in his jaw twitches as he waits for Shaw to talk.

"What kind of relationship did you have with Mr. Dawson?" Shaw asks.

Pickler gulps. His voice cracks as he answers, "Good."

"You were friends?"

He bites his lip, staring down at his hands in his lap. "We were friendly enough, I guess."

"The kind of guy you'd borrow a rake from?"

"Yeah."

"Maybe share a beer, watch the game together?"

"You got it."

Shaw leans forward, elbows on his knees. "What kind of neighbor was he?"

"What do you mean?"

"Was he the music too loud, trashcan sitting out all week type?"

"No." Pickler shakes his head. "Rick, well, he kept to himself, mostly. He was kind of shy, but always willing to lend a hand. He was a real good guy."

"Did you know him long?"

"Three years now. I bought this place right after my divorce."

"What made you decide to call the police?"

He glances up at Shaw, his expression filled with grief, his eyes watery. "I was worried. Wasn't like him not to answer."

"Did you see anything? Hear anything concerning?"

"No."

"Did the two of you have plans?"

"What? No."

"Then why were you over there?" The couch creaks as Shaw sits back.

"Huh?"

"Knocking on the door. I know he didn't answer, but if you went over there twice, you must have had a reason, right? What was it?"

"Oh." Pickler rubs the back of his neck. "Yeah. You're not going to believe me."

"Why not?"

"Because I was there to borrow a rake."

*****

As Detective Shaw introduces himself to the victim's sister, she seems lost, disoriented. She offers her hand for him to shake, pulls it away before he can make contact, using it to rake through her hair instead. It reminds Shaw of the game he and Jimmy Kraktow used to play. And while he usually managed to smack his fingertips across Jimmy's palm before the other boy could successfully jerk it away, he feels like he's lost some of that speed, that today he'd indeed be too slow.

He clears his throat. "I'm very sorry for your loss, ma'am."

Tears shine in her eyes. She swallows hard, her voice breaking as she says, "I still don't really believe it. He was supposed to come over for dinner when he got back in town tomorrow."

"Hey, mom. Is Uncle Rick really dead? Can we see his body?"

Shaw wonders what Jimmy would have done if he'd been alone with the corpse. And his stick. The way, after they'd called for help, the police had made Jimmy go home after they questioned him, while Shaw himself had been allowed to stay, forgotten or perhaps just tolerated, backed into a corner at the edge of the yard.

"No. Sit down and put your seatbelts back on. Now. And put the window up." She tugs on her hair. Turning to Shaw, she grimaces. "Sorry. They're always so hyper when they get out of school. Don't supposed you have an extra pair of handcuffs or two?"

"None that would fit."

The boy who asked the question jerks back from the window as his brother grabs him by the neck. Shaw winces, watching as two pairs of pale arms thrash like an angry Kraken in the backseat of the minivan. Their mother appears oblivious to what's occurring behind her back. Or maybe she's beyond caring.

Trying to keep his focus, Shaw asks, "Do you have any idea why he cut his trip short?"

She bites her nails, staring down at her shoes as she shakes her head. "No. He didn't say anything to me about it."

"Do you know if he's been having any trouble with anyone lately? Any threats? Enemies?"

Her hand drops from her mouth long enough to say, "He was having issues with one of his neighbors letting their dog use his yard as a toilet, but I don't think he said anything to them about it. He didn't think it was worth making a fuss. He was real easygoing like that. As far as I know, Rick got along with everyone."

"What about work? Any issues there?"

She shrugs.

"A girlfriend?"

"Not that I know of."

"Boyfriend?"

Her left eyebrow quirks up and she shakes her head.

"And the two of you?"

Her expression turns sharp, edged with anger. Her hands ball into fists as she sears him with a scathing look. "What about us?" Her voice is cold, hard.

"How did you get along?"

"He was my brother."

"And?"

"And...I loved him?"

She doesn't sound too sure to Shaw.

"What about the rest of your family?"

"There isn't any. Just us. Our mom passed away several months ago."

"Has the estate been settled yet?"

She narrows her eyes. "It's still in probate. Listen, if you think I did something to my brother to get his share of the inheritance, you're wrong. He was the only . . ." Shaw watches as her face crumples. "Oh, God. It's just me now, I guess." She wraps her arms tight around herself.

"Is there anyone I can call for you, ma'am?"

She shakes her head, sniffing hard as she stares at the ground by her feet. Her body shudders as she draws a deep breath.

"One last question. Did your brother own a rake?"

"A what?"

"A rake. A lawn rake?"

"Rick? No. He hated yard work. Had a service who took care of anything like that. They came out once a week. Why?"

"No reason. I'd like to thank you for your time, ma'am. I have your number if I need to reach you, but for now, I better let you . . ." Shaw gestures to the minivan.

"Oh, Jeez. Jason! Let your brother go!"

Jason removes his foot from his brother's throat. His brother lowers the window like he wasn't just being strangled. "Hey! Can I hold your gun?"

"Not this time."

"So next time then?"

"Jeremy, put the window up and get your seatbelt on. We're leaving."

"But he said -"

Shaw turns and hurries away while he has the chance.

*****

Detective Shaw drags himself through the door, crosses the room, and lets himself collapse into the recliner. It's been a long day, and it's not over yet. He leans his head back and shuts his eyes. Sees the Hawaiian print shirt from his memory. The rigid form of his neighbor sprawled across the grass, his errant baseball laying against the man's shin. Vacant, sightless eyes seeming to stare into Shaw's own.

The air shifts against his face, churning like the wind of a summer storm. He hears the flurry of feathers as the clawed feet grip his knee.

"Hey, Little Buddy. What's up?"

His parrot, Gilligan, cocks his head to the side and inspects him. Like a good bird butler, Shaw curls a finger beneath the feathers at the parrot's neck and scratches, waiting until Gilligan's head stretches forward and his eyes shut before resting his own eyes again. He's found out enough times the hard way what the punishment is if the bird feels ignored.

But birds are simple creatures. Easy to read. Unlike humans.

He thinks back to the people he interviewed today. All of them were hiding something. None of them were completely honest.

It's more common than you'd think – people lying to the police – even when they aren't guilty of the crime in question. But Shaw's a good cop. Human nature, their body language and reactions, the lies they choose to tell him and the truths they choose to hide, give him most of what he needs to know. And the obvious scenario isn't always the correct one.

All those years ago, he'd stood against the fence in that yard, watching as the police processed the scene. Somehow, some of his hair had gotten caught under a splinter in the wood plank, and it slowly yanked those strands, one by one, from his scalp by the root. But he'd barely felt it, barely breathed, as his eyes took everything in.

A ladder lay on its side in the far corner of the yard, beneath an oak tree. The fragments of a broken bird house peaked out of the grass near its base. An officer in a uniform squatted next to Mr. Kirkpatrick, a wad of dirtied gum stuck to the bottom of his shoe. He'd looked at the puddle of blood that had seeped from beneath the man's head and said, "Better call homicide."

But Shaw didn't think that was right. He looked again to the tree, the ladder, the birdhouse, the body. And he knew what had happened. His voice was timid, had wavered as he said, "He was on blood thinners. He told me once when he cut his finger helping me fix my bike chain."

The cop looked at Shaw over his shoulder, annoyed. "That's great, kid."

"And head wounds bleed a lot," Shaw continued, even though he knew he was three words away from being banished from the yard. But it was true. It's what his mother told him every time the towel pressed to his scalp became soaked in red on the drive to get him stitches.

But no one paid any attention to him. They'd seen what they wanted to see. Homicide. A murder. Much sexier than an accident, a man falling off his ladder in his backyard while trying to hang a new birdhouse. Yet sometimes it's the places we consider safest, where we're most comfortable and let our guard down, that prove the most dangerous.

Shaw had made it all the way over to Mr. Kirkpatrick's oak tree before anyone noticed. "Hey. What do you think you're doing, kid?" the cop barked at him. "You can't just go play in the yard at a time like this. Can't you see this is a crime scene?"

"But it's not." This time, his voice was confident. He pointed at the ladder, to a dark splotch on the sharp top step. "Look. Blood. There's even hair. Mr. Kirkpatrick fell."

"Well, if he did, it was probably because the killer startled him."

"No." Shaw shook his head, stomped a foot for emphasis. "I told you, he was on blood thinners. He fell and hit his head. It was an accident. I don't think there was a killer at all."

"What's he even doing here? Someone find out where he belongs and take him back. I don't need some kid -"

But by then one of the other officers had approached him, had seen what he'd seen. "I think he's right, Rodge."

"Huh?"

"The kid. I think he's right."

It was at that moment that he knew he wanted to be a detective. And he knew he'd be a good one, because he wouldn't look for the easiest answer. A sister waiting for her inheritance, who stood to profit from her brother's death. The neighbor who called the police in the first place, who lied about the reason he was there. The nervous neighbors with the dog who had an asinine vendetta against him because of a stupid hedge. Even the old lady across the street had her reasons.

Shaw would have to wait for the data to support his theory, but he'd wager a wagyu fillet dinner at the city's finest steak house that he's narrowed his suspect pool down to the guilty party. IT is already working on the computer. The victim's phone records have been requested. And Shaw made a few calls of his own earlier, speaking with Dawson's employer himself. It shouldn't take long before he can prove his suspicions.

*****

Shaw settles on the uncomfortable couch at Gerald Pickler's house. Not much has changed in the days since he was last here, yet the place seems gloomier, Pickler himself more despondent. After declining the offer of a beverage, he waits for the man to settle into the seat across from him.

"You may wonder why I'm here," Shaw begins.

Pickler shrugs, like he already knows.

"I wanted to tell you that we're making an arrest in the murder of Rick Dawson."

This seems to surprise him. He straightens up, looks around as if taking in his surroundings for the first time.

"I also wanted to express my condolences for your loss."

Pickler looks at Shaw, tears welling in his eyes. His face turns red as his shoulders start to shake with contained sobs. "How'd you know?"

"When we met, you looked like more than just a man upset by his neighbor's death. And you said you were worried about him. Why would you worry about a casual acquaintance?"

He smiles sadly. "Was I that obvious?"

"Well," Shaw says. "That, and Mr. Dawson didn't own a rake."

Pickler laughs sadly. "I knew that was probably pushing it." He wipes his eyes. "We weren't ashamed, you know. About our relationship. And I figured you'd probably find out the truth when you started investigating the details of Rick's life."

"There were an awful lot of calls and texts between you two. And we were able to discover that he cut his trip short, so he'd be home for your birthday."

"That's what I thought," Pickler whispers. "When I saw his car in the driveway. But when he didn't answer, I knew something was wrong. And it was, and then you were asking all your questions, I was just in so much shock. And I thought that maybe if I pretended we were only neighbors, that it wouldn't hurt so bad. But I was wrong."

Shaw nods as he reaches inside his jacket pocket, withdrawing an envelope. Pickler stares at the bulge as Shaw holds it out to him. "His sister asked me to give this to you. It was Mr. Dawson's watch. She wanted you to have it."

A bubble of emotion catches in Pickler's throat.

"She also wants to know if you'd be interested in talking to her, and if you'd like any of his other belongings. Her number's in the envelope."

Pickler takes the offering with a trembling hand, nodding, tears streaking down his cheeks. "The killer. Was it someone who knew him?"

"It was."

"Was it that couple in the house on the other side of his?"

"No. They still harbor hard feelings over a hedge that was taken down, but they were getting their retribution out by letting their dog use Mr. Dawson's yard as a restroom."

"Then who?"

Shaw's phone buzzes with an incoming text. He slips it from his pocket, reads the message, and stands, gesturing for Pickler to follow him. "You'll want to see this."

Pickler follows the detective out of the house, almost running into the back of him when Shaw stops on the porch. Across the street and one house over, police lead one of his neighbors, handcuffed, from her house. "The old lady across the street?" he asks. "Loretta Herndon?"

"I'm afraid so."

"What? Why?" The word breaks into two syllables.

"She an addict. Been struggling with it for a long time, apparently, she's up to her neck in debt and is about to lose her house. My guess is she figured that Mr. Dawson, being a pharmaceutical rep, might have had some samples on hand that would interest her."

"But Rick would never have given her any," Pickler says.

"I don't disagree. And she might have known that, too. So, she helped herself. According to his supervisor, Mr. Dawson had a briefcase dedicated solely to holding his trial boxes for when he met with doctors. There should have been dozens of samples. But we couldn't find a single one. She cleaned him out."

"But how'd you know it was her?"

"A lot of little things that added up. Like, in my initial conversation with her, she never asked if he was dead. She knew. She also told me that she knew which neighbors were home the night before, even though I hadn't told her when the crime occurred. So, I assumed she knew because she'd either been the one to commit the crime or she knew more than she was telling me."

Shaw watches the squad car with Loretta Herndon drive off. Turning towards Pickler, he says, "I think she left a note for Mr. Dawson to call her when he returned. We matched her prints to an empty envelope in his house. She'd probably been watching the other neighbors so she'd know when she could go over there unseen."

Pickler gapes at him.

"The weapon that was used matches the one missing from her knife block, so we'll get her for premediated murder. She had his sample case hidden under her bed. We even found Mr. Dawson's keys in her possession. Apparently, she took them so she could lock up after herself when she left the house."

"But Rick. He wasn't a small guy. How could she have managed to overpower him like that?"

Shaw swallows hard and takes a deep breath. That had been his own question. And the hardest of the answers. He looks towards the house next door even though he can't see the new addition in the backyard.

"Did Mr. Dawson have a birdhouse?"

"A what? No. I mean, I don't think so."

Shaw nods. "Well, we found one hanging in his tree out back. Looks brand new. We think that Herndon brought it over for him, waited until he was hanging it, and stabbed him in the back."

Shaw had left the little nesting box where he'd found it, lodged between two low hanging branches. Decades late, but the job's finally done. Something for the birds.

And like that, the ghost slips back into his past.

Sneaker on the Beach
Tom Sheehan

Jadon Calix was complex and complete, yet here was dawn teasing him out and about in the universe, along with a lone *Adidas* sneaker. In one bright shaft of light he had seen the sneaker on the beach, harsh as an old idea. The toes of the sneaker faced the sea, as if the supposed late owner had been at departure, or at sincere contemplation.

Calix loved the beach in the morning when the Gulf was quiet. He'd been up much of the night, knowing that in a few days he'd have to leave Louisiana and head back north. Two months hardly seemed enough. The generosity of the Bredens had been overwhelming. Their son Paul had been his comrade, had died in his arms on the Iraqi desert. He had been able to tell Paul's parents his last words. "Find my Louisiana, Jadon, you'll love it."

He loved the endless beach because he had known terror on the desert. Amazement overpowered him when he realized sand was the one constant in both lonely places. Now, he fully contemplated the differences of the sandy geographies.

An inner message told him the day itself was different too. Earlier, the sun had come on slowly, like a surprise was at hand. The rim of the sea, at the eastern horizon, bloomed the way a new orchid comes, first purple and then an orange-purple and then, in an attempt at utter beauty, a slow gracious lavender. It banged him right between the eyes when he saw the lone sneaker.

His handsome face erupted with intrigue. He had deep eyes that sought and delivered messages in quick instances. Mrs. Breden, at their door, saw the attractive young man on the porch from one of her windows, telling her husband, "I swear this is Paul's friend, Jadon Calix. He's about the handsomest man I've ever seen, with all due apologies, my dear, a few years removed." She chuckled immediately, knowing he would somehow bring some new life back into their darkened lives. They rushed him into their home with a gracious welcome and thanks.

Now, on the beach, the combers coming slowly, he wondered if the sneaker belonged to a one-legged, one-footed beachcomber. Did such a man play the drums? The piano? Gamble? Tap time with one foot? Share shots and beers? Bull his way in bed in spite of an infirmity?

Three or four times that morning, gulls calling, air sweet and salty, he passed by the sneaker. Once it must have been a gaudy, outspoken type, styling for all it was worth at a hundred and twenty bucks a pair. Times change, he argued.

Calix could not remember all the nights when Paul's words came to him again from far off, thin and narrow and weak, escaping from a star wobbling on the horizon. It haunted him like a promise not kept. He could not go back to sleep. It was meeting barbed wire in the dark.

Paul often said, "There's so much adventure there, Jadon. Don't miss out on it. Between the Gulf and the bayous there's a whole lot of crawl space. Find some of it. I did. I loved it. You will too."

That probably started it off. Calix got up early, called his boss telling him he was going to Louisiana. In three days he knocked at the door of Paul Breden's parents.

They had given him the run of their summer home for two months. "Down on the Gulf, son. Paul loved it there."

Now, on his final morning, he was recounting all of it.

Something took him back to the sneaker, as if Paul was directing him. He heard him say, for the hundredth or more times, "There's so much adventure there, Jadon. Don't miss it."

He picked up the sneaker. Had not been in the water in for long. Maybe an incoming wave had tossed it higher on the beach. Jadon looked for the mate, for a footprint. The beach was pristine.

He put his hand inside the open heel. He felt queasy. He felt the shape of something inside, jammed into the toes. The lacing was tied tightly about the object, as if to keep it inside the sneaker. Intrigued, he felt a small round container and pulled out a plastic pill bottle, with no prescription label.

The little plastic bottle had a tight white cap on it and a note inside. The note was dry and said:

Whoever finds this: My name is Carlton Maxwell. I was visiting in Chapacteau.

I was looking for a canoe that got loose and floated off downstream. I saw some men kill a man and carry him on their boat. They caught me and took me too. I found this container in the water. I am alone among these men. I'm afraid I can't be saved. I have seen nobody for days,

These men stole something and carried something aboard along with the dead man. They carried me off with them and tied me up and later made me work. They said they'd kill me. I don't remember how many days it's been. Two or three times they locked me below the deck during daylight hours. But one night, when they thought I was sleeping after they were drinking a lot, I got my hold of a small can of paint. If you find this, my fingerprints in paint are on the underside of many surfaces on the boat. The gunnels, the bottom of a door, on the hinge side of hatch cover. I've hidden them there as proof of my abduction. I know they will throw me overboard when they are done with me. They tossed the dead man overboard, when we were far out.

If I jump off I will drown. I'd do it if I saw a boat, but they lock me up when a boat appears.

I know the sneaker will float. The medical bottle carries air. I threw both sneakers overboard.

The man they killed and threw overboard was Black Martin. They talked about him and something about the Carousel Lounge and another murder they had committed there but he got in the way. His fingerprints are in paint on a note I hid below deck under an emergency container.

If anyone finds this, the boat has a number on the side that says LA 9176 WZ but I could tell that some of the figures had been swapped because of the background marks.

If you can find them, please find me. If my friend had not died in Iraq, I bet he would be the one to find me.

That last bit crushed Calix.

He read the note at least a dozen times. If he went to the police with it, they'd laugh him out of the station. A note in a bottle in a sneaker! How ridiculous! Don't bother us! It's a joke.

He wished that Paul was standing by. "Hey, old buddy," he said a number of times, "wish that you were here. I know you'd believe this."

The police, of course, didn't laugh him out of the station, but did say it was far-fetched. "A sneaker?" the sergeant at the desk said. "When's the tap-off for the next game? We'll get back to you, son."

"Can you check to see if this Maxwell guy is missing?"

"Right to it, son. We'll have it checked out. We'll look for him, you can bet on that. That's a promise."

Nothing made the papers, not a word surfaced about a missing person. No face. No person. No memory. Calix was alone in the matter.

Of course he never saw Maxwell, who never rose up any place in the Gulf. Three months later, Calix came back to Louisiana, Paul Breden constantly after him to "find" his Louisiana. And he kept thinking it meant to find Maxwell.

The Bredens, knowing of his plight, allowed him use of their summer home again, and another turn at the beach. He started policing boatyards, the old boat registration number and all its possibilities computerized at first and then locked into his mind.

One day, at a boatyard lunch counter near, he met a girl working at a painter's easel. Her black hair hung over her eyes and he wondered how she could be making much of what she was looking at. She was painting a scene of a boat at a pier. It was pretty good, he thought. She was a pretty and her name was Judi Pless. She had known Paul Breden in grade school. Interest was heightened in both directions when he told her Paul's last words. She liked Calix immediately thereafter.

Judi was very curious about him. Her intrigue grew quicker over lunch and coffee. "Where up north do you come from?" she said, brushing hair out of her eyes, letting him see the sparkle suddenly residing there, the interest coming focal. The shape of his face pleased her, the eye of the artist making measure, finalizing acceptance.

"From a little town north of Boston about a dozen miles."

She liked how he looked at her when he talked, as though his eyes were hungry.

"It's called Saugus, but just a few miles away, on the ocean, is a place called Nahant.

She also liked his juxtaposition of interest points. "Once, I saw an exhibition of paintings there by a marine artist. All of them of huge ships and derricks and wharves and gantries and stevedore gear of all kinds, from ports all around the world, like energy at rest in busy harbors. Your work reminds me of his work, but of all of his paintings there was one simple one with a few dories tied up loosely at the ocean's edge, at a place in Portugal, by the mouth of the Aveiro River. Ropes were tied from the dories to branches driven into the sea bottom. It was the difference from the huge gantries and ships that haunted me at first, and then I saw what he had left out of the picture, and what he *wanted* me to see, I was convinced of that.

Judi Pless nodded her understanding. "Now I see what you meant by capturing the energy in my paintings." She, in that short moment, had been captivated herself, could feel it working through her body, making strange demands in its own right, leaving a trail her mind would follow later in the night. "You're the first one ever to say that, how I felt about a stand-still. Now tell me what really brings you down here to Louisiana again, whatever it is beyond Paul Breden."

She was expecting something entirely different from this man, a kind of intensity that enveloped him, that was broadcast from him in spite of his most handsome profile. She admitted he had taken her breath away with her first look at him. The depth in his eyes was new to her. All he said in the following moments still came as a total surprise. This stranger, this Jadon Calix, had a way of creating interest. She almost said how interesting he was, the words being tasted on her tongue.

He read Carlton Maxwell's note to her, his voice steady, his eyes as riveting as anything she had seen.

Then, an angelic light falling on her face, her hair suddenly in place as if set forever, she made him read Carlton Maxwell's note a second time. She kept nodding as if each scene was being set for her mind, keeping it for later contemplation. "There are things in the note that grab and twist me. Like I'm seeing things he did not say." He thought her to be in that trance-like attitude she called on when she was studying a subject to paint.

Calix felt her deep resonance searching for meaning or resolution. "The police won't help?" she said. "They don't care? How can that be? They should pursue all possibilities. Every damned one."

They talked about other things that interested them, the sea, how it touched in harbors, how harbors touched her, and, lately, touched him on the Gulf. They spoke about the Pacific Rim and Pacific Platelets and the California Faultline. It was a classroom filled with interests. *The Old Man and the Sea* came and went, along with *South Pacific* and *Moby Dick*. She was stunned when he told her that Michigan had the longest shoreline of any of the original 48 states, where she thought it would be Florida or Maine or California.

Calix, despite all his other interests, was smitten with her, drawn continually to her good looks, the way her hair would often seem to catch itself in a very special light, as if those shared lights were setting up her pose.

"I think Carlton Maxwell is saying find the missing boat, find the missing fingerprints. I think he's really saying 'find the missing men who killed that man and dropped him at sea,' and," she paused, brushing her hair back, staring at Calix as if she was looking through him at another scene, "'find those men that killed me.' I think it's pretty obvious that he's been murdered. They couldn't and wouldn't keep him around this long, not with the slightest chance of him getting loose. We have to find that boat. It all boils down to that."

"There's a lot of water out there, a lot of boats in ports, and hundreds of miles of shoreline. How do we do it?" He was torn in his attention span; Judi Pless was working all the secret places in his body, all of them, and it began to unnerve him.

He was, at one moment, about to kiss her, thinking how good it would feel, how good she smelled, the way she could look at him as if he could be, would be, a subject for a new painting. And in that one moment of indecision, when he felt at a total loss for all that he felt, Judi Pless leaned over and kissed him right on the lips. "I never do that," she said, "never. I think something might happen here. I'm hoping that it does."

He almost caved in at that kiss. He remembered Paul Breden out on the Iraqi desert, the mortars, the car bombs, and he could smell the scent of death. But this marvelous woman had cut through something a long time ignored with a simple yet not so simple kiss.

"I hope so too," he said, feeling his mouth drying up, a choke catching in his throat, a bubble threatening to burst in his chest, his fingers gone itchy. The dawn from an earlier day came back to him in its lavender touch; he could smell the lilac bush his brother had planted some twenty years ago, how a spring evening in the backyard could almost fracture him.

But Judi Pless left that alone for one second more.

She tossed her head nonchalantly, the dark hair bouncing about her face, masking something. "Would you like to come up and see my etchings?" she said, and without waiting for an answer, took his hand and walked off toward her small studio at the head of the marina.

He was amazed at what Judi had accomplished in her painting. The studio, to the walls and shelves, was full of paintings of all sizes, and all bordering in or on the sea. Boats. Shorelines. Rocks with a sea pounding at them. Silent sand under the sun. The paintings leaned on baseboards, lay piled on shelves, were hung indiscriminately on three of the walls. Three harbor scenes at dusk hung on what he presumed to be the bathroom door. When he flipped the paintings over, like others he had turned, he saw the legends. "There's so damn much here. You've recorded all data on the back, just like a newspaper caption, like a journal or a diary of every painting. Your whole life is here. You could spin your whole life right out of these paintings, flip them and make a movie. Still life to action, let the energy loose again. God, you're ingenious. You're thorough. You're so beautiful at what you do. How old were you when you started painting?"

"My father was painting when I was a kid, he always painted. He'd paint a scene and sometimes throw it away the next day. He was not very good at it, but he was happy mixing and slopping and making crude angles in scenes. My mother yapped at him a lot. Painting was, I think, a way to get away from her. Out in the garage he'd paint anything, whether he liked the scene or not. I wanted to tell him for years, to suggest things, changes, other ways, techniques I could see very early on but I couldn't do it. I wanted to talk about color mix and shading and linear stuff at an angle, but I couldn't bring myself to do it."

Her confession went the whole route, pouring out of her, her face lit up from a mysterious halo. "When he was dying from throat cancer, he said, 'You always knew, didn't you? I knew it and you never said a word and I loved you for that. Now take every damn one of my paintings and burn them before your mother thinks she can sell them. I don't want them seen by anybody. I don't ever want them connected to you in any way. I know that you knew, even when you were a kid. You were special then. You are special now. You will become very special. Find your place in all of this and then kick the hell out of it. Promise me that, that you'll kick the hell out of it all.' He died holding my hand."

In love! In love! Calix knew he was in love with this painter with the dark lashes and the dark hair and the light leaping in her eyes. He knew incandescence, the mysterious halo burning about them. He knew what ambience was, how it was meant to be. Was this Paul Breden's Louisiana? Was this part or all of what Paul knew he'd find in his Louisiana? He kissed her without another second's hesitation and she trembled and nestled in his arms and then, abruptly, tried to say something, but he was holding her the same way he had held Paul at his dying breath. The end or the beginning was on top of him, around him. The heat of the desert had been overpowering, burning right down through his throat, into his guts at turmoil. He could taste the acid of gunfire, of shrapnel almost in flight, the dust ready to bury both Paul and him. But in his arms she was struggling, whispering, "The numbers. The numbers. I remember the numbers!"

He could not let go of her. He wanted to hold the moment forever.

But she kept saying, kept scratching at reality, "The numbers! The numbers!" Finally, she broke loose, then came back into his arms and kissed him again. It was a long and passionate kiss and then she struggled anew. "I know those numbers, those letters," and with that broke free of him again and started tossing paintings aside after looking at them.

"Help me, Jadon, help me!" she screamed. "I remember those numbers! I remember the numbers, the boat."

There were hundreds of paintings stored in her small studio. It was as if they were old magazines or newspapers to be discarded, the way the two of them tossed paintings aside, off the walls, off the shelves, from piles against the baseboard. And in a moment of serene triumph, her hair thrown back over her brow, her eyes full of fire and knowledge and final resolution, she held up Carlton Maxwell's boat. The alphas and numbers were there, caught forever on the prow of the hull, even to the distorted shading of the background where the registration numbers had been switched around.

Judi Pless had listed the date, marina, the slip number, the harbor, the city. The whole scene came leaping back at her; the masts and bowsprits of other boats at the marina, a small sloop out on the bay, a boy standing in a nearby dory while holding a fishing rod, a whole ball of energy at an utter and complete standstill.

Jadon Calix could almost see the painted fingerprints on the underside of the railings that dipped down the length of the boat. "Let them duck this one," he said, as he kissed her again.

Unsolved Mystery

Wil A Emerson

Murder comes easy for me. Either I see an opportunity to advance an agenda, strike an agreement and follow orders or I go the traditional route and kill to right a wrong. A snake in the grass or a soldier? Doesn't a farmer strike with a shovel to chop off the head of a venomous beast?

Not long after my tenth year as a pro, I was asked to alter the daily routine of a member of congress. The well-schooled but non-conforming fellow often referred to himself as Stardust. Fairy tale believers thought it meant he could make dreams come true. As his following grew to exponential numbers, the down and outs on the street, along with adversaries, understood why he often used slang to describe his endeavors. 'I'm lit', a favorite. Or 'busted' when the polling numbers didn't work his way. When a bill he promoted got overturned, he'd say 'my frenemy let me down'. Somehow in the end, it all worked in his favor.

Saved by a recount, he retained his congressional seat. Then his nefarious bill got tweaked at the last minute. Victory.

Among other things, a well-healed group of opposites were aware this designated fellow was 'bi-polar'. His moods shifted like the tides. It wasn't from eating jam and jelly. For the record, his family became tremendously wealthy by selling a variety of jams and jellies on the international market.

What the public didn't recognize was the fact this notorious family had paid for their son's seat in Congress by aiding transformational political zealots who wanted nothing more than to change the face of the United States and American democracy. Campaign reform, they called it.

The opposition knew why and how this dynamic, dangerous family intended to gain power. One mayor, one governor, one congressman. Godly men do the right thing...and others just follow a false promise.

So, I signed a contract with the opposition. Not because I had it out for Stardust, not that I hated Mr. King of Stardust Jams and Jellies—it was because I hated drugs and knew most of those imported jelly jar boxes were packed with heroin grown in distant lands from which the family had their origin. Thus, in the underworld, in their very lucrative business circle, they were the Kings of Stardust. Their drugs had caused far too many problems on our streets.

It seemed like the right thing to do: stop this Congressman's dirty habits and improve his overall health condition, too.

I didn't hesitate when the designated time arrived. I dressed for the occasion, not my usual attire, either. A simple outfit, worn by dozens on the street. Black and gray running gear, white and black sneakers, sweat band, ear plugs and drug store sunglasses. Run, I can do. Jog or walk and observe my surroundings within a moving crowd.

Two pops. Four blocks from Stardust's condo as he waited for an Uber driver. Discreet. I'm a pro. Trained by experts, work for experts.

How many trash cans along a city street? Enough to toss a muzzled weapon. Next block discard black and gray shirt, bright red tee underneath. Alley, pull on the shorts stashed earlier in the day.

Only two minor incidents had the potential to interfere in the stealth get away: first, another jogger, similar black and gray spandex, treading in the opposite direction, who tripped and staggered to recover. I lent a helping hand, pulled him to upright position. A quick thank you. But I remembered every nuance of his face, his hands, what he wore. Ray-Bans from the Ferrari collection. Habit of mine to mentally catalogue every encounter. Second intrusion: a dog walker, three blocks from my apartment. The red shirt must have triggered the bulldog demeanor. It growled. I skirted around the nasty brown and white, four-legged creature.

The owner, female, gray curly hair, queen size blue jeans, green tee-shirt with daisies on it, called out, "Oh, Oscar is very friendly."

I decided, why not. Not wanting to be perceived as an unfriendly stranger, a suspicious one due to what had occurred not too far from this meet and greet spot. Safety first. Don't attract unwarranted attention. I returned her smile and offered the back of my hand to let the mutt take a sniff. I'd have kicked the dog to high heaven if it bit me but that might have caused more attention than I wanted.

So, as I jogged the last blocks to home, I planted pictures of the encountered people in my mind. Perhaps one of my back-ups. Accident or intended. I might never know.

After the event, I went home and fell into a deep coma. Nothing to aid me, just the satisfaction of a job well done. It happens that way. An honest person knows the difference between duty and global destruction.

When the doorbell rang, I adjusted my pillow to ignore the intrusion. I'd never had a visitor. The wrong address, quick finger, mistake. A drop-in? Couldn't be. No long-lost friends would track me down in this unlikely neighborhood. If anyone had received an invitation to foster a friendship, it had been in the far distant past.

Another adjustment and I was back to hugging the pillow.

But, like the mailman, the doorbell rang twice. I glanced at my watch. Not even midnight. I needed at least seven hours straight to feel refreshed, spiritually renewed, enough to tackle the day. And whatever job awaited me. Could be immediate or a many weeks delay.

But then the mind I'd groomed, nurtured to be on alert and super speculative, wasn't trained to let go easily. Late UPS delivery? Impossible. Like a data collection system, neurons buzz and dendrites whirl. It took a few more seconds to focus on the intrusion and conclude there might be a matter of importance on the other side of my door. Another ring, bing, ding.

Okay, grab a cover up, glasses on. Enough. Get rid of the intruder.

Like a few other renters in my apartment building, I'd hung a green wreath on the door. Picked up at Hobby Lobby, it represented the 'friendly' neighbor persona. But I'd never had the occasion to consider the effect it had on the inside of the door.

To my chagrin, I suddenly realized I'd created a problem. The peephole was covered and left no visual access to the person only inches away from a straining eye.

A big mistake. Not that I feared anything, but awareness is preparation for the unexpected.

There wasn't a single reason in this world or the next for anyone remotely connected to my professional job or day job to be at my door. Logic worked at full capacity. The person whose knuckles rested on the wood, who wrapped and fingered the little button could only be there for one reason. Trouble. Capital T.

I braced my back against the wall, next to the door jam and waited a few seconds. To add to the suspense, I deftly removed my slipper and pressed it lightly but with surety on the door. As if I'd approached and leaned into the peep hole.

A nanosecond and two ping, pings. Silencer. Rapid fire. Right through the peep hole.

I heard the scuffle of feet in the hallway. The sound carried to the stairwell at the north end closest to the subway station, closest to throngs of people out for late night pleasure. An easy exit and one would be lost in the hoopla of frivolity.

I slide down to the floor, my palms sweaty, my heart rate at NASCAR speed. The attack nearly shattered the essence of my Charlotte, North Carolina upbringing. If you lived an honest life, worked hard, did the right thing, you'd be protected by a higher power. Like Bubba Wallace on a winning day, though, I was relieved and happy beyond belief that I'd followed my instincts, mimicked an eyeball gander with the shoe trick and denied my intended assassinator's victory.

There wasn't much I could do to right the injustice of the moment. By making even a small gesture, like calling the police, my cover would be blown. I did the next best thing. Altered the tale tell signs of the event, dug the pellets out of the wall, patched the spot with some toothpaste and baking soda, hung a picture over the area and went back to bed.

I would still get in a full seven hours of necessary slumber if I cut breakfast short.

The next morning took a little ingenuity to not make it obvious the assailant had failed at the mission. Like the professional I am, I rearranged my hair, adapted a style with different clothes, a cane, orthopedic shoes, and a small oxygen tank and snuck out the door. My apartment is near the stairwell, so I gingerly took a flight down, walked the length of a lower-level hall, took another stairwell down to the next floor, walked to the middle of the hall and pushed the elevator button. At six in the morning, few people wandered those halls or stairwells. It made walking in and out of the confines undetected very easy. Unlike many in my building, a multitude of techies working at home, I was a steady on-sight employee.

But I did have to be on high alert. The unthinkable had happened. Was this revenge for my earlier dastardly deed? I had taken a human's life. Everyone involved in the process had taken great care to not leave a trail. Not the slightest, most remote, unlikely piece of evidence left at the scene. There was a designated sweep-up crew before the police arrived. If the weapon was found during the investigation, all recognizable ID had been destroyed. Preparation had taken several months, coordination, tracking, security measures of the highest level. Approval had come from the top.

Why was I chosen for this particular job? Because I had an untraceable profile, a persona depleted of wrongdoing. It worked so well, it afforded me and the organization the opportunity to perform a string of duties as never before imagined.

But someone decided, I concluded during my unfashionable, disabled person's walk to my workplace, I needed to be either eradicated or used to teach a lesson. The intention had been to murder me. Murder the professional who had just assassinated a member of Congress. Murder the professional who had erased the vile person who led a duplicitous life, who had no concern for his constituents or any other American citizens. However, what I had done was essentially an act of treason or at the very least, a federal crime.

Caution, as never before, needed to be my best friend.

I entered the walkway that led to a seldom used back door in a small garden area behind St. Cecelia's rectory. Yes, I'd kept an eye on my back even though the street was empty as I shuffled along the two blocks to the sanctuary. I unlatched the bolt, twisted the handle, and then slide the key into the keyhole. Done in that sequence or the door would not open. Rigged by a special locksmith who also worked for the organization. Inside, I slipped into a small closet, pulled the cord for the ceiling light, squirmed out of the frumpy apparel, salt and pepper wig and folded all the items neatly to store them in the footlocker which had a combination lock. After smoothing out my day wear, I pulled out a pocket comb and rearranged my hair. Normal attire, ready for the day.

At some point, the garments in the footlocker would be taken out and replaced by another nonthreatening, uninviting, unassuming outfit. I often delighted in the artistic ingenuity of my clever, unknown dresser. Bless their soul, everyone has something to contribute in the effort to keep the United States of America a free and decent place to live. I can't reveal all the personas assumed by wearing these intriguing outfits, but imagine what you'd see at any time on a major city street. Where every type of entertainment is available along with every type of cuisine, every fad to buy or sell, every religion to represent. So many assumed characters.

Before sitting at my desk, I fully opened the slated blind over the largest window in the office. After each assignment, I adjusted the individual slats of the blind to an exact specification to reveal what message needed to be conveyed to my team. At the day job, I signaled either task completed, general communication, pertinent information, help, or SOS. Six modes of transmission.

This time, due to the late-night incident, I debated what should be passed on to the higher ups. My task master, of course, should be first on the chain of alert. But I had to consider the risk. What if I was no longer deemed worthy of the required tasks? With all the information I carried in my mind, would I just be retired to become a veteran of these *special forces*?

Who could I trust? Mistake number one. I'd never formed a cohesive bond.

Mistake number two. I didn't plan ahead for the personal long gray road. What would I do when nerves gave way, sight filtered through milky gray eyes, foggy recollection or when heaven's reward, the overwhelming goal was reached, and pockets were full of money? What if the United States of America was no longer a target for the zealots, idealists of reform, the dangerous power-brokers whose only desire is total control of the world. What happened then?

In this select institution, of which most my adult years had been spent, where did all those old warriors go? Retirement on a beach or permanently retired?

As I studied options, it came to mind that, other than an occasional encounter with my task master, I had no real knowledge of who my superiors were, their rank and file in this clandestine service—or their routine employment. Not all were doctors, lawyers, business moguls, in a work environment where they acquired retirement benefits and lived securely ever after. What happened to the undercover librarian, metal welder, bus driver, teacher, the grocery store clerk, those with full-time jobs but at a moment's notice could be reassigned?

It was known, after being vetted, proven trustworthy, one could achieve what they desired in the organization if time and good graces were on their side. Move higher on the chain of command? A fellow professional with a strong constitution and expert-level talents, would be given priority when a call for advancement came. Those select people were then supposed to be protected with lifetime status. But what about those, such as myself, who preferred to remain at the expert level? Those who wanted to be embedded in the web and full of critical information but didn't sign a lifetime commitment?

At present, during the day, I performed as an assistant in a rather small rectory office. An inconsequential assistant who on any given day could/would be moved to a different location, adapt to a new boss, and still provide crack-shot expertise as the organization deemed necessary.

Was I really a critical member of the team? Or had my experience become the sword in my side? Too much knowledge, a great risk?

Whoever rang the doorbell the night before could have been of the same mind-set.

Beware. Caution must be taken.

More questions loomed. Why now? Outlived my usefulness? Retirement pending? As required, no matter the assignment, my routine had to remain stable.

My day boss rarely arrived before eight-thirty which gave me time to alert my task masker via the code method about the recent event and if a call came through after my signal, I would attend to that undercover business. If there were an emerging problem, I'd receive a response within a half hour. If I displayed the abominable SOS, help would arrive in less than five minutes. Lucky for me, I had never tested the extraordinary service

During the waiting period, I tuned out and switched into a form of complete concentration, the opposite of mindlessness. Every aspect of mental control was used to train this invaluable organ, gray and white matter, which so many individuals neglected. I thrived on constant adjustment and training. As exercise, I played out previous tasks performed. Each step of preparation, execution and the finale revisited. Around each curve at an exact speed, eye on the counter-intuitive obstacles, also alert to tailgaters. Out for the win. Nerves of steel, ready, aim, fire. No mistakes.

If no response arrived from my task master, I could then review the calendar of events for my day boss. Assume the ordinary and do the work for what I was paid.

But on this day, this very unusual day, the day after a congressman had expired by my hand, I had an unresolved dilemma. It had to be dealt with. Which made me hesitate a couple minutes longer than usual.

What exact signal should I send to my task master? General communication? Pertinent information? Help? SOS seemed far too radical. No harm had come my way but…and it was a big what if.

Who could I trust? I decided to go with number two signal. Task completed. Simple. No red flags raised. The mode: Two of the slats angled in the opposite direction. No specific slats, just two. Random mishap for the outdated mode of limiting light into the old rectory office. A rustic form of air-conditioning. When I first sat down at that desk, I would have appealed to my benefactor to replace the hideous blinds. Funds limited in the church coffer for updates.

And now the thirty-minute wait. Eyes on the clock, mind centered on routine. I decided to forgo the review of my previous accomplishment. That vivid picture would remain for some time. Savor it later. I went back to an earlier task, performed two months before. It had required more dexterity, more clever concealment, more diversionary tactics. The target wasn't a political figure but a member of the spoilers. In an appealing, more feminine attire, I'd carried out the task. That, too, had been risky, when factoring in no extra cover for the weapon I carried. The steps used to achieve the required outcome were firmly fixed, like gorilla glue, in my mind.

Tick, tock, tick. Thirty minutes went in a flash.

Because I had not taken time for breakfast, I went to our break room, a converted office space used on occasion for counseling sessions. A nice tufted blue couch, an antique table with wrought iron legs and four high-backed wooden chairs with blue and white checked pads on the seat. All donated items from a generous parishioner. A bookshelf and a gray metal file cabinet were in a corner. On top of the file was our eight-cup coffee pot and a wooden wicker basket that held the accouterments for the more adventurous coffee aficionado. Water for the coffee maker was carried from a utility room at the end of the corridor.

I or my boss brought in the supplies, no schedule as to who or when, as the need arose. One or the other refilled the basket with creamers, flavored syrups, sugar substitutes and an assortment of designer coffee brands. Donated, of course. First arrival brewed the coffee during the week, last to leave washed the cups. On the weekend, I had no knowledge of who did what but I knew the room was often used. On Monday, coffee was still in the pot and several unwashed cups or paper plates sat on the scarred table. Why be concerned about who left it there? It felt good when the room was tidy, so clean-up satisfied my thimble-size domestic need and offered a few minutes reprieve from phone calls, calendar, or ledgers.

On more than one occasion, I found the day boss taking a nap on the couch. I'd never be one to deny him quiet time. The lord he answered to knew what had been required of him during the wee hours, rain or shine. As a matter of fact, I never inquired as to whose funeral he attended, the weddings he performed, the hospital visits he made. His calling; to each his own.

While in the coffee room, I heard the rattle of his office door. Earlier than usual, I thought, but went about my chore. I waited for the coffee to brew and rummaged through the first drawer of the cabinet file to see if any cookies or treats had been stored away. Those items were seldom left in sight. Temptations in a sugary form led to an increase in his waistline, he said too often. The food chain was never ending, though, as matrons of the church seemed to be on a constant mission to nurture the faith leader who stood between them and the pearly gates of heaven. I gathered by my timeline as his employee, if this continued, a few rungs on the ladder to heaven would collapse by undue stress if strict avoidance wasn't practiced.

Preacher, I am not, though. Everyone left to their own devices or vices. I just wanted one cookie or, perhaps, a donut to provide a little sustained power.

A bag of luscious home-mades, the bag itself, was caught between the first drawer tract and the drawer below, so I fiddled to unleash it. I smelled pecans and peanut butter. Would this be a double lucky find? A few jiggles, wiggles and the second drawer slide out. Ready to grasp the zip lock bag and breathe a sigh of relief, I was halted by the sight beneath the bag. Resting between two files in the second drawer was the butt of a black metal weapon.

I know my weapons and while I would never pick up an unknown firearm to investigate its lethal potential, loaded or unloaded, I also knew not to leave fingerprints behind. This was not my business. Perhaps the day boss felt justified in defending himself. Although a hidden gun wasn't much of a deterrent to crime, this wasn't my business.

Hunger pains needed to be satisfied. I picked up the goody bag and gently closed the drawer. The light on the coffee pot blinked green so I added sweet-and-lo to a large mug and filled it to the brim with the dark brew. Two bites of the sweet treat and I was ready to move on. Two steps and I heard the phone ring. Someone in need. The day had officially begun.

The phone abruptly stopped ringing. Unheard of. The boss never answered the phone. A cardinal rule. It could set him back an hour if the person on the other end had a tale of woe to share. My job, one of many, was to be the screener.

I heard a voice and shook my head. Time to juggle meetings.

As I reviewed his schedule, I finished the delicacy, rested back in my desk chair, and sipped on the delicious coffee, a brand sent via express mail from Vermont by a wealthy parishioner. This sanctuary leader had good taste buds and appreciated a nice gift. Especially, coffee, baked goods and whatever other delicacies that kept his waistline in a constant distended state. Happy man. Bless his soul.

However, I still had a serious problem playing havoc in the back of my mind. Two slugs through the peephole at my apartment. Someone after me.

Who could I trust?

I needed another cookie. So, I went back to the break room, munched on one and then pocketed another for a later time. I happened to glance at my watch again. Exactly eight-thirty, the time when day boss usually entered his office.

Ah, but he had already arrived. Okay, habits formed are meant to be broken.

I entered my office and sat at my desk in the high-backed wood chair, a donated relic from the past. The phone rang and before I could push the on button, it stopped. The day boss taking another call? Wonders never ceased. And then I looked at the window. The largest window in the room, the one with the blind that conveyed my recent message. The slats were now a new variation. My number two signal, *task completed*, had been changed. Someone had deliberately adjusted the blind over the largest window in my office to the number three signal. Three in a downward angle. In my organization it only meant one thing, Pertinent

Information.

WTF. Another topic? Who altered the blind?

Under any other circumstance, I would have concluded it had been done by a shift in the air. If not, a ghost had altered the air flow. But in my profession, there are no coincidences.

Beware. Caution. The opposition at work?

No mistake about it, the window covering with its separated cords, open, close, adjust height, had been altered. Pertinent Information?

I slowly rose from the chair, took a deep breath, and went to the doorway, a quick peek toward the boss's office. Two voices. I pressed against the wall and started to move stealthily down to the first exit door. I turned just in time to see my day boss, dressed as usual in his black pants and white shirt with the black collar, come from his office and stop in the middle of the hall.

"Good morning," he said. His most chipper voice.

"And to you, too," I said. Should I stay or should I go? Never blow your cover: high on the top ten of a long list of rules. Very close to the top. Safety first, sits as number one. Fight or flight, number two, then a matter of circumstances.

"A little off schedule," he said. He looked at the watch on his wrist.

Was he lying, covering up? "Five minutes at the most," I said.

"Not sure you were in." He stepped toward his door.

A strange comment I thought. Although he seldom greeted me on his arrival, I usually made a point to acknowledge him after he'd settled at his desk for a few minutes. Habit, nothing more. And then I'd be right back on the phone. If he were unusually late, he still would have settled behind his desk and greeted me only on my approach.

And then his office door opened. We both turned at the sound, the appearance. Cookie lady, the matron nurturer who supplied the sweet treats. The chubby matron who was known to frequent the parish Sunday services and hall social gatherings, one of the most devoted members of the church. The one member who did her best to make sure the faith leader had a full, round belly.

"Mrs. Lafferty, an early morning pleasure."

She looked at him and then her dark eyes turned on me. Suddenly open, wide, surprised like a deer caught in the headlights, as if she had seen a ghost. No mistake about it.

"Good morning, Mrs. Lafferty," I said. "Thanks for answering the phone earlier." I smiled.

I had to give her credit; she didn't overreact. She just nodded as the color drained from her face.

It had been a clever disguise, the one she wore on the street. And the added bulldog as a confirmation of her status. A clever prop. Unique.

Remember, I never forget a face. Never. A talent I didn't share with my trainers or the public. No professional reason to do so.

A decision had to be made. Leave immediately or resolve a dire situation. I had been discovered, tracked by the opposition. They, she in particular, had failed the mission.

I decided to go about the expected routine and left the two *faithful* friends in the hallway, went back to my office and adjusted the slats one more time. SOS. I walked nonchalantly to the small break room, opened the second drawer of the file cabinet and, drew out the black metal weapon. A Bonds Arm Derringer. Yes, I know my weapons. I held it behind my back for safety reasons.

A few more steps and I was at my day boss's office door. I smiled, fired. Pop, pop, pop. Loud, no means to silence the Derringer, and stepped back. The faithless matron fell flat on her traitor face. My day boss made the sign of the cross.

"Have a nice day, Father. I actually did this for your safety." And then I left the room. Went to the front entrance of the historical neighborhood church and got into the blue sedan idling at the curb. As promised, they did respond in less than five minutes. A lot less than five.

Gone, gone, gone. Out of the picture. On to another location.

The incident received a lot of media coverage. A hideous murder took place in the once quiet neighborhood. Church relics had gone untouched, the murderous thief took the poor box, though. A representation of how disenfranchised people, ravaged by drugs, were infiltrating our United States of America's streets. Killed the innocent to steal donations that probably only amounted to a few hundred dollars.

The opposition was in a tight place. Too much hoop la about the demise of one of their own would bring in a lot of unwanted investigators. The faith leader, with his black pants, white shirt and black collar, would be transferred in the near future. Publicity, good or bad, can be too much for any institution to bear.

How I'd blown my cover never came to light. Relocated to a sunnier location and with new, certified credentials, I found the new day job a little more interesting than the previous one. As a copy editor for a small newspaper, the written word does become a sword. The pay isn't very sufficient but a few letters, lines here and there can alter the intent of an article. My nature thrives on doing the right thing.

They tell me, via messenger, there's a possibility I'll be given a higher rank in the organization. Something to consider.

Time catching up with me? It has been more than ten years of intermittent stress. It can wreak havoc on the eyes, this professional work I've done. No glasses needed, yet. Perhaps in the future, a professional instructor in the organization will fit my needs. Let another generation solve the problem if it still exists.

Are instructors allowed to retire? Or is the only way out permanent dismissal by someone who believes in the importance of protecting democracy? The reality is, I carry with me from job-to-job extensive knowledge on how the face of this organization operates. Am I still a valued employee or a potential risk?

Then it hit me. Had my cover really been blown? Was it the opposition who rang the apartment doorbell, ring, ding, ding on that one exceptional night? Or a fellow professional?

Unsolved mystery. A lot to ponder while waiting for the next assignment.

Vanity and Innocence

Peter Trelay

I sat staring at the searing lava vaporizing the water as it extended the land mass of a little piece of forgotten rock in the vast Atlantic Ocean. It made me think about the millennia lost to human consciousness and the infinite future. It evoked that sense of calm that comes from realizing how insignificant we are in our petty little struggles for self-affirmation and glory; struggling to make a mark on the sliver of time we call modernity.

I turned off the T.V. and went to check on the baby. She was so angelic; a blank page not yet messed up by the world around her. I returned to bed where her narcissistic mother lay snoring, and watched the diffused neon light fracture as it flickered through the mottled glass of the floor-to-ceiling window. For a brief instant, I had the urge to scoop up her near anorexic body and throw her out the window onto the pavement eight floors below.

That's it, I thought. *Time to go.*" Breaking points still take you by surprise no matter how anticipated they may have been. I thought the time had come to book a ticket out of the nightmare she had so carefully constructed.

But where to go? Anywhere but here in Buenos Aires. I wasn't going to kill the mother of my child, however convinced I was that it would be doing them both a favor in the long run. Eventually the baby would grow up and realize what a self-absorbed, little tyrant her mother was. Then she would have to decide whether to abandon her or suffocate.

What is it that drives some people to try to dominate every aspect of another person's life? Ah, yeah, of course, I know. A deep seated insecurity, combined with low self-esteem.

Doctors think everyone is stupid, but I knew what she was doing.

Softening her stance and making me think everything would get better, but only when she thought she was fertile. Then lying-in bed afterwards with her pelvis elevated by a pillow. I should have left then. *So why didn't you?* Hesitation; the worst of all sins.

Narcissists have the incredible ability to reinvent the past, by believing the lies they tell themselves and others. She insisted that she had not been trying to get pregnant, and then told me, "Don't worry; I know you're not up for this, I'll get an abortion." The next day she rang everyone we knew with the wonderful news of the baby, and then assured me that she would stop being a bitch. Like a deer caught in the headlights, I hesitated.

In the end, I decided to see it through for the sake of the baby and to wait and see. *Who knows,* I thought. *Maybe becoming a mother will make her grow up.*

She thought she had finally managed to get me under her thumb. What a shock it must have been for her to realize that there are people who cannot be enslaved, regardless of the cost. Although I didn't know at the time, it would mean three years of sleep deprivation, and a lifetime of waking up at two in the morning. But it wouldn't have changed my resolve.

I was trying to remember some quote along the lines of 'Women possess like despots and dispose of with the same fervor'. There was no point in extending this farce to the bitter end. In any case, narcissists don't believe in bitter ends, they prefer endless torture. They keep coming back to see if their victims have forgotten the lesson. I looked over at her, above her half open mouth her large nose was rattling with each snore. How much more ugly than usual she now appeared, like that day in the kitchen when she was still pregnant and stuck her infuriated, contorted face into mine, screaming. Forever the drama queen, as I pulled her away from me, grabbing her blouse from behind, she collapsed like a sack of potatoes, as if she'd been violently struck.

Latino women always try to attack the manhood of their partners when they're angry. She never realized that I was oblivious to this, not being even remotely patriarchal. No wonder Latino men are so macho.

I got up, went to the kitchen, and made a cup of coffee.

I felt a little more at peace and slightly less guilty, knowing that my daughter would be taken care of, physically at least. Although being raised by a neurotic is never easy, something I knew from personal experience. My partner was an ophthalmologist and only child, heir to a few pieces of valuable real estate from her aging parents, so she could cope financially. Being an only child undoubtedly contributed to her neurosis.

I had only eked out a living teaching English there for five years; so it was a relief to know it might soon be over, and I could find somewhere that paid a decent salary. It made me depressed to think about leaving behind my daughter and the few good friends I had made in that time. The random thought of faking her suicide had brought home the necessity of getting out. That insane impulse had been a shocking revelation to me, one that had never sprung to mind before. I realized that the pain of leaving behind my daughter had made me capable of contemplating it.

I wanted to find a way to remain close to my daughter, even if separated. Then came the thought of how impossible she would try to make life if I did. I put this to the test by moving out and staying with friends, and then renting an apartment nearby. Already thinking it would give me a little space to decide where to go if it failed. Each time I came to visit the baby she would provoke a fight. As I left, my daughter would cry and pull at my shirt. So she took to leaving her in the crib when I was leaving, but she would jump up and down screaming, rocking the crib by pulling furiously at the bars. It was doing more harm than good, and convinced me that leaving was better all round.

I dithered still about where to kick-start my life again. The frontier between transitions is a delicate moment. It sets in motion an entirely new sequence of largely unpredictable events. Getting it right, is at least partially determined by intuition. Because my hand had been forced, it made arriving at a quick decision that much more difficult.

Forced into exile after the months of stress that our deteriorating relationship had created, I decided to go somewhere lush and warm to lick my wounds. Costa Rica came to mind. Short on money, I found a cheap flight that meant flying first from Buenos Aires to Los Angeles and then south again to San Jose in Costa Rica.

When the customs officials in Buenos Aires saw that I had overstayed my visa by five years, they reacted with the pompous indignation so typical of government officials. I pointed out to them that even without a work permit their government had insisted that I pay taxes at all the places I had worked. They didn't seem to understand the duplicity or hypocrisy of this, and demanded that I cough up a fine of $2000. When I told them I didn't have it, they threatened to detain me, which even I knew was illegal. In the end, with piqued self-righteousness they registered me as *persona non grata* for five years and let me exit their sovereign land.

When my daughter turned six, I would return to that airport, and be charged $100 for a 70-day visa, in spite of having a daughter who is an Argentine citizen. The cynical excuse they gave me was that Argentines are charged the same amount for a Canadian visa. The 'tit for tat' diplomacy of national governments reminds me of children in the playground who say; "He hit me first." Why is it that more often than not, people elect the biggest babies with fragile egos to run the country?" He was ignoring the obvious. No Canadian would come to work illegally in a country with an average year on year inflation rate of 190 percent.

I had gone hoping to settle there again, and to get to know my daughter. It would turn out to be a waste of time. Initially, her mother permitted me to see her one day each weekend for a few hours. When she realized I did not intend to become her obedient lap dog, she began cancelling the visits, with the excuse that her six year old had to study for a test. I would leave again after the 70 days.

In L.A. while I was waiting for the connecting flight to San Jose, I left the terminal and sat on a bench outside to smoke. An Arab looking man sat down beside me for the same purpose. We began the kind of brief conversation that people have in airports with complete strangers to pass the time. He was in the fabric business, and had had a successful meeting to produce material for an American clothing manufacturer.

Now he was on his way back home to Turkey. I was looking down at his phone as he showed me some photos of his family, and the factory in Istanbul, when two pairs of gaudy-looking stilettos appeared on the pavement below. Looking up past the fishnets, miniskirts, belly piercings and tube-tops, I arrived at the lurid makeup and big hair of a couple of stereotypical L.A. hookers. One of them asked for a light. My Turkish friend was more intensely disgusted than I was amused. They stood there a few minutes humming and hawing and then moved on. I remember thinking that neither my smoking companion nor me looked in any way like possible clients.

Still chatting, we got up and strolled back into the terminal, where we were met by four oversized TSA agents who invited us to come with them. They separated us. I was taken to a small room and found my luggage, which had already been removed from the plane. It was being examined next to a curious looking machine that looked vaguely like a photocopier. An officer emptied the contents of my bag, and began wiping down things with a square cotton swab and then continued by swabbing the empty backpack. He put the piece of cotton into a small drawer on the machine, pressed a few buttons and waited. In the meantime, another officer flipped through the pages of my passport and asked me around twenty questions related to what I had been doing in the recent past, and what I planned for the near future. Satisfied that I was not a terrorist and that my belongings had no traces of bomb making or explosive materials, they let me go and check-in my baggage again.

Prompted by a racist outlook, I think they assumed that two strangers, from such diverse ethnic backgrounds were unlikely to enter into casual conversation at an airport. They had sent the two undercover agents made up like prostitutes to get a closer look at us. I suppose they thought if we were true fundamentalists, we would overreact to the sinful women accosting us. My smoking partner, who looked obviously Arab, had set off their radar and made them think that the two of us were planning to blow a plane out of the sky.

*****

Surrounded by mountains, San Jose, Costa Rica, lies nestled in a valley at 1,200 meters above sea level, and it's chilly in February. I bought three newspapers and examined the classified job sections while overdosing on some of the world's best coffee. The *Ticos*, as the natives refer to themselves, take their coffee seriously, and forbid the planting of anything but Arabica seeds in the rich volcanic soil.

I found an advert, 'English teacher needed afternoons and evenings-accommodation provided'. The job was in a very small town on the Nicoya Peninsula on the west coast, only 7km from the Pacific. I rang one 'Jorge Crespo', who was quite vague and almost certainly inebriated.

I set out on a bus the following morning regardless, heading due west for 60 miles towards the coast. After an hour of skirting blue mountain ranges on a winding narrow road, we began our descent to sea level.

In Puntarenas, I took a ferry ride to southern end of the peninsula. From there I got another bus, arriving at the address just outside the tiny town of Cobano by mid-afternoon. In less than half a day, I had travelled half the breadth of the country.

Jorge sat, drink in hand, on the porch of a dirty bungalow surrounded by tall weeds, both of them looking derelict. He was about 60, though he doddered like an octogenarian when he got up slowly to shake my hand, and then immediately collapsed back into his folding beach chair. He was a small man, with dyed black hair and thick glasses that made him look like an aging owl. The sagging skin on his face and the back of his hands was covered in spots. In spite of this outward appearance, he seemed to be in denial, with a pathetic air of bravado about him. He was dressed in matching white patent leather shoes and belt, cream-colored polyester pants and a loud shirt of primary colors. Within minutes of greeting me, he asked what I thought of the, "Las hembras Ticas," or Costa Rican "females."

He seemed pleased to have someone to talk to, and I felt compelled to get a taxi back to the ferry, but the state of my finances would not allow it. I sat down next to him on a folding beach chair while he continued imbibing cheap rum. On his invitation, I entered the kitchen to get a beer, which I removed from a twenty-year-old refrigerator that hummed loudly. I took a sip and looked out through the mosquito screens in the back of the kitchen. A little stream ran along the edge of the backyard, disappearing behind the neighbor's house. On a tree branch a heavy-set iguana, easily more than a meter long, stopped munching on a leaf and stared back at me. It had a long crest of spines running from the back of its head to the tip of its tail, and black stripes around its torso. It gave me a bored expression that said, "I've been around for ten million years, and you were born yesterday."

I went back out to the front porch, to get a better idea of what I had got myself into. He had been evasive on the phone about where exactly I would be teaching and staying, and now I learned why. Tomorrow I would teach two classes from 5 to 8pm in the local community center. There was no school, he organized groups in community halls and churches, and the 'accommodation' was a dingy room in his dilapidated bungalow. A company had sponsored him to come here, and even rented the bungalow for him. If he could get enough students signed up, they would open a branch of the academy in Cobano.

Judging by the look on the faces of the women as they stared in our direction walking into and out of town, I imagined that Jorge had been accosting them whenever the opportunity arose. I felt a kind of embarrassed, guilt by association, and with difficulty got him to move himself into the kitchen to continue talking.

He was from the capital where his wife and kids lived, and every two weeks they would come out and stay for the weekend. He told me that he had to make sure none of his girlfriends came round during that time. I took a closer look at him. His eyelids were sagging and flakes of dandruff stuck to the thick lenses of his glasses, between which his bulbous red nose was covered in purple capillaries. He was wheezing with each breath, and the index and forefinger of his right hand had burnt orange stains from chain smoking. My immediate thought was, *How much longer can this guy go on living?*

Needing some space to assess my bad luck, and come to terms with my failed intuition, I told him I was going to walk into to town and take a look. He was not too drunk to realize that I was blowing him off, and was sulky and dismissive as I told him I would be back in an hour. I dropped my bag in the room and headed out the short distance to Cobano.

In the field across the road, a cow with long fluted ears stood staring at me blankly. It was also an unfortunate immigrant. Originally from India, Brahman cows were imported because they could withstand the heat better, but here they ended up on people's dinner plates instead of being venerated. Our neighbors to the left had a smaller, bare brick bungalow with a corrugated tin roof. They were all in the yard, busily chopping wood and preparing for the evening meal. A teenage boy smiled and waved at me. Against the side of the house, a long rectangular piece of iron plating sat on two large stones, between which a man was setting a fire. They had set out aluminum pots with black beans and rice, and a woman was slicing plantains, all of which are staples of the Tico diet. Nearby a man of at least 80, flayed at some weeds with a machete. Another elderly woman, with an impressive under bite stood by him, and after seeing me, gave a disgusted looked at the meter-high weeds surrounding Jorge's bungalow.

Next to their bungalow was a warehouse. A large signboard on the roof was painted with a logo and the words; 'Tu Casa' or 'Your House'. A group of workers, wearing T-shirts with same logo, were unloading timber and roofing tiles and moving them into the store. I looked inside from the road and saw a black, Cherokee jeep with fat, flashy, chrome wheels, and an inflated rubber Zodiac boat leaning against the wall beside it.

At the entrance to the warehouse one man stood out, he was much bigger than the others, with a shaved baldhead. He was just standing there with his arms crossed overseeing the proceedings, wearing a tank top and a bandana folded in a wide band around his forehead. I looked at him, and he gave me what could only be described as a snarl, before reaching for a plaid shirt on top of the stack of tiles next to him. Before he could put it on, I noticed he had a tattoo of the 'Santa Muerte' or 'Holy Death', on one shoulder, and on the other, the red cross of the 'Knights Templar'. Having lived in Mexico I knew a little about the

'Caballeros Templarios' cartel. Like the mafia, the cartels have strict codes, and there is no such thing as a living ex-member.

As the rainforest became a black silhouette on the horizon, I wandered into the town center huddled around a crossroads, where there was one of everything except hotels, bars and places to eat. One bank, one supermarket and one gas station. Cobano, was really only a distribution point for the coastal resorts of Mal Pais, Santa Teresa, and Montezuma. These three beaches could be found at the ends of tortuous muddy tracks through the rainforest. Sometimes during the heavy rains in September and October, the roads to the resorts became impassible due to landslides. Then their only connection to the outside world was by boat.

There were a fair few cowboys in town preparing for a bull-riding rodeo, so technically it wasn't a one-horse town. I sat briefly in a dimly lit bar with no walls, under a thatched roof with a dirt floor, listening to violins and trumpets. 'Rancheras', are basically Mexican country and western songs with guitars and horns, but they have the same predictable chord progressions and hound dog lamentations in the lyrics.

Returning home, I found Jorge sitting in the kitchen looking demoralized as he stared at some numbers on an Excel sheet. He seemed to be hoping they would spontaneously change for the better. I told him I needed to prepare classes and went to my room. I Googled 'Knights Templar Cartel'. It was run by an ex-school teacher turned gangster, who recruited poverty-stricken teenagers with a mixture of pseudo-religious, nationalistic propaganda set out in a 22-page code of ethics. I thought of Mao's little red book.

'El Tuta', or 'The Tutor', described himself as a 'necessary evil', fighting government corruption. Like most cartel leaders, he fancied himself a defender of the poor, a kind of delusional Robin Hood. Narrow, single-mindedness is a recipe for success, and nothing is more dangerous than a psychotic who believes he is fighting for justice with God on his side.

*****

I woke early in a state of desperation bordering on panic, with my heart falling through the mattress. Since sometime before leaving Buenos Aires, this had become a daily routine. I went to the kitchen to make coffee. The cooking area was windowless, but sealed from the waist up with mosquito screens.

I heard manic chirping and a low-pitched buzzing sound that wasn't coming from the 1960's era fridge. At less than arm's length, a hummingbird was extracting nectar from a flower. It was a mixture of shimmering green and cinnamon colors. I stood there transfixed by its magic, thinking how exquisitely delicate it looked. My trance abruptly ended when a butterfly landed on the flower and the bird instantly skewered it with its sharp beak, leaving it mortally wounded. We love to romanticize nature but it can be as barbarous as we are. In the yard beyond the flower, the neighbor's son again waved at me, I smiled back and raised my coffee cup in salute.

With nothing to do till evening, I decided to walk down to the village of Montezuma, about 7 kilometers to the ocean. I left a note for Jorge, who I could hear snoring through the closed door of his bedroom, and headed back to the crossroads in Cobano. Turning south to the coast, my T-shirt began sticking to me; it was already in the low thirties. Along the roadside, the vegetation was covered in a thick layer of dust thrown up by the cars and trucks, but just beyond it were lush green meadows and forest. In the depressions, it was muddy, with deep ruts cut by the streams that cross the road in the wet season. A band of four coatis crossed the road scurrying in hops into the forest.

In an area of dense forest, a large house had been built, clearing a view to the sky. A thick, insulated, electric power cable ran across the open space, disappearing again into the canopy on the other side. I heard the deep bellowing roar of howler monkeys approaching and the cable began moving up and down. As they drew nearer their calls sounded more like gorillas or some sort of monster from a horror film. The alpha male appeared first, followed by two younger males, then some females, piggybacking the very young. They all emerged from the canopy crossing the open space on the cable. Towards the end of the troop, a young monkey stopped and froze. With nothing to grab onto if it fell, it became too nervous to continue. Behind it a large female began howling and bobbing up and down shaking the cable. This only frightened it more, and it strengthened its grip, obviously terrified. Its larger companion at first insisted. Realizing it wasn't working she moved slowly towards it, making softer moaning sounds and pushing it very gently from behind. With a larger companion ready to grab her, the young monkey finally inched its way across the cable to the safety of the canopy. The whole interaction struck me as being more human than primate.

The Pacific Ocean finally came into view from a cliff 300 meters above it. The sweeping scope of it gave me a rush that blew my anxiety away. A snaking gravel road led down into the village with its many small shops and stalls selling souvenirs, clothes and handmade jewelry. It had a definite, laid back, hippy vibe. I scored some weed, which I had been looking forward to since leaving Argentina.

On a terrace restaurant overlooking the small, idyllic beach bordered by rocky outcrops, I sat down to get something to eat. At the table next to me, a young fat, balding guy, was staring wistfully out to sea. He was dressed for the beach, but like a tycoon, with everything including his moccasins, sunglasses, and watch being expensive designer made articles. He suddenly turned towards me and blurted out, "You on vacation?"

"Not really, I came here to teach; you?"

"No, I live here; I have a place near Mal Pais."

"Ah, what do you do here?"

"At the moment nothing."

"Good for you, I can't afford to do that."

"Not so great my friend, I'm in exile out here."

Without further prompting, he launched into an exhaustive explanation of his woes, making me feel like a priest in a confession box. He was the son of an Israeli military commander, and had been convicted for selling arms to some African dictator. It was decided he would move here to be out of sight and largely forgotten, to reduce the shame he had brought upon his family back home. I listened patiently, tutting and shaking my head at the appropriate moments, but all the while thinking he had actually been very fortunate. He had only served 2 years of a 7-year sentence thanks to his father's connections, and was living on a nice little estate in paradise. By the sound of it in a palatial villa, bought with the money he had managed to launder and conceal during his short career as an arms dealer. It made me wonder how many other criminals in hiding there might be in this corner of the world. He invited me to see his villa, but I declined, telling him I had to get back to Cobano shortly, and bade him goodbye.

I headed southwest along a path overlooking the rocky coastline interspersed with shallow coves and white sand beaches. At one point, it led down almost to sea level. Through the trees, I spotted a jeep with a small triangular trailer parked just off a dirt road. As I drew closer, I recognized it as the one I had seen two doors down from Jorge's bungalow in the warehouse. I passed by it, and the path began to climb again up another embankment until again I could see the Pacific in all its glory. I sat down gazing at the view and rolled a joint. There was nothing but sand, rocks, sea and sky, and no sound apart from the low, muffled pounding of the surf and the wind rusting the trees.

The tranquility was interrupted by the droning sound of a powerful motor that came wafting on the wind. A large speedboat was galloping towards the coast, as it pounded up and down on the waves. Another smaller motor started up below. I leaned over the precipice and saw quite clearly the baldhead and bandana of the guy from the warehouse in Cobano, he was heading out in the Zodiac. There were two figures in the speedboat. It stopped dead in the water about 300 meters out, just before the Zodiac pulled up alongside it. One of them took out two bales from a hatch in the floor, and hoisted them over the side to the open arms of the man in the Zodiac. Then both boats started up again, and headed in the directions they had just come from. I laid behind a rock and peeked down, watching as the man in the bandana dragged the boat up onto the beach. He grabbed the two bales wrapped in plastic by the ropes that bound them, and hurried, hobbling into the brush back to his jeep. He made two more trips, first for the motor and then the boat, which he heaved up onto his back and maneuvered it back inland.

I'd read about this the night before when I Googled *Knights Templar*. Costa Rica, with no standing army and only 10,000 cops, had become a staging ground for moving drugs from Colombia to the U.S. With so many tourists now, there was even a local market. The speedboat had probably come from Panama less than 150 kilometers to the south. The Ticos export bulk shipments of agricultural products, which are perfect for smuggling drugs by land, sea and air.

When I got back to Cobano, the next-door neighbor's teenage son was washing the Cherokee jeep outside the warehouse. He dropped the hose he was holding, ran up to me and asked if I would teach him how to play Frisbee. Some foreigner had given him one in town. We went to the parking lot of the community center just up the road and I showed him how to stand, knees bent, like riding a skateboard, and to rotate his whole upper body not just his wrist and arm when he threw it. Within minutes, he had it down. I asked him whose jeep it was; he said his name was Paco, but everybody called him Oso. He was a friend of the man who owned the building materials outlet. Enrique or Quique as his friends called him earned a few dollars now and then washing his jeep or unloading materials.

When I got back to the bungalow Jorge was sitting on the porch snoring, his neck folded over the back of his beach chair with his mouth wide open. I woke him, as it would soon be time for him to introduce me to the class in the community center, and went to shower.

By the time I was out, he had composed himself for his P.R. role and we strolled up the road so slowly that it made walking difficult for me. He introduced me with great pomp and ceremony, as if I was a guest speaker in a college auditorium and then promptly left. There were twenty or so students mostly young, and a few curious housewives. They had wide-ranging abilities in English, which I had accounted for beforehand, and had come equipped with photocopies of varying degrees of difficulty. They focused mostly on Hospitality English because in that area most new jobs were tourism related, but it was a sham trying to accommodate them all in the same class. Despite this, they were all very appreciative and grateful. After the second class, a single mom in her late thirties tried to invite me to dinner, with her teenage daughter rolling her eyes right beside her.

*****

Life quickly fell into a routine as it inevitably does. I travelled to Santa Teresa twice a week to teach in an auditorium attached to the local church. The rough trail cut through the forest was less than twenty kilometers, but in such a raw state that it took an hour and a half to complete the journey. If it rained, the first two kilometers back to Cobano were so steep; I would have to stay with a friend overnight. No taxi driver would run the risk of getting stuck in the mud sliding down the embankments. In the mornings and early afternoons, I hiked along paths in the rainforest, which became something an obsession. With so much flora and fauna it was never boring, though I'm sure in part it was just to avoid Jorge, and the atmosphere in the bungalow. Apart from his ever-increasing anxiety, he was now becoming morose. I decided that once I got paid I would be out.

Cobano's restaurants and bars were overflowing into the streets. The rodeo was about to begin, and the town was bursting at the seams. There were no hotel rooms left, and people had come in RVs or camped out in fields. For the opening night, classes in the community center were cancelled.

The thought of watching a bunch of screaming locals taunting a confused bull did not appeal to me, but Quique showed up and roped me into it. I told him I'd take a shower and be over at his place in half an hour, instead he sat on the porch with Jorge and waited. As I emerged from the house Jorge was handing him money. Surprised, he blurted out; "Quique here is going to cut the weeds for us." Looking back, it was strange, and things might have unfolded differently if I had said something, but Quique was so excited I left it for later.

We headed out and caught up with his family at the fair. There were floodlights set up around a reinforced bullring surrounded by bleachers. Fireworks lit up the night sky, and people were running around waving sparklers. Everywhere stalls were selling beer and food, but when I tried to pay for anything, one of Quique's family members would slap my hand away.

In the ring, 50 people ran circles around each bull as it was released, trying to hit it on the head between its horns. Each time someone managed to do this the crowd roared. At least the bull didn't end up bleeding to death on the ground. When it became too tired to react, some cowboys on horseback would guide it back through the gates to the holding area. Sometimes they would release one with a bronco rider, most of whom hit the ground hard in less than a minute. If they managed more than this, the crowd cheered them on enthusiastically.

After nearly two hours, I'd had enough, but didn't want to seem ungrateful. I looked around for Quique, but he had disappeared. His family were too caught up in the spectacle to notice, so I was sure I could do the same. I wandered back into town, already there were men stumbling around the streets holding each other up and singing out of tune. From the terrace of a bar, I heard two or three voices shouting out my name. A group of students from the community center were waving at me, and I joined them for a few drinks as they partied hard. This too began to wear on me after an hour, but by then, it was easy to fade away because everyone was more or less pissed.

Arriving home, I found Jorge on his knees under the sink. He had lifted a tile from the floor that gave access to the plumbing beneath, and had one arm deep inside the hole. He looked back at me startled, replaced the tile, backed up on all fours, and laboriously pulled himself up using the counter for support. Brushing off his clothes, he mumbled something about leaky pipes. He grabbed two glasses and a bottle of rum, sat down at the kitchen table and insisted I have a drink with him. He seemed different. Still very edgy, but no longer depressed, almost excited.

I thought it would be a good moment to tell him I was going to leave at the end of the month. I made up a story about a school in Colombia that had offered me a full time job. To my surprise, he took it very well. He told me that in fact he was thinking of packing it in himself and going back to San Jose.

The following morning, I left early for Santa Teresa to hang out with a friend at the beach before class. Sebastian and his family had been banana plantation owners who were forced out of Santa Marta, Colombia, by the F.A.R.C. or Revolutionary Armed Forces of Colombia. They destroyed their machinery, executed some of their workers, and threatened to kill his whole family. He had witnessed the massacre of some of the farm laborers in a field near his home. It had traumatized him, and that, along with a few too many acid trips, had given him a passive and reflective way of thinking and speaking. His family now ran a restaurant, and his mother managed time-shares for tourists. Rain started pelting the tin roof of the meeting hall next to the church while I was teaching. It got so loud we abandoned the class early, and I spent the evening with Sebastian listening to music and smoking weed in a time-share no one had rented that week.

Around noon the following day, I caught a ride in a 4 x 4 capable of surmounting the steep grade of the muddy road out of town, and was back in Cobano around two. As I passed the warehouse, I noticed the jeep wasn't there, and then saw Quique's mother coming out and hurrying to the roadside to speak with me. She looked worried but not distraught, as she asked me if I had seen him. He hadn't come home last night and she hadn't seen him since noon yesterday. It wasn't the first time he done this though, the last time he'd gone fishing with his cousins and didn't bother to tell her. She asked me to tell him to come home if I saw him, and she joked about killing him when he did, but you could see the concern written on her face.

I was surprised not to see Jorge on the porch getting quietly smashed. The door was closed, which was also unusual. I thought maybe he was with one of his mysterious girlfriends I'd never seen. It wasn't locked so I entered, and saw the entire house had been turned upside down and ripped to pieces. I froze. The contents of every cupboard and drawer were strewn across the floor and the sofa had been shredded with a knife.

There was so much chaos; it took me a second to notice Jorge in a chair in the kitchen facing away from me. His head was folded over the back of the chair, as it had been when I found him sleeping on the porch. As I moved towards him, I saw his eyes were open, and a thick, dried stream of blood along the floor leading towards the cooking area at the back of the kitchen. The whole room was abuzz with feasting flies. Coming around to face him, I saw his head was almost severed, and his entire chest and pants were covered in blood. I stumbled back hit the wall, and slid down till I was sitting on the floor, dry retching and holding my mouth. I sat there staring at him for a moment paralyzed and stupefied by the sheer gruesomeness of it. Only a machete could cut like that. When my brain kicked in again, a series of confused thoughts and images flashed through my head. He said he was leaving. Quique had disappeared. I saw him handing money to Quique. He was staring in dismay at numbers on a spreadsheet. He was kneeling under the sink. He is dead. I followed the coagulated stream of blood towards the sink; it led towards the tile he had lifted to get at the plumbing.

I got up and closed the front door, went over to the sink being careful not to step in the blood. I lifted the tile with my fingertips, put my arm in, grabbing at anything I touched, and pulled out two packages wrapped in plastic. They were a bit wider than VHS tapes. Instantly realizing what they were, all the little pieces came together for me. My first thought was that Oso or his people would come for me next. The police would assume I was a suspect in a murder case, and if I somehow avoided these threats, I was also nearly broke. I thought about trying to give them back their coke, but knew that wasn't going to work. They'd just kill me anyway. Jorge knew that. I pictured him sitting in the chair pleading with Oso, and hoping he would finally believe he didn't know where it was. He would have continued like that, right up to the moment Oso swung the machete into his throat. I thought about taking the coke and running: *They'll never stop looking for you.*

So, if you're screwed if you do and screwed if you don't, then do a little of both, and maybe you'll end up only half screwed.

I wiped down one of the bricks and put it back in the floor under the sink for the police to find, thinking this would lead them to believe I hadn't killed Jorge. I took the other, and left by the screen door at the back of the kitchen. I went through the trees and up along the stream, until I could see the clearing of the parking lot next to the community center. I found a large rock on the bank of the stream, rolled it over, dug a little earth out from under it and threw it in the water. Then I placed the brick in the space and put the rock back on top of it, washed my hands in the stream and went back to the house.

Now at least I had something to bargain with or run with. I called the cops and waited.

*****

As the atmosphere inside the bungalow was a little heavy, I sat on one of the beach chairs on the porch, and looked at Jorge's empty chair. Next to it, on a small circular table was a half-empty glass of rum and a package of cigarettes. They were placed on top of a magazine with a photo of a villa overlooking the sea. I imagined him daydreaming about sitting on the terrace of his villa drinking better rum, surrounded by bikini-clad girlfriends.

I looked across the road and stared at the Brahmin cow staring back at me. My distracted mind drifted back to my youth, and a farm I worked on near Montreal. A friend of friend told me about someone who had graduated from agricultural studies, and had bought a forty-acre farm. He had turned it into one big experiment, and had a menagerie of animals. I worked there unpaid; helping him construct a greenhouse heated by methane from the animal dung. I remembered thinking how stupid the cows were compared to the pigs, but right now, I half wished I could be that cow; so vacant and so calm.

I still had a little weed in my room and entered the house to flush it down the toilet. The smell of blood hit me. Earlier, in my terrified panic I hadn't smelt anything. There were so many flies now that the room seemed to vibrate. I was drawn by some morbid fascination to look at him again. It still sent a shock through me, and made me recoil. What sort of animal would slaughter another human being in such a macabre way?

The distant chirping of sirens sounded like exotic birds. A police car and pick-up truck appeared on the roadside with their lights flashing in front of the house. I had told them directly on the phone that someone had been murdered and they came in force, five of them in total. I went out on the porch. Two of them walked around the sides of the house and waited outside, the other three entered with me. One was a lieutenant, one was wearing surgical gloves and carrying an aluminum case, and another had a camera. The lieutenant asked what time I had arrived at the house, and wanted to see my passport. As he did this, he kept scanning the room as if expecting to see something in particular. He posed a few other basic questions, without really listening to the answers, and then shouted loudly to the two men outside. They came back around to the front of the house. He gave my passport to one of them, and said in a dry, hurried voice; "Please go with them."

At the station, they sat me in a room with no windows, a table and three chairs. There were two small cameras near the ceiling in opposite corners of the room. Two men entered, one in plain-clothes, the other in uniform. The uniformed man stood in the corner by the door and the plain-clothes one sat at the table opposite me.

"Do you want to make a statement?"

"You want me to make a statement."

"Yes, that's true."

"You're supposed to tell me that anything I say can be used against me, and ask me if I want a lawyer present."

"Yes, that is also true."

"So say it." This obliged him to repeat what I said.

"I don't need a lawyer; I haven't done anything wrong, so I'll give you my statement."

With that, I launched into it, explaining where I'd been in the last 24 hours and what I'd been up to. He interrupted with the occasional question about locations and names, which he took note of on a little pad. The whole time I was speaking, I didn't take my eyes off him, and by the time I was finished, I felt reasonably sure that he had believed what he heard. Although he took great pains to remain expressionless throughout. They got up and left. About 15 minutes later a female officer came, gave me a bottle of water, and told me I would have to wait for at least a couple of hours. She asked me if I wanted something to read, I said sure, so she brought me a fascinating magazine about angle fishing.

Two hours later a different plain-clothes detective entered with another man in uniform with O.I.J, or Judicial Investigations Organization printed in large letters on his polo shirt. Again, the uniformed cop stood near the door and the other sat down in front of me. He introduced himself as Detective Romero and shook my hand. He already had a clipboard with a synopsis of my previous statement. They had obviously come from some larger town and were responsible for more serious crimes. We went back through the same series of questions, with a few more added. He asked me why I spoke fluent Spanish. Then he wanted to know what my relationship was to Enrique Rojas. Until that moment, I didn't know Quique's surname. I remembered his mother was looking for him.

"Is Quique alright?"

"He's been listed as missing. When was the last time you saw him?"

The image of Jorge passing him money on the porch flashed again, and set off a feeling of dread in my stomach. "Last night. We went to the rodeo together, but he left before me."

They left, and I waited again. As with the other interrogation, I felt satisfied. He seemed to have believed what he heard. Finally, they escorted me from the room, and took me to see the captain. He was a fat, jovial looking character, who explained that they were going to put me up in a local hotel with a guard detail for "my protection."

I asked him directly if I was a suspect, but they didn't have enough to arrest me. He almost chuckled, and then unconvincingly denied it. Then he added; "We would appreciate it if you remained in town a few days while we conduct the investigation. When we know more, we may have some other questions."

Making a run for it with so little cash seemed more dangerous than waiting till they had scared away any cartel members from around Cobano. I told him I wanted to ring the company in San Jose that rented the bungalow, because I needed to get paid. He said that they would be contacting them and he would look into it for me. All this made me think they were still suspicious of me, and perhaps even the people Jorge was affiliated with.

They installed me in the hotel room where they had already delivered my pack with most of its contents. From the way it was repacked, I could see they had carefully examined its contents. One cop sat in a chair outside my room, and another in a cruiser across the road. They told me to order room service from the restaurant but I was too wound up to eat anything. I opened the doors of the tiny balcony and sat on a chair inside the room looking out onto the street. I sat there trying to calm myself enough to think clearly about the whole, convoluted messed up story. Especially the events of the last few days. Maybe I did need protection. Oso knew I was friends with Quique, who had probably been stupid enough to steal the coke for Jorge with the promise of more money later.

I flipped on the T.V. to see if news of Jorge's murder had broken, but there were only game shows and Mexican soap operas. I turned down the volume and lay on the bed watching the ceiling fan rotate. Images of Jorge sitting in the kitchen with his head hanging off kept coming to mind, in between detailed images of the bungalow, Quique's house and the warehouse. I remembered looking past the jeep in the warehouse, on my first walk into town. There was a door at the back with a heavy padlock on it. One day Quique and his family had invited me to lunch. As I washed my hands in the stream at the back of the house, I saw on the other side of the fence, a small, added room, attached to the rear of the warehouse. It had a flimsy, corrugated tin roof. The first night of the rodeo Quique had probably pried the roof up and taken the coke. I regretted not asking him about the money Jorge had given him; I knew it wasn't to cut weeds. If he had told me what he was planning, I could have explained to him what kind of people he was dealing with. Until now, people like that had never come to his little town.

I looked over at the T.V. and saw the local news anchor was speaking. I jumped off the bed and turned up the volume.

"...a Mexican national has been detained in San Jose for questioning in connection with the murder of a 62-year-old man and the disappearance of a 16-year-old boy from Cobano, on the Nicoya Peninsula."

It had to be Oso. I felt sick to my stomach, and my brain went into overload trying to work out who else could be involved in this ghoulish shit fight. The owner of the building supplies outlet had to have known what was happening under his nose. I saw Jorge's head hanging over the back of the chair again as I stood staring at the T.V. weather forecast.

I really needed to switch-off for a while, so I started by switching off the T.V. I dug out a notebook full of passages I had written for a play. It was going to be about a man alone in his studio apartment each night, arguing with an apparition who he believes is the Devil, but turns out to be his alter ego. I opened it randomly and read the Devil saying; 'When you're forced to play among the vicious, you have to be willing to do what's necessary to protect yourself, and to wield your weapons with precision, even when wounded. You need the shrewdness to discern the motives and thoughts of your rivals. On the other hand, danger is often accompanied by opportunity. You must find the way to use your astuteness more effectively'.

How fucking appropriate, I thought.

*****

The following morning the guard outside my room knocked on the door and gave me a tray with breakfast laid out on it. About an hour later, there was another knock and he asked me to follow him downstairs. I thought he was going to take me to the station for another round of questions. As he led me to the cruiser, I saw the other guard standing on the pavement, and the lieutenant, who had come to Jorge's bungalow, was sitting in the back seat alone. My escort opened the rear door, motioned me in and then closed it again. The lieutenant turned towards me putting his arm up along the back of the seat and said; "Good Morning Peter, how are you today?"

"Fine thanks, when do you think I'll be able to leave?"

"Not quite yet I'm afraid, there are some loose ends that need to be taken care of first."

"Uh, uh, and what would those be?"

"Well we have recovered a kilo of cocaine from the bungalow, but we understand that there is another kilo still missing."

"I see. And how do you know there's a kilo missing?"

"We have our sources, Peter."

"Well lieutenant," I stopped to read the rectangular nameplate above the breast pocket of his freshly pressed shirt. "Lieutenant Torres, I'm afraid I don't know anything about that, I'm just an English teacher. Perhaps Jorge stashed it some other place."

He shifted forward looking through the cage screen and out through the windshield, and spoke more softly and slowly.

"You know, you are a stranger in a foreign land, and through no fault of your own you have been caught up in a very dangerous situation here. So it would be better for you to be completely honest with me, that way, I can protect you."

"Uh, uh, well, you are right about that Lieutenant. It seems that it was very dangerous for my neighbors' son. Have they found Quique?"

"Not as yet, but we believe he may still be alive."

"Hmm, and what leads you to suspect he's okay?"

He turned towards me with an expression of contained fury, realizing that I had been parroting his syntax all along. "The police do not share information about ongoing investigations with gringos who come here to hang out on the beach!"

"Well I'm not a gringo Lieutenant. My father was French and my mother Irish. Apart from that, I speak your language, and I didn't come here to hang out on the beach."

"You're all gringos to us."

We sat for a moment in silence. Then I said, "Maybe we can find some common ground Lieutenant. I learned a fair bit about Jorge during the month I stayed with him. If Quique were to miraculously return home to his family, I think I might have some information that could be useful to you. It might even help you recover what you're looking for."

He breathed in sharply through his nose; I could see he was losing it. "If you play with fire, fuckwit, you get burnt!" With that, he put his arm through the open window, pulled up on the door handle and kicked the door open. Then he walked to the corner and disappeared. When I stopped having to pretend I wasn't afraid of him, my blood pressure rose from a mixture of fear and rage. His abrupt exit did not bode well for the fate of Quique. The guard opened the door for me and I returned upstairs with him.

I sat down on the bed staring at the floor. It dawned on me that I needed protection from the cartel and the police. He was dirty, and our little talk was obviously off the record. There were so many moving parts it was becoming impossible to predict where it would go next. The whole police force couldn't be behind it. The way the cops guarding my room behaved towards me gave no hint of collaboration with him. The lieutenant had balls, or maybe he was afraid himself. When a cartel makes you responsible for protecting their product, there is no valid excuse for losing it.

Voices in the street drew me to the balcony door, a van had pulled up downstairs and a T.V. crew started to get out, I stepped back quickly from view. The guard outside told them to move on. I turned on the T.V. again without volume, and left it on a channel with news updates. It didn't take long.

"…in the continuing investigation into the death of Jorge Crespo in Cobano, our sources indicate that it may have been perpetrated by the Knights Templar Cartel, from Michoacán State in Mexico. We understand that businessman, Mr. Juan Belmonte, the proprietor of a local building supplies outlet, has been arrested in connection with the drug smuggling ring. Two other men employed by Mr. Belmonte have also been arrested. Meanwhile, the search continues to determine the whereabouts of sixteen-year-old Enrique Rojas, a neighbor of Mr. Crespo, who disappeared two days ago."

I took a pad and pen from my pack and sat down to write at the table.

Esteemed Detective Romero,

I would appreciate it if you could find

the time to come and speak with me at the hotel.
I believe I have some information that you will
find useful for your investigation, but I do not
want it officially recorded.

Thanking you in advance,

Peter.

In Spanish, they use *Esteemed*, instead of the equally ridiculous *Dear*. I folded a piece of cellophane tape, stuck it along the lower edge of the note and brought the top of the paper down onto it. I handed it to the guard in the hallway and told him that only inspector Romero should receive it directly in his hand. I was expecting him to say no. To my surprise, he entered the room, went to the balcony, and whistled at his partner, signaling him to come up. He handed it to the other guard and repeated verbatim what I had said. Maybe these guys had sniffed a rat themselves. It was still before noon. I waited, and again tried to distract myself, but whether reading or watching inane daytime television, I continued counting the minutes.

As the light faded, I began to think he wouldn't show, at least not that day. Around seven-thirty he arrived, he was shorter than I remembered him, but solidly built.

With a calm and patient air about him as we sat down at the table he said; "I want to tell you that all the details you gave us have checked out, and I'm writing a preliminary report recommending that your passport be returned to give you freedom of movement. That should be sometime tomorrow afternoon, and we will escort you to the mainland." He seemed to want to assure me so that I would feel free to tell him whatever I knew.

Then his mood darkened, and with a slightly choked voice he said; "I'm sorry to tell you this, but last night we located your friend Enrique Rojas. A man living just outside of town on the road to Santa Teresa heard dogs fighting in the forest near his house. He found Quique hanging from a tree. His abdomen was slashed open. These sons of bitches have no mothers."

My vision blurred, and I licked the salty taste from the corners of my mouth. For the past three days I'd been pretending that he would return home to his mother. It threw me, but almost simultaneously, it raised my hackles and infuriated me. I got up and went to the open door to the balcony, wiped my face, and returned to the table looking down at him. My voice came out splintered and weak; "I have some information that could help you cut the head off this snake. I'm telling you now, but I'll disavow all of it if you ask me to make a formal statement. I'm not going to appear in court to testify against a cartel, and sign my own death certificate. You just said it; these cunts have no mothers. I don't really have a dog in this fight, but for Quique's sake it would give me enormous satisfaction to see them all fall."

There was a pause. He seemed a bit worried, like he'd read something into what I'd said that wasn't intended. "Alright, as long as it doesn't directly incriminate you, you have my word."

"The first officer at the murder scene, Lieutenant Torres, came to see me unofficially this morning, he told me you've recovered a kilo of coke from Jorge's house, but that he thinks there's more still missing."

"Yes, given the people involved, it seems unlikely that there is such a small quantity at stake."

"I'm sure there is, but he was much more specific than that. He told me there should have been precisely one more kilo in the house. He seems to think that I know where it is, and went so far as to threaten me if I didn't tell him."

"And do you?"

I stared straight at him, "If I did, I wouldn't be stupid enough to tell you now, would I. No, I'm just an English teacher with extremely bad luck."

"What exactly did he say to threaten you?"

"He told me; 'If you play with fire, fuckwit, you get burnt.' And judging by what happened to Quique and Jorge I have no reason to doubt him. I just want to leave here as soon as possible."

He sat for a moment staring at the table, pinching his lower lip between his thumb and index finger, then rose abruptly. "Thank you for letting me know—it is indeed useful. I'm sure that shortly we can arrange for your departure; please bear with me for one more day." He shook my hand and left.

*****

The third day in the hotel room was the longest. I found myself pacing from the balcony door to the bathroom and back again like a caged dog. I imagined it all backfiring. These people were capable of anything, and I had no idea how deep the corruption ran. If Romero were to disappear suddenly, it would not have surprised me. I read, paced, and kept the T.V. lit waiting for news.

The image of a news anchor standing in front of the Cobano police station appeared on the screen. "…lifeless body of 16-year-old Enrique Rojas has been recovered from the forest near this small, rural town, leaving its residents horrified. One officer said; 'it was the most gruesome crime scene he had ever witnessed', but refused to give further details." Later the full story would come out, complete with gory details. Enrique's body was found hanging by the wrists between two trees, with a bunch of dogs fighting over his entrails, which hung down to the forest floor. "In what police believe to be a related crime, Francisco 'El Oso' Varela, has been formally charged with the murder of Jorge Crespo, which took place four days ago here in Cobano. Yesterday Mr. Varela was detained at Juan Santamaria International Airport attempting to board a flight to Mexico City. A police spokesperson has informed us that DNA evidence found at the crime scene and blood traces found in Mr. Varela's abandoned jeep, led to his formal indictment on murder charges. Although the murder weapon itself, believed to be a machete, has not yet been recovered."

His arrest would send the cockroaches scurrying into hiding. I waited hoping that someone would arrive with my passport, but night fell and there was no sign of them. Around seven, the guard knocked on my door. He handed me a large, clear plastic bag, in it were the few things that had not been in my pack when I came to the hotel. These included some clothes I'd hung on the line that were obviously too big to be Jorge's, some books in English, and my hiking boots. He told me that Detective Romero was coming tomorrow morning at 9am, we would travel to Puntarenas on the mainland, where I would be asked to give a final statement and my passport would be returned to me.

It seemed too good to be true. I felt a little disgusted with myself because the next thought that came to mind was what I had left by the stream. I could always return in a few weeks and pick it up if I decided to. Then the rationalizing began. Quique's arrangement with Jorge had cost him his life. It had also brought down an entire cartel smuggling ring. I think he would be pleased to know that it was me, and not his killers who had profited from the unimaginable price he had paid for his mistake. I would have told Torres where to find it without thinking twice, if he could have arranged for his release, but he was already dead when I spoke to him. I had never smuggled coke in spite of its obvious advantage in value per gram over hash. In part, because it's addictive, and it can turn a likeable person into an asshole with just a few months of sustained use.

In the morning when I switched on the T.V. I saw the silly, half smirk on the face of the Captain of Cobano police station. He was standing behind a table with his colleagues on either side, proudly displaying 39, one-kilo bricks of cocaine recovered from the septic tank behind Lieutenant Torres' house. The next video segment showed the lieutenant being led away from his residence in handcuffs, looking like any other drug-trafficker, without his uniform to give him the guise of a public defender.

At 9am, Detective Romero appeared at my door with two other men, all in plain clothes. One took my pack and the other gave me a hat and a pair of sunglasses before they led me downstairs. We went through the kitchen and out to the delivery area behind the hotel, got into an unmarked car with heavily tinted windows and swept out of town. Two hours later, we were in Paquera on the coast, and took the ferry to Puntarenas on the mainland. They made me remain in the car for the crossing.

The police station was only a few blocks from the ferry terminal, so soon I was sitting in an interrogation room not unlike the one in the Cobano police station, but in better condition. They had prepared a statement for me to sign, that was nothing more than what I had already told them. There were a few added clauses stating that I had remained in Cobano of my own free will to aid them in the investigation. Although this wasn't exactly true, I happily signed it.

Detective Romero produced a zip-lock pouch with my passport from the inside breast pocket of his suit and gave it to me. He picked up the paper; I smiled and nodded at him. As I turned on my chair to stand, he said; "Just one more thing Peter, one the bales of cocaine we found in the septic tank behind Lieutenant Torres' house had been resealed. It contained 18 bricks each weighing one kilo. The other bale had 20 bricks in it. It was obvious from the packaging that both had originally contained the same number. So, Lieutenant Torres was right when he told you that one was missing." I realized he had prepared this comment for the unlikely event that I refused to sign the statement.

"Well, maybe you should investigate any contacts Jorge had in Cobano. He told me he had some girlfriends, though I never met any of them."

"Hm, yeah, maybe we'll look into that." I stood up; he smiled and reached across the table to shake my hand, all the while observing me fixedly. After the intense fear I had been through over the past week, it didn't even begin to faze me, I kept my cool and didn't flinch. He offered to take me to the bus, which I politely declined.

Stepping out of the station felt like escaping execution, like a fish returned to water.

A Lovely Place to Die

Philip Pak

Jackson Blast pulled the door closed behind him on his way out of the Blast Detective / Employment Agency. It was late May, and finally with a few bucks in the bank, he decided to close up shop and take a few weeks off. There was nothing cooking with the Detective end of his business, and the Bank, his sole customer for the employment end of the business was closed for a two-week audit.

On his way to the elevator, he encountered the building's janitor.

"Hi Lenox, you won't be seeing me for a couple of weeks. Do me a favor and don't let the Chinese restaurant menus pile up in front of my office door."

"Where you going Jack?"

"Madeira."

"Where the hell is that?"

"It's a small Portuguese island of the coast of Africa."

Lenox pondered for a moment. "What's there?"

"Who knows? Global Airlines is running a special rate on certain seats to that destination."

He continued through the lobby, down the elevator and across the street to where his 1993 Dodge Daytona was parked. Pat Martinez, of *Martinez Motors*, had assured him it'd been the very last to roll off the production line. After the third twist of the key the engine finally caught and, pulling out into traffic, he headed home to his Brooklyn brownstone.

Traffic was heavy as usual, and what should have been a half hour ride took over an hour. Add another half-hour looking for a parking space.... But the hassle was worth it. The brownstone that his father left him was far better than he could afford on his own. His mother was still alive, however she was in a nursing home and getting crazier by the day.

Prior to the brownstone, he'd been holed up in a fifth floor studio that he swore had once been a walk-in-closet.

That's what a divorce does to a guy.

Oddly, he was taking the reason for his divorce with him on vacation; Taffy

Dux, the sister of his ex-wife.

Their affair ended not only his marriage, but also his partnership with his ex-wife in what had been a lucrative employment agency.

Having picked up his PI licence prior to his marriage, he was torn trying to decide which business to pursue, so he opened an office that did both. And so far he wasn't making much money with either. A winning Trifecta ticket on the Kentucky Derby was the only reason he could afford this trip.

Since he wasn't going to be around for a while, he felt a touch of guilt, and thought he should visit his mother before his flight.

*****

The Datona pulled into the circular driveway of the *Gate to Oblivion* Senior Center. The smell of old people filled his nostrils as he headed to mom's tiny apartment. There she was, staring out the window as usual. He briefly wondered if someday this would be his fate, only in his case he doubted there would be any children to come and visit him.

"Hi mom."

She turned towards him. "Hello Jack, is dad with you?"

Somehow, she was never able to process that he was dead. Jack gave up trying.

"He couldn't make it, mom."

"What's his excuse this time?"

He felt like saying, *the usual, he's dead.* But he remembered the last time he'd reminded her, and she'd started to wail and cry. This time he decided to spare both of them that.

"He's traveling."

"Any idea when he'll be back?"

He muttered: "When Gabriel blows his horn."

"What was that, Jack?"

"Nothing mom. Anyway, how are you?"

"I spend my days sleeping and looking out this window. How the hell do you think I am?"

This sudden bust of lucidity startled him.

"Is everything okay, mom?"

He barely finished his sentence before she turned toward the window and that blank stare reappeared. She was back to her old, out-of-it self again. He figured that it was a good time to make his exit. As far as his mother knew, he could have spent half the day with her.

A quick check to make sure she had everything she needed, a soft kiss on her cheek and he was off.

*****

The next day, Jack pulled the Dodge in front of the Dux residence. He got out of his car, walked up the two steps, and rang the bell. Mama Dux opened the door.

"You again!"

He couldn't really blame her. He cheated on her favorite daughter Effie with her other daughter Taffy. Effie's money paid the family bills, and Mama never forgave Taffy. God knows how they lived under the same roof.

"Taffy's expecting…" He never got to finish the sentence.

"I'll tell the bimbo you're here." She then slammed the door in his face.

Jack got back in the Dodge and waited. He kept checking his watch; it was her habit to always be late. Finally, she came down the front steps with a trunk large enough to fit a body into. She parked it in the middle of the sidewalk, so Jack could lug it into the back seat. Their initial romance had been hot, but it'd cooled somewhat after the divorce. Taffy had this strange attraction for married men.

"Oh, Jack, I'm so excited," she said as she arranged herself on the passenger seat. "I'm so used to you taking me to those two-for-one restaurants, and the romantic discounted rerun movies. I can't believe we are actually going to Madeira. By the way, where is Madeira?"

"It's a lovely island in the Atlantic."

"Where is the Atlantic again?"

"Never mind, you'll love it."

He wondered how she could manage to pack considering she had no idea where they were going. Judging from the size of the trunk, she packed for every conceivable climate.

The traffic made the ride to JFK take longer than it should have. After Jack had steered the Dodge into the airport parking lot, he almost got a hernia dragging Taffy's trunk from the car. A youngish looking man saw him struggling and stepped into help.

"Excuse me, Sir. Let me give you a hand with that."

Even though they kept bumping into each other until they finally figured out the best way to carry it into the airport building.

*****

Two hours later, they boarded the plane. Jack had been lucky enough to purchase two of the few remaining discounted seats left, unfortunately they were situated 10 rows apart. Taffy's seat was on the isle and as luck would have it, Jack got a middle seat between two very large gentlemen. When he sat down, he wasn't sure his ass was in contact with the seat. It was more like he was wedged in above it. Both of these guys should have chipped in and bought his seat in the middle. They needed it.

Just after take-off he'd started to feel his shirt dampen, and the longer the flight went on, the more their sweaty bodies oozed into his space.

That was when he decided that it was going to be the kind of flight one prays for the plane to crash.

Relief came a gruelling seven hours later when the plane coasted to the terminal, and Taffy and Jack followed the signs to the baggage area. This time he hired a person to take their luggage to the waiting hotel van.

As he put his wallet back in his pocket, Jack's phone rang; it was his mother. He told Taffy that he would meet her later in the van while he took this call.

"Hello mom?"

"Gustav, is that your?"

"No, you dialed me, mom."

"Call Gustav and tell him to call me."

"Is everything okay?"

"Yes."

"Alright mom, will do."

One of these days, he's going to have to get through to her that her husband was dead. She'll forget she called in a minute, anyway. It was a pleasant May day, and Jack stepped outside the small terminal. He felt a drill like poke on his back. It was the fat passenger that had been seated to his left. A giant of a man looking more menacing than he had on the plane.

"I'll make this quick. Give me the thumb drive in your left jacket pocket."

Puzzled, Jack reached into his pocket, and to his surprise, pulled out a thumb drive.

"How did this get here?"

"The guy who helped you with your trunk in New York slipped it in your pocket. Give it to me!"

The giant grabbed Jack's wrist and tugged, but his hand slipped off Jack's still sweaty arm and he tipped backwards. Then, losing his footing on the uneven curb, he dropped like a ton of bricks into the street. There was the almost immediate sound of screeching tires, but the breaks were not applied quickly enough and an approaching taxi's right front tire rolled over the giant's head. The driver jumped out of the cab in a panic with the cell phone to his ear. A crowd started gathering and airport security followed. Jack, now in a half panic himself, backed away from the crowd and boarded the hotel van, still trying to fathom what had just happened. The doors of the van started to close behind him, but reopened to allow the fat guy, who tortured his right side on the plane, to enter. Coincidence? There was the faint sound of police sirens as the van pulled away toward the hotel.

*****

A half hour of winding mountain roads took the van to the Ocean Cliff Hotel. Jack and Taffy stepped off the van and walked through its bleached white entrance. There were fresh flowers everywhere. The hotel brochure did not lie. The place was beautiful. An attentive concierge staff took care of all Jack and Taffy's necessities before they followed the bellhop with their luggage to room 701. It was spacious, bright, and came with a king sized bed. There on the table was a welcome bottle of the island's famous wine, Madeira. Obviously named after the island itself.

Once settled in, Taffy pulled aside the drapes, revealing a beautiful view of the bay side of the island. "Now that's nice." Taffy opened the balcony door, letting in a cool fresh ocean breeze.

"You could knock me over with a feather, Jack. Somehow, I thought this place would be one of your usual overrated dumps, but you delivered the goods this time. The place is gorgeous. We are in the right room, right?"

"Of course, you know I've always been a sport."

"I remember you always were with my sister's money, but since the divorce, not so much."

They uncorked the Madeira, and carried their glasses to the chairs on the balcony. After the rigors of the trip, the sound of the bay along with the smooth mellow Madeira wine calmed them to the point where they could barely keep their eyes open. They called it a night.

*****

The following morning a buffet breakfast was being served in the hotel dining room. Jack and Taffy chose an outdoor table facing the bay. Taffy was a light eater, probably why she kept her school girl figure. She looked younger than her 34 years. Taffy got 80 percent of the looks, her sister, Jack's ex, Effie, got ninety percent of the brains. Jack, 36, is one of those guys who never seems to change. His six foot frame was athletic, his hair was a bit unruly, and he had this energy about him.

"Jack, I'm going upstairs to put on my bathing suit and sit by the pool. Coming?"

"I'll meet you there, I have some business to take care of."

She laughed. "You barely have any business when you're sitting in your office. What kind of business could you have here?"

"Never mind, see you by the pool."

He watched her leave, then made one more trip to the buffet table. After the last cup of coffee, he headed back up to the room. When he got there, Taffy had already left. He went into his jacket pocket and pulled out the thumb drive that the guy on the plane wanted so badly. Apparently, he was set up to transport this drive, but why? Were they afraid that there was a possibility the carrier would be stopped by customs, or worse? He put it in his pocket and headed to the business center. Leaving the room, he noticed the still alive fat guy from the plane entering the room next to his. He was a lot friendlier than the guy who's head had been rolled over by the taxi.

"Good morning, sir. I believe we were seated alongside each other on the plane."

"Your right. Nice to see you. Have a good day."

Jack smiled and continued on his way. He wondered if this guy next to him in room 702 has anything to do with the thumb drive.

After finding the business center and an unoccupied computer, he slipped the drive into an empty port. A dizzying array of numbers and equations flashed across the screen. Jack couldn't make heads or tails out of what he was seeing. Obviously, its contents were important to someone. He wondered how and why he'd become involved in this? Was he randomly chosen? Was his other fat bookend from the plane, now in the room next to his, specifically there to keep an eye on him? He had a lot of questions, but the pressing one was, what to do with this drive? Go to the local police and waste expensive vacation time being questioned in some hot office, or just throw the damn thing in the ocean and be done with it? He decided to hide it in his room for now and join Taffy by the pool. He could use a swim.

*****

Alfonso Lopez walked into his study and closed the door behind him. His wife was in town shopping and his house cleaning staff had just left. Excellent. He needed privacy for the call he was about to make. The Lopez house was one of the larger homes on Madeira's island. He was old money. However, his import/export business hasn't been nearly as profitable as it had been when his father left it to him. In fact, lately it was in the red. Luckily, he found a more profitable way to support his expensive tastes, smuggling drugs. The deal he had with the New York syndicate was a sweet one. Madeira was the new hub for drugs coming from Columbia on their way to Europe — the island was perfectly situated, and Lopez's business was ideal for transporting them. The instructions on the upcoming shipment would be hand delivered on an encrypted thumb drive. The reason the instructions were not transmitted electronically was simple: the shipments contained millions of dollars of pharmaceutical grade product, and there was always a chance an electronic message could be intercepted and decoded.

Well, it stood to reason that if the US Government could be hacked, anyone could. One would never know of the leak until the shipment arrived, only to be impounded by the DEA, or whichever department was in charge of the operation. By then millions of dollars would be lost, and the cartels made sure they never lost.

Plus there was no way of really knowing who has gained access to your computers. The CIA, Middle East, the Chinese and the Russian mob – all had very talented and well-paid hackers.

By putting the instructions on something like a thumb drive, a physical device which could be kept in total control from one person to another, there was less of a chance an unwanted party could become aware of their plans.

Should the drive be intercepted, as it was this time, the breach is immediately known, and the plans aborted before the product is sent, and new plans put in place, making the information on that drive useless. Nothing really lost except maybe a life or two in the process.

*****

Lopez sat behind his desk and slowly rotated toward the window. There was a non-obstructed view from his cliffside villa to the sea below. He picked up the satellite phone and dialed a New York City number. The terminal at the far end rang four times before it was answered.

"Who's calling?"

"Alfonso. I need to talk to your boss. I take it Ethan Ellis is there?"

A short silence, then another voice came on the line.

Ellis sounded like he gargled with hot vinegar and had a 3-pack-a-day habit.

"I've been expecting your call. It looks like we have a problem. We're still trying to figure out who this guy is who's giving us grief. Originally, we thought he was just some random schmuck we used to get the thumb drive past customs, but now we're not so sure. He appears to be some kind of private detective, but we believe he's something more. After all, he took down the guy we had on the plane to watch him — one of our toughest guys too. Also, he's staying in one of the island's more expensive hotels, and from what others have said, that's totally out of character."

There was a pause. Mixed with the sound of stubble rubbing against the receiver, then: "To be honest, we don't know what to make of him, or who he's connected with. We have too much to lose so we don't want to make any rash moves until we know exactly who we're dealing with. It could be something we can salvage by offering him a cut of the action."

"Do you think Mendoza is involved?"

A second pause, then: "You have a point, this guy could be working for Mendoza. He's always trying to cut into our business for some time now."

Alfonso's turn to pause. "What about my money?"

"The IP address for your digital payoff is on that drive, but don't worry, we've terminated that payment portal. You're money's safe and everything will be rearranged once we know who we're dealing with. All you have to do is sit tight and you'll get you your money."

"I hope so, because at the moment I'm no longer happy with our arrangement. I'm taking all the risk here. I want a bigger cut."

"We can talk about it after we clear up our problem and get things running again."

Alfonso heard the 'burp' as the far end hung up.

*****

Blast was returning to the room after his swim, leaving Taffy still sunning by the pool. Walking down the hall, he noticed a maid's cart in front of his open door. He walked in and saw the maid and the guy from room 702. Blast was about to ask what he was doing in his room, but the fat man beat him to the punch.

"I'm sorry, I needed to speak to the maid, and when I saw her in your room, I approached her with my problem. Seems I don't have any soap."

He smiled and stuck out his hand.

"My name is Tombs, Harry Tombs. Sorry for not speaking on the plane. Flying always makes me sleepy."

Jack was suspicious of his motives, but he didn't let it show.

"Nice to meet you, again. I'm Jack Blast. What brings you to Madeira?"

"The beauty, the ocean, the mountains. This little island has it all. I've been coming here for years. Is this your first time here?"

"Yes."

"I'm sure you'll love it." He looked at his large wristwatch. "Got to get back to my room. See you around."

Jack noticed he had left without the soap.

Moments later the maid nodded silently, spritzed some more freshener into the air, then smiled and left.

Almost gagging on the scent of hibiscus, Blast decided to air out the place, so he lifted open the large shuttered window that was on the side of the room. Behind the glass were colorful heavy wooden shutters that looked like they were a tight fit.

Leaning back, he slammed both palms against the wood, forcing the shutters open, and in the process, pushed the man standing on the other side over the small Juliette balcony.

Leaning half out of the window, Jack watched the man fall seven stories before landing in the pool area, causing a panic with the guests.

Naturally, the hotel immediately called the police. Jack, meanwhile, stepped back into the hotel room, bewildered and in a half daze, barely making it to a chair. He just sat there in shock, unable to move. He just killed a guy. Who was he? A window washer? A burglar? Whatever the answer, he was having severe difficulties in processing what had just happened.

*****

Jack didn't know how much time had passed, but Taffy came into the room. She was crying and speaking in an animated manner. The body had landed about twenty feet from her chair. Still in shock, Jack just sat there with Taffy's chatter filling the void in the room. A knock at the door brought Jack somewhat back to his senses. He never got a chance to open the door. The bellhop let Detective Busto in. He flashed his badge.

"Sorry to trouble you, Mr. Blast, but witnesses say the body that fell to the pool below came from your room. What happened?"

Jack shook his head as if clearing his thoughts. "I don't know. I came up to my room after having a swim, and I decided to open the window and let some fresh air in. When I pushed out the shutters, I saw a man fall. I had no idea he was there. I had no idea this tiny balcony, or whatever it is, was even behind the shutters."

Busto sighed. "I'm afraid I'm going to have to ask you to come to the police station and make a statement."

Jack turned to Taffy.

"Go and have dinner. I don't know when I'll be back."

They left.

*****

In the northern forested part of the island sat a ranch house with several smaller cabins and surrounded by wine vineyards. This was the Mendoza compound. Julius Mendoza had originally grown up in the slums of Porto. An incorrigible petty criminal with a record a mile long, he'd arrived on the island quite by accident ten years before.

After serving a year in a Porto prison, he was able to get a job as a dishwasher on a cruise ship traveling to Madeira, only he was fired before the ship reached port. Broke, he bounced around the capital city, Funchal, working both as a dishwasher and waiter for the local restaurants. Mendoza was a handsome and charming man, which masked his loathsome character. Not long after, while drinking in a bar, he met the only daughter of the widower who owned the vineyard where he would eventually reside. A plain woman in her late forties, she took a shine to the younger Mendoza, and they married after a short courtship.

Her father died two years into their marriage, and Mendoza became the co-owner of the land. He eventually became the full owner when his wife had a fatal accident two months after.

Some people are just born with a black heart.

Even though Mendoza made a decent living with his vineyard, he was still drawn to crime. His compound housed some of his old friends from his lawless days; pickpockets, burglars, and worse. And Mendoza always made sure he got his cut.

Carlos Pérez, the man Blast had accidentally killed, was a second story man in Mendoza's employ. Mendoza was well aware of Lopez's drug transport business and sent Carlos to try and find the seemingly missing thumb drive. He had been watching Lopez's every move and planning for a way to cut him out and take over the operation himself.

When news of the death reached him, he'd immediately called what he termed as A Council of War.

In a sombre tone, he opened the meeting.

"We lost one of our guys today." There had been a mumble around the table, but no one said anything aloud. Mendoza continued, "We have to find out who this guy is who killed Carlos. We know he's the courier for Lopez's mob. Carlos went to search his room for the thumb drive with the information on it. And apparently this guy Blast, or whatever his name really is, found him in his room. The fact that Carlos was thrown out the window was no accident."

He let that information sink in before continuing. "Whoever this guy is, he's a dangerous professional. Our contact at police headquarters, says Blast is claiming it was an accident, though I don't know if the police are buying it. We've been making penny ante sucker money with our low level business around the island. The real money is in the drug transportation business, and I want in."

Around the table heads nodded in agreement. As he stood, he said: "Everyone into the cars – we're going downtown."

*****

After a grueling several hours of cross-examination, Blast, unsure if the police bought his story, was finally allowed to leave the police station. As he walked toward the taxi stand, he was addressed by a man standing in front of a black Mercedes.

"Mr. Blast, may I offer you a ride back to the hotel?"

"Sure, thanks."

Blast got in and the car pulled away.

"It was nice of the hotel to send a car to drive me back. It's been a rough day."

"We are not from the hotel, Mr. Blast."

"Who are you?"

"I'm someone who wants to offer you more money than you're making now."

"I don't know what you're talking about Mr..?"

"My name is Mendoza. Look, I'm going to lay my cards on the table. I know about the contraband drug importation business. I know you're from the States, and I'm willing to pay big if you can put me in contact with someone in charge of the operation."

Blast was totally lost, he had no idea what this guy was talking about.

"You can't mean the President?"

"Fine, if that's what you want to call him. I know you are the guy who couriered the USB drive containing information regarding the up-coming drug deals. I'm no longer interested in the drive, I want to talk to the guy that sent it. I have a proposition for him."

Now things were starting to make sense. So that drive held information for a drug shipment – and by the sound of the conversation, this had to be the guy who sent one of his men to the hotel room to retrieve it.

"Was that your guy who accidentally fell from my room?"

Mendoza smiled. "If you want to put it that way, that's also fine by me. I believe in letting bygones be bygones. Get me a meeting with your head guy and I'll make it worth your while."

The car pulled up in front of the hotel. Mendoza handed Blast his card.

"I'll be in touch, Mr. Blast."

*****

That evening, Blast and Taffy decided to have dinner in the hotel's main restaurant. For once the décor didn't annoy him, and the other more important thing was it was a public place. No real chance of any confrontation, and that knowledge meant he was able to really relax for the first time since their arrival. Taffy was her usual beautiful self, and things were finally starting to feel normal again.

After dinner, they walked into the bar and took a quiet corner table. They ordered their drinks and enjoyed the piano players' romantic melodies. Blast finally felt like he was truly on vacation, until a waitress came to their table with a note on a platter.

"Mr. Blast, the gentleman at that table..." she nodded toward Harry Tombs "...asked me to deliver this to you."

The note read: *Your life is in danger. Come to my table, I'll explain.*

His first impulse was to crumble the paper and go back to his serenity, but the *your life is in danger* part made him nervous, so he excused himself and walked over to Tombs.

"Please sit down, Mr. Blast. I owe you an explanation."

He reached into his wallet and pulled out his FBI badge.

"I'm assigned to this case. I am not sure what you know, or don't know, so let me fill in the blanks. We found out about this drug smuggling operation some time ago. We were already trailing the guy who slipped that thumb drive into your pocket, and then we followed you."

He took a sip of his drink. Blast suspected it was a virgin Cuba Libre. It could have been worse. Like a Shirley Temple....

His throat lubricated, Tombs got back to his explanation.

"We know you just happen to be just a random guy they chose out of nowhere to transport that drive. We know that now. The man on the plane to your left was there to make sure the drive got through customs, and if it didn't, report it back to the New York syndicate run by a man known as Ethan Ellis. The Bureau arranged for my seat on your right. Things were going smoothly until their watchdog got killed. By the way, if that had been intentional, then it was neatly done."

Another sip of the coke and ice, then: "Needless to say, that screwed both Ellis and ourselves completely. Forcing them to alter their plans also set us back. A guy name Alfonso Lopez is the person here who arranges the imports and exports for the mob. To make a long story short, the drive you carried contained the specifics such as what ship the drugs are coming in on, which crates and which boxes contain the drugs, what country those boxes were to be routed to, etc. Since the info never got to Lopez, we had to abort and let you go about your merry way."

Blast let his fingers play with a napkin. "So if the shipment has been abandoned, who sent the guy to search my room?"

"Julius Mendoza. He's not a nice person to know, even if he's your friend. The thing is this guy plays rough and you could wind up dead. As you're an American citizen, the last thing the FBI wants is to put you in any kind of danger."

Blast didn't quite stifle a snort of derision, but Tombs just shrugged his shoulders in a 'what do I really care' attitude.

"I spotted you getting out of Mendez's car earlier today. What did he want from you?"

Jack leaned back and quickly repeated the conversation that had taken place in the car. Tombs appeared worried.

"No doubt Mendoza is going to want to talk to you again, and before that happens I think it would be best if we took you out of the equation and got you the hell out of here. When Mendoza contacts you, tell him Mr. Ellis is in town and is keen to arrange a meeting with him. I'll give you a time and place that Mendoza will consider safe, and will probably be all the more happier to know you're stepping away from it all. Tell him things have become too hot for you here and you're going to make a quick exit before the local police start digging into background checks. From then on, you stay out of it, and we'll take over. We'll make it so you're no longer a factor to him."

Tombs stood up, put his hand into his jacket pocket and pulled out his hotel room keycard. "For now, go back to your girlfriend, relax, and keep me in the loop. Remember," he waved the keycard several times. "I'm going to be right next door."

Blast went back to Taffy, his drink, and the romantic music. But the serenity was definitely gone.

*****

Blast was sitting in his room when the call from Mendoza came.

Two days had passed since his conversation with Tombs. True to his word, the FBI operative had provided a time, date and place for the meeting. Tombs requested the he play it as if he was in it for the money. The receiver was picked up on the third ring.

"Hello?"

"Mr. Blast, Mendoza here. Have you made any headway with my request?"

"You're in luck. Mr. Ellis has flown in from New York to meet with you. He's been unhappy with Lopez, and the whole organization lately and he's willing to talk. Are you familiar with the Malas Tierras Bar on the edge of town?"

"That dump? Yes, I know where it is."

"Be there this afternoon at 2pm. You'll be taken to a back room."

"I'll be there."

"By the way, what about my money? I did what you asked."

"Don't worry, you'll be taken care of."

There was something in the way Mendoza said it that sent a chill down his spine. Taffy came out of the shower.

"Jack, you've been so busy, you haven't had much of a vacation."

"I know, but all that is about to change. I've arranged for a car to take us to Porto Moniz today. They have these lava pools we can swim in, and then we'll have lunch at an expensive restaurant."

"What are lava pools?"

"They are natural swimming pools that were formed by volcanic lava millions of years ago. The sea fills them with crystal clear calm water. The island is famous for them. You'll love it."

"You are the best, Jack!"

She impulsively kissed his cheek.

"This vacation is changing my opinion of you. I've always thought of you as this scheming cheap-skate bullshit artist, and always wondering, what the hell did I ever see in you? But now, I'm seeing you in a different light."

She put her arms around him. There was a look of admiration in her eyes. A look he's never seen before.

However it was short lived.

Suddenly, Detective Busto entered the room without knocking. There were two other policemen with him.

"Mr. Blast, you are under arrest for the murder of Carlos Benito, the guy you threw out the window. And you Miss Dux, are under arrest as an accomplice."

Taffy's expression and body language took on a more familiar look.

"You two-bit no good son-of-a-bitch! I should have known this was all baloney! What the hell did you get me into now?"

She lunged at him, but was pulled away, kicking and screaming by one of the local policemen. But there was no stopping her and she seemed to find new strength from somewhere, and she lunged again. Thankfully the second constable stepped in to help, but even so they both had a hard time restraining her.

Eventually the two of them were led out of the hotel in handcuffs, bundled into separate cars, and taken downtown.

*****

It was late afternoon, and Blast was sitting in his cell when there was the sound of an angry commotion at the front desk. To his surprise, he saw a group of cops walk by and in their control was a handcuffed Harry Tombs. When Tombs saw a puzzled looking Blast stare at him, he stopped and yelled:

"I'll get even with you for this, you son of a bitch! You're as good as dead."

He was forced to keep moving to a cell further down the hallway.

Next one passing through was an angry Mendoza. The cops had to constrain him.

"This is not over Blast! Your death is going to be slow and agonizing."

It took some tugging, but they were able to eventually move him along.

The last one in the parade was a sobbing Alfonso Lopez, who paid no attention to him. Very puzzling. It wasn't long after that Blast was taken out of his cell and brought into Detective Busto's office.

Taffy was already seated in front of his desk. Busto motioned for Blast to have a seat next to her.

"I have to apologize to the both of you for putting you through this. We have been onto Lopez for a while. But, thankfully, because of your involvement, we've been able to successfully round up the whole gang here on the island."

Blast responded.

"You locked up one of the wrong guys – Harry Tombs is with the FBI."

Busto smiled. "Mr. Blast, Harry Tombs is not the gentleman's real name. Nor is it Leon Gallo, the name he used to fly to the island alongside you. He is better known as Mr. Ethan Ellis. Lopez thought he was talking to New York when they spoke, but Ellis had that fake New York number patched directly to his cell phone, so he appeared to be in New York no matter where he was. Lucky for us, he came here from the States to get a better look at the way the island side of his operation was performing. We had his room bugged and got all the formation we needed to be able to set up our trap."

Busto leaned back in his chair, smiling a little. "We also had your room bugged, so we know that Carlos' death was a genuine accident. Originally, we didn't know what to make of you two. Frankly, we still don't. The fact that Mendoza got involved was lucky. We suspected he was somehow connected with the island's organized crime, and now we also have him for conspiracy as well. We were waiting out of sight from them at the Malas Tierras Bar. When we had all the information we needed on record, we moved in. The reason you two were arrested was to protect you in case something went wrong with the bust."

"I don't know if you know it, Detective Busto, but I was threatened by Ellis and Mendoza when they walked past my cell."

"I'm not worried about that. When your plane leaves tomorrow, you'll be out of my jurisdiction and no longer my problem."

Taffy just rolled her eyes. Busto stood up and offered his hand to Blast.

"In a screwed up way, you did us a great service. Thanks. You're both free to leave."

*****

And so, with their vacation over, Jack and Taffy were on the plane heading back to New York. This time they were seated next to each other. Blast tried to make nice to Taffy, but all he got back were nasty remarks and dagger stares. He was beginning to wish he was seated between the two fat guys again.

The Usual Unusual Suspects

Anthony Diesso is originally from Bridgeport, Connecticut, although he ended up in California and later Arizona, probably due to confusion over the interstate freeway system. He has been telling stories since grade school, where his first fictional narratives tried to explain why he hadn't done his homework. This might also explain why so many of his later tales show an interest in myth and criminal behavior. More recently, some of his adventure stories have appeared in online magazines; in tone, they're a bit like American explorer Roy Chapman Andrews getting stuck on Mr. Toad's Wild Ride. Mr. D currently teaches 5th grade at a local elementary school, which can also resemble a Disneyland ride at times (heading for Tomorrowland, but getting lost in a jungle of bad jokes and fake animal noises). He has a wife and two children who continue to inspire his stories, such as the epic tales of why he didn't take the trash out, empty the dishwasher, or remember a birthday.

Brandon Barrows is the author of several novels, most recently 3rd LAW: MIXED MAGICAL ARTS, a YA urban fantasy, and over one-hundred published stories, mostly crime, mystery, and westerns. He is a two-time Mustang Award finalist and a 2022 Derringer Award nominee. He is also the editor and driving force behind *Guilty Crime Magazine* (https://www.guiltycrimemag.com/) – also find Find more at http://www.brandonbarrowscomics.com and on Twitter @Brandon Barrows

E. James Wilson is a 20-something 70-year-old, born in Brazil to English and American parents. At the age of 15 he taught himself to type because most of his school teachers stated that his handwriting was, at best, atrocious. From that point on it was a rapid descent into cheap cigarettes and lurid prose, to the point where his parents bought him a book tutorial on Pitman Shorthand and told him to become a journalist. Fifty-five years later he is still writing fiction, but it's no longer printed in newspapers as fact.

His *#27 **The House Special*** appeared in *Crimeucopia – It's Always Raining In Noir City*.

At present he is living on a small farm in Patagonia, with some chickens and half a dozen goats. We don't ask about what happened to the llama.

James Roth is a writer of fiction and nonfiction. His work has appeared in several magazines and journals. His first novel, *The Opium Addict*, is forthcoming from Hear Our Voice, LLC. A second novel, *A Prayer for My Daughter*, set in modern Japan, is a noir/literary mystery that should be out in 2024. He has taught in Japan, China, and Zimbabwe and likes to say he was "Made in Japan." His parents lived there during the American occupation but he was, to his and his mother's lasting regret, born in a military hospital in the U.S. He is presently a fellow in the U.S. State Department's ELF Program at the Jordan Media Institute in Amman, Jordan. www.jamesroth.org.

Jesse Aaron served as a police officer in New York City and Connecticut for over five years and also worked in the field of private security/investigations. His first novel, *Shafer City Stories* is available on Amazon.com. Jesse's short story *The Leaky Faucet* was featured in *Crimeucopia – It's Always Raining In Noir City*.

Jesse has two more short stories on the way to publication and he is currently at work on his upcoming serial killer thriller *Harlem Hipster Homicides*." Jesse's style is dark and gritty, and his stories focus on the underside of the police and private detective worlds. Jesse has a love of all things Noir, Science Fiction, and Fantasy.

Jim Guigli is a student of many interests: SCUBA diver, auto-mechanic, and gunsmith, served as an Army Security Agency Russian Voice Intercept Operator in Japan, studied Judo, played basketball, was a career mechanical designer for National Labs LBNL, SLAC, & LANL, trained at Gunsite with pistol & shotgun, designed and supervised firearms competitions, toured Quantico as an FBI Citizens Academy graduate, designed a 400 sq ft kitchen addition to his house, and earned BFA and MA degrees in Art/Photography. Jim is an active member of SMFS, PSWA, & Sacramento CWC.

Publishing History: Won 2006 Bulwer-Lytton Fiction Contest Grand Prize. The Grand Prize sentence and one other were published in *It Was a Dark and Stormy Night*, by Scott Rice, Friday Books, London, 2007. Self-published 2013 Kindle Bart Lasiter novelette, *Bad News for a Ghost*. Other Bart Lasiter appearances include *Looking for Mishka, (Rock and a Hard Place Magazine, Issue 7, Winter 2022)*, and *Cane Mutiny (May 2022 Pulp Modern Flash). Listen to the Gunsmith* appeared in the *July 2022 Guilty Crime Magazine*. Two new non-Bart pieces – *Ben Hurt* and *Not Funny* – are due to appear in *Guilty Crimes Magazine* during 2023. His *Blood on the Stairs* appears in *Crimeucopia – We'll Be Right Back – After This!* He has also written various articles for the *PSWA newsletter* and NorCal Chapter newsletters of MWA and SinC. Website: www.jimguigli.com

John M. Floyd's short stories have appeared in *Alfred Hitchcock's Mystery Magazine, Ellery Queen's Mystery Magazine, Strand Magazine, The Saturday Evening Post, Best American Mystery Stories* (2015, 2018, and 2020), *Best Mystery Stories of the Year 2021, Best Crime Stories of the Year 2021*, and many other publications. A former Air Force captain and IBM systems engineer, John is an Edgar finalist, a Shamus Award winner, a five-time Derringer Award winner, and the author of nine books. He is also the 2018 recipient of the Short Mystery Fiction Society's lifetime achievement award.

Kevin R. Tipple reviews books, watches way too much television, and offers unsolicited opinions on anything. His short fiction has appeared in magazines such as *Lynx Eye*, *Starblade*, *Show and Tell*, and *The Writer's Post Journal* among others. He's also online at such places as *Mouth Full Of Bullets*, *Crime And Suspense*, *Mysterical-e* and others. *Mystery Weekly Magazine* published his story, *The Damn Rodents Are Everywhere*, in May of 2021 and soon had to change their name to *Mystery Magazine*. His short story, *The Beetle's Last Fifty Grand* appears in the 2022 anthology, *Back Road Bobby and His Friends*, and everyone involved seems to have survived the experience unscathed. He hopes the same for *Crimeucopia*.

Fully trained before marriage, Kevin can work all major appliances and, despite a love of nearly all sports, is able to clean up after himself.

Maddi Davidson is the pen name for two sisters: Mary Ann Davidson and Diane Davidson. Together they have published several novels, a non-fiction book, and numerous short stories. Their tales range from the murder of a deranged scientist resurrecting the dodo to a spurned wife hacking the pacemaker of an ex-husband who richly deserved it.

News and updates can always be found at https://maddidavidson.com/.

Michael Grimala is a journalist who lives in Las Vegas. He spends most of his free time with his dog, Lucas, and his short fiction has appeared in *Crimeucopia – As in Funny Ha-Ha, Or Just Peculiar*, *Ellery Queen Mystery Magazine* and other publications.

Robert Petyo is a Derringer award finalist whose stories have appeared in small press magazines and anthologies, most recently in *The Black Beacon Book of Mystery*, *Asinine Assassins*, *Now There Was a Story*, *Whodunit*, *Mickey Finn 21st Century Noir*, and *Stonewall Detectives*. He has also appeared in the following Crimeucopias - *We're All Animals Under the Skin*, and *Careless Love*.

He writes primarily mysteries, but also SF, fantasy and horror and an occasional mainstream piece. He lives in Northeastern Pennsylvania, is happily married, and is recently retired from the Postal Service, which allows him more time to read and write. Unfortunately, there never seems to be enough time to read and write.

With degrees in Crime Scene Technology & Physical Anthropology, Florida author **Shannon Hollinger** hasn't just seen the dark side of humanity - she's been elbow deep inside of it! She's the author of the psychological thrillers *Best Friends Forever* and *The Slumber Party*, and the forthcoming *Chief Maggie Riley* series (November 2023, published by *Bookouture*). Her short fiction has appeared in *Suspense Magazine*, *Mystery Weekly*, and *The Saturday Evening Post*, among a number of other magazines and anthologies, and her story *Lady Killer* was a finalist for the 2021 Al Blanchard Award sponsored by the New England Crime Bake. To see where you can find more of her work, check out www.shannonhollinger.com.

Shannon's short *Money Talks* appears in *Crimeucopia – It's Always Raining In Noir City*.

Tom Sheehan is now more than halfway through his 95th year, (31st Infantry, Korea 1950-52; Boston College 1952-56). Coping with macular degeneration, he was named Saugus Man of the Year, 9/10/22, and has had multiple works in *Rosebud*, *Copperfield Review*, *Literally Stories*, *Frontier Tales*, *Green Silk Journal*, etc. He has one self-published book, a winner, and a second self-published book in the running. He has 18 Pushcart nominations, and 6 Best of Net nominations (one winner). Latest books released are *The Townsman*, *The Horsemen Cometh*, *Jock Poems and Reflections for Proper Bostonians*, *Ah, Devon Unbowed*, and *The Saugus Book*. His book count is 58. He's retired 30 years.

Tom first appeared in *Crimeucopia – Tales From The Back Porch*.

Wil A. Emerson has been on the writing path for approximately fifteen years. While not fresh out of college to write the Best Seller, she spent her early years as a Registered Nurse. Now on the fringe of being overlooked due to the inconvenient late start, she's successfully published in anthologies and has one novel under her belt. *Taking Rosie's Arm*, a Five Star, Thorndike publication, recounts the story of an elderly woman who befriends a troubled, but determined young girl. Writer, artist, traveler, cook: soup's on.

Wil's recent work is mainly mystery and women's fiction, and her first *Crimeucopia* appearance was in *Careless Love*, with her piece, *The Driver*.

Also a struggling artist, her art can be viewed on her website. www.wilemerson.com

Peter Trelay was born in England to French and Irish parents, and has lived in many countries in the Americas, Europe and Asia, teaching English over the past thirty years. He is currently living and teaching in Myanmar.

Vanity and Innocence is an extract from an unpublished novel called *Jaws of Life*. It recounts some of the experiences Peter has had while pursuing his other occupation, which involved surreptitiously moving items across borders.

Philip Pak is a retired NYC police officer who has been writing comical mysteries for the past 7 years. His stories often include offbeat characters who find themselves in absurd situations with deadly consequences. Who said murder isn't funny? His books include, *The Every Other Day Detective*, *Mystery Shorts*, *Death is on Deck*, *Dead Mimes Don't Talk*, *Murder at the Lowdown* and *Stop the Music, He's Dead*.

CRIMEUCOPIA

The Lady Thrillers

16 Countesses of Crime recount tales of Murder Mayhem and Revenge

Karen Skinner - Hilary Davidson - Pauline Gostling -
Linda Kerr - Kate Miller - Tiffany Lindfield - Lena Ng -
Ginny Swart - Sandrine Bergèss – Michelle Ann King -
Amanda Steel - Kelly Lewis - Paulene Turner-
Claire Leng - Madeleine McDonald - Joan Hall Hovey

*16 stories ranging from the 14th to the 21st Century,
all from women authors whose forte is crime.*
Paperback Edition 9781909498198
eBook Edition 9781909498204

CRIMEUCOPIA

We're All Animals Under The Skin

Featuring: John Gerard Fagan, Nick Boldock,
Weldon Burge, Chris Phillips, Dan Meyers,
Jeff Dosser, Eve Fisher, Emilian Wojnowski,
Fabiyas M V, Lamont A. Turner, Edward Ahern,
Robert Petyo, Al Hagan, Caroline Tuohey,
Steve Carr, Bobby Mathews, Michael Bracken,
and June Lorraine Roberts

18 authors take time to look under the skin of the people who
sometimes inhabit their heads, and put what they find down on
paper.

Paperback Edition ISBN: 9781909498235
eBook Edition ISBN: 9781909498228

CRIMEUCOPIA
The Cosy Nostra

A Crimeucopia Family Gathering

17 writers take us on Cosy journeys - some more traditional,
while others are very much up to date.
Eve Fisher, Alexander Frew, Tom Johnstone, John M.Floyd,
Andrew Humphrey, Joan Leotta, Gary Thomson,
Eamonn Murphey, Matias Travieso-Diaz, Madeline McEwen,
Lyn Fraser, Ella Moon, Gina L. Grandi, Louise Taylor,
Judy Penz Sheluk, Joan Hall Hovey and Judy Upton.
Paperback Edition ISBN: 9781909498242
eBook Edition ISBN: 9781909498259

CRIMEUCOPIA
Dead Man's Hand

Featuring

Redemption
John M. Floyd

Rebel Seed
Alexander Frew

For the Honor of the Family
Jim Doherty

Murder at Bullet Pass
Bruce Harris

Wild Yellow
Brandon Barrows

The five writers here have very respectable track records in the Western genre, and are old hands when it comes to telling compelling stories.

So join

John M. Floyd - Alexander Frew - Jim Doherty - Bruce Harris and Brandon Barrows

and let them take you back to a time of six-guns an' whiskey, an' wild, wild fiction.

Paperback Edition ISBN: 9781909498266
eBook Edition ISBN: 9781909498273

CRIMEUCOPIA

As In Funny Ha-Ha

Or Just Peculiar

Murderous Ink
Press

Putting the Outré back into OMG are
Jesse Hilson, Gabriel Stevenson, Maddi Davidson,
Brandon Barrows, Robb T. White, Regina Clarke,
Martin Zeigler, K. G. Anderson, Andrew Hook,
Ed Nobody, Jody Smith, Michael Grimala,
W. T. Paterson, James Blakey, Emilian Wojnowski,
Andrew Darlington, Lawrence Allan, Ricky Sprague,
Bethany Maines, John M. Floyd and Julie Richards

Paperback Edition ISBN: 9781909498266
eBook Edition ISBN: 9781909498273

CRIMEUCOPIA

CARELESS ♥ LOVE

You're driving me crazy
You're making me mad
'Cos the only way of lovin' you
Is with a good love gone bad...
(Vicky LaPerso – The 1956 Ventura Tapes)

Fifteen writers tell us about affairs of the heart – some with humour, some with a darker intent, and others that are never quite exactly what they seem. Is it all about manipulation? Can there be more than one agenda? And does Love really conquer all, even when it's supposedly blind? Or maybe Love is just an old Devil, looking for mischief?

Steve Sneyd, Ange Morrissey, James Roth, Michael Wiley, Gustavo Bondoni, Matthew Wilson, Peter W. J. Hayes, Wil A. Emerson, Brandon Barrows, Bern Sy Moss, Michael Anthony Dioguardi, Russell Richardson, Robert Petyo, Sam Westcott, Bryn Fortey and *Vicky LaPerso* – all of whom take us on roller coaster rides through a fictional Tunnel of Love.

Paperback Edition ISBN: 9781909498303
eBook Edition ISBN: 9781909498310

CRIMEUCOPIA
The 👁's Have It

*Featuring: Mike Job, Jill Hand,
Joe Giordano, Michael Thomét,
Michele Bazan Reed, Paul R. Paradise,
M. C. Tuggle, Edward Lodi, Lynn Hesse,
Kelly Zimmer, John M. Floyd
and Shannon Lawrence*

Investigators and investigations are the mainstay of most Crime fiction sub-genres. Everything from the original *Golden Age* of country houses and the amateur sleuth, through to the high tech ultra-modern 21st Century – a place where the cyber investigators sometimes appear to be baffled by old-fashioned motivations of power and greed, and human foibles such as love and revenge.

So is there any real difference between the Private and the Public Sector investigators? Not much, if writers are to be believed, and the two can often be found straddling both sides of the 'what's legal procedure?' fence.

Of the twelve authors contained within, eleven are voices new to the world of Crimeucopia - and although the theme is *Investigators*, the material ranges from Cosy, through to not too Hardboiled - and most are touched with a vein of humour, be it light or dark. Rather like a box of chocolates...

Paperback ISBN: 9781909498327 eBook ISBN: 9781909498334

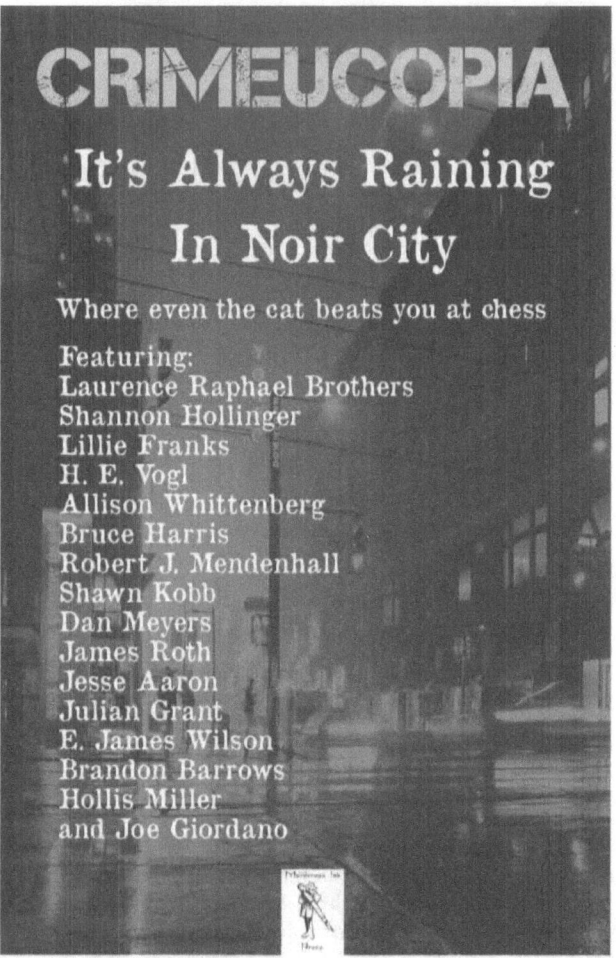

CRIMEUCOPIA

It's Always Raining
In Noir City

Where even the cat beats you at chess

Featuring:
Laurence Raphael Brothers
Shannon Hollinger
Lillie Franks
H. E. Vogl
Allison Whittenberg
Bruce Harris
Robert J. Mendenhall
Shawn Kobb
Dan Meyers
James Roth
Jesse Aaron
Julian Grant
E. James Wilson
Brandon Barrows
Hollis Miller
and Joe Giordano

Is the Noir Crime sub-genre always dark and downbeat? Is there a time when Bad has a change of conscience, flips sides and takes on the Good role?

Noir is almost always a dish served up raw and bloody - Fiction bleu if you will. So maybe this is a chance to see if Noir can be served sunny side up - with the aid of these fifteen short order authors.

All fifteen give us dark tales from the stormy side of life - which is probably why it's *always* raining in Noir City....

Paperback Edition ISBN: 9781909498341
eBook Edition ISBN: 9781909498358

CRIMEUCOPIA

Tales From The Back Porch

Telling tales are:
Penny Hurrell, Teresa Trent, Wendy Harrison, Maroula Blades,
Tom Sheehan, Jan Christensen, Bryn Fortey, Michele Bazan Reed,
Carol Willis, Madeleine McDonald, Adam Meyer, Nikki Knight,
Regina Clarke, J. W. Wood, Deb Merino and Alison McDonald

Small town, big city, watercooler or the back of that 1950s beat-up
Chevy Bel Air with the leather back seat that your parents told you
never to get familiar with. It doesn't matter where you hear it, gossip
is 100% pure ear addiction – and knowledge is, after all, power when
all's said and done.

So why don't you settle down, get yourself comfy, and pour yourself
a drink – long and tall, or just short and nasty, the choice is yours –
and let these 16 story tellers spin their tales as only they know how.

Paperback Edition ISBN: 9781909498365
eBook Edition ISBN: 9781909498372

CRIMEUCOPIA

When the theme is no theme at all, you've just got to ask the question

Say What Now?

Featuring:
Peter Ullian,
S. E. Bailey,
N. M. Cedeño,
Edward St Boniface,
Jan Glaz,
Eleanor Luke,
Momodou Bah,
Eve Fisher,
John M. Floyd,
Joan Leotta,
Glen Bush
and DL Shirey

Sometimes editors are forced to reject submissions through no fault of the author. It could be a wonderfully written manuscript, but if the editor cannot place it, then what do they do?

MIP has been lucky in its flexibility and its "Can we start a new project with this?" attitude. Some of the dozen authors contained within are seasoned professionals, having been published in the likes of Alfred Hitchcock's, Ellery Queen's, or other notable publications, while some are making their publishing debuts as Crimeucopians. And while the quality throughout remains exceedingly high, the subject spectrum is the widest we've published so far. But that's only fitting when you consider that the theme of this Crimeucopa is that of No Theme At All.

And in true Murderous Ink fashion, with a dozen authors to choose from, you're bound to find something you'll like, and something you didn't know you'd like until you've read it.

Paperback Edition ISBN: 9781909498389
eBook Edition ISBN: 9781909498396

This is the first of several 'Free 4 All' collections that was supposed to be themeless. However, with the number of submissions that came in, it seems that this could be called an *Angels & Devils* collection, mixing PI & Police alongside tales from the Devil's dining table. Mind you, that's not to say that all the PIs & Police are on the side of the Angels....

Also this time around has not only seen a move to a larger paperback format size, but also in regard to the length of the fiction as well. Followers of the somewhat bent and twisted Crimeucopia path will know that although we don't deal with Flash fiction as a rule, it is a rule that we have sometimes broken. And let's face it, if you cannot break your own rules now and again, whose rules can you break?

Oh, wait, isn't breaking the rules the foundation of the crime fiction genre?

Oh dear....

CRIMEUCOPIA
ONE MORE THING TO WORRY ABOUT

Featuring
Gerald Elias, Bob Ritchie, Michele Bazan Reed,
Terry Wijesuriya, Aran Myracle, Alexei J. Slater,
Nikki Knight, Issy Jinarmo, N. M. Cedeño,
Wendy Harrison, Andrew Darlington, Larry Lefkowitz,
Jesse Aaron, Madeleine McDonald, Joan Leotta,
H. E. Vogl, and Vinnie Hansen

New Crimeucopians *Aran Myracle, Alexei J. Slater, Gerald Elias, Terry Wijesuriya, Issy Jinarmo, Larry Lefkowitz,* and *Vinnie Hansen* smoothly rub literary shoulders with a fine collection of familiar Crimeucopia old hands: *Bob Ritchie, Michele Bazan Reed, Nikki Knight, N. M. Cedeño, Wendy Harrison, Andrew Darlington, Madeleine McDonald, Joan Leotta, H. E. Vogl* and *Jesse Aaron.*

All 17 tell tales that will make you realise there's always going to be One More Thing To Worry About....